THE DECISION

KC SAVAGE

Edited by Writing Evolution
Front cover image by Carter Cover Designs
Formatted by Carxander Publishing

Printed by Amazon Inc., in the United States of America.
First printing, 2022

Lyla D Creations LLC
24445 Painter Drive
Land O Lakes, FL 34639
www.lyladcreations.com

DISCLAIMER

This book contains lying,
sexually explicit scenes,
and strong language.
Please read at your own risk.

Table of Contents

For me.
Through all the obstacles and delays,
I persevered and made my dream come true.

The forbidden will always be desirable.

- Unknown -

CHAPTER 1

"Jack, please try calling your parents again." Emma grabbed his forearm as he walked by her in the kitchen, her eyes coming together. She wanted his parents to attend their wedding, which was set to take place in a month in New York City. She'd not met them yet, but wanted them there, for Jack.

With his head lowered to his chest, he took her hand in his and brought it to his lips. Kissing it softly, he said, "Emma, I'll try again, for you. But please, love, don't get your hopes up. My dad is a stubborn man, and my mom won't go against his wishes." Jack drew Emma in and surrounded her with his embrace. "I'll do anything for you."

She pressed her cheek to his firm chest and wrapped her arms around his waist. "Thank you." She tilted her head up and smiled at him.

Leaning down, he kissed her tenderly. "Let me get my phone and I'll text Mom first to be sure they're home." Jack turned and walked toward their bedroom.

During the past six months, Emma had asked Jack to reach out to his parents more and more. But his mom had made excuse after excuse of why they couldn't meet. They'd been on vacation. His dad had a business dinner. They'd both been sick.

Hopping onto the barstool, Emma waited patiently for Jack to return with his phone. She'd prepared herself for his parents to refuse to attend, but she felt asking them was the right thing to do; regardless of how they felt about her. Jack was their only son. They should put their dislike of her aside for a day and be there for him.

She knew she'd win them over if given the chance. She'd show them how much she loved Jack and be the best wife to him. She had her poem paintings about him that she wanted to share with them.

Feeling her heart begin to race, she rubbed her hands down her slacks. She hopped off the stool and walked into the kitchen. Instead of a whiskey glass, she reached for a mug. She filled it with water and placed it in the microwave. While her water heated, she went to the pantry and found a teabag. She made herself a nice lavender and chamomile tea to help calm her nerves.

"Okay, Em." She turned at Jack's voice behind her. "My mom said they are home. Are you sure you want to try this again?" Jack raked his hand through his hair and rubbed his mildly scruffy chin.

After taking the few seconds to make her tea, she walked toward him. She placed her mug on the bar and held out her hands to him. Wiggling her fingers, she took his hands and intertwined their fingers. "Yes, baby. I want them there. We have to try and ask." She squeezed his hands tightly, then released them and embraced him. "I love you and I want them to know how much. I want them to see us and how happy we are. I want them to feel how much we love each other, and I hope that'll bring them around to accepting me as their daughter-in-law. I know it will, Jack." She released her embrace and stepped back.

Waking his phone, he placed it on the counter and pressed Mom, then placed it on speaker. Jack brushed Emma's cheek and smiled weakly at her.

Her heart pounded fiercely inside her chest as the phone rang several times before a woman's voice answered. "Hello, Jackson." Emma brought her hand to her mouth, her eyes filled with tears as this was the first time she'd ever heard Jack's mom's voice. She sounded kind to Emma. She hoped she was right.

"Hi, Mom. Is Dad there with you?" Jack asked. He glanced at Emma and held his hand for her. She slipped her hand in his and sat quietly by his side. Butterflies filled her stomach, a drum major leading the band in her chest. She tried to keep her breathing steady as she sipped on her tea.

"Yes, son. We're both here," a deep groggy voice said. Emma's heart stopped and she pinched Jack's hand. His gaze met hers. He leaned toward her and kissed her softly.

Whispering in her ear, so his parents couldn't hear him, he said, "I love you."

"Jack, why did you call?" his mom asked.

"Mom, Dad." He cleared his throat, then pulled in a deep breath and closed his eyes tight. He squeezed her hand. "I want…, No, *we* want to invite you to join us in New York City next month." Jack paused and drew in another deep breath.

Before he could continue, his dad said, "Who's 'we'?"

Emma's head fell to her chest. She yanked her hand free from Jack's and covered her face with both hands. Stifling any sound that tried to escape her, she breathed deeply, then raised her eyes to Jack. He cupped her chin in his soft hand and spoke to his dad. "You know, Dad. So, stop acting like you don't. We want you to come to our wedding. It's time for you and Mom to meet Emma. I—"

"No," Jack's dad interrupted him.

"Why, Dad? I love her. She's going to be my wife. She wants to meet you."

"Because she ruined your marriage to Jenna. She nearly ruined your career. She—"

"Stop, just stop. Emma didn't ruin anything. I fell in love with her. I pursued her. My marriage to Jenna was over. Emma didn't break up that marriage." Jack stood from the stool and embraced Emma. Her legs went weak as she listened to his dad say those awful things about her. She shook in Jack's arms. He held her tightly, kissing the top of her head over and over.

"Jackson, we should go," his mom said.

"Why? You don't want to hear the truth? You don't want to be a part of my life anymore?"

"We love you, Jack—"

"If you love me, then show me by coming to our wedding next month. Meet your future daughter-in-law. Because Emma will be your daughter-in-law whether you like it or not. I love her. We're getting married. We want you both there to celebrate with us. Please, Mom. Please, Dad." Jack's voice cracked as he pleaded with his parents.

"We have to go." Jack's phone went black. Emma slumped to the floor, her head in her hands, her tears flowing freely.

Feeling Jack's strong arms around her, she gazed up at him with red, puffy eyes. "They hate me, Jack. They hate me." Her body shook as she leaned against his.

He caressed her as he comforted her with his words. "What they think doesn't matter. I love you, Emma. I don't need them. I only need you. It's their loss if they refuse to join us in New York City. I don't need anyone there with me but you." Jack leaned against the bar and pulled Emma's tiny body between his legs. His arms brought her to his chest and engulfed her. Rocking them from side to side, he kissed the top of her head. He did his best to calm her and convince her that she was all he needed.

"I'm sorry," she whimpered as she leaned against him. "I wish I could convince them to be there with us next month, I want them to see how much I love you, I—" Her body shook again as Jack held her tighter.

"Emma, please calm down. Please, love. Breathe." He held her face in his soft palms and wiped her tear-stained cheeks with his thumbs, then leaned down and kissed her tenderly. "I love you. No one else matters." He gazed deeply into her bloodshot eyes.

"Oh, Jack. I know you do but having your parents there would've made the day perfect. My family and friends will be there but all you'll have with you is John and his wife. It doesn't seem right to not have your parents there." She sniffled hard as she held his gaze.

"Yes, I'll only have John there for sure, his wife may not make it, but we don't need any of them. We can fly away tonight and be married. But I know you want to go to New York City. I do too, but I don't need all of that. I only need and want you." His lips covered hers as she began to speak. She welcomed his tender kiss and slipped her arms around him.

Emma decided the only way to win his parents over was to be the perfect wife to their son. She'd make sure that Jack kept in touch with his parents, despite his father's stubbornness. And kept them updated on everything happening in their lives. She'd give them the time they needed, all the time in the world for them to come around and accept her. They didn't have to love her, just like her, even just a little, so they could be a family. She knew Jack wouldn't ever become his father. His heart was too full of love.

CHAPTER 2

As Emma stepped out of the limo, her eyes sparkled as she took in all of Times Square. Twirling around, she grasped Jack's bicep and met his blue eyes with hers. Her heart warmed and filled with all the love she'd held within for him. The pitter-patter and butterflies inside her were loud and wild; she wondered if those feelings would ever diminish like they had for Matt. But unlike her ex-husband, Jack always put her first, never left her wondering about his love for her. He made her the happiest woman on Earth.

"Thanks," Jack said to the limo driver, then he turned toward her. "Are you ready, love?"

With her slight frame tingling from head to toe, she smiled brightly as she threaded their fingers together. "Yes, I am." Pulling her long, black wool coat tight as several dried brown leaves swiftly flew by them, she snuggled against Jack. Releasing her hand, his arm embraced her as he led her into the hotel lobby.

After checking in and settling into the suite, Emma walked out onto the terrace. Still in her wool coat, she took in the extraordinary views of New York City. "Oh," she yelped when Jack swept her off her feet.

Spinning them around, he walked back into the warm suite and placed Emma down. "It's cozier in here." Jack reached for her coat as she slipped it off her shoulders.

"Thank you," Emma said and followed him to the bedroom. "This suite is beautiful. I may not want to go home." She fell onto the king bed and patted the space in front of her for Jack to join her.

His sinful smile revealed what he wanted, and she craved. Crawling into bed with Emma, Jack kissed her knees, sliding his warm hands up her thighs. "We're almost husband and wife. Maybe we should wait until we're married to make love." Jack's grin turned from sinful to innocent. Then he kissed her before she could protest.

Squirming under his firm body, she feathered her fingers through his dark-brown hair. "If that's what you want, I can wait." Biting her cheek, she prayed silently that he was kidding.

"Okay." Jack stopped his foreplay and laid on his back, locking his fingers behind his head.

Her eyes grew wide, her mouth opened as she began to protest. Changing her mind on how to convince him, Emma crawled onto him, straddling him, her wet center sitting on his rock-hard cock. She wiggled her ass against him, her lips curving upward. Slipping her hands under his polo shirt, she glided them up his firm chest. Lifting the navy-blue cotton polo shirt, she planted kisses along the way. Feeling his dick throb, she licked his nipples.

"Oh, Emma," he moaned, reaching for her, and stripping her blouse from her body.

"Still want to wait, baby? I can stop." Emma's seductive smile filled her face as Jack pulled her to him and covered her mouth with his. Diving her tongue into his delicious mouth, playing with his velvety tongue, she moaned. "Take me, Jack. I want you now."

Flipping them, Jack yanked Emma's skirt from her petite body. He slid her lacy panties down her sleek legs and stripped off the rest of his clothes. Her phone chirped as Jack crawled onto the bed. He reached for her purse, but she grabbed him.

"Ignore it." As she pulled him closer, her legs fell open and he slowly made his way between them. Arching her back when his rigid shaft touched her clit, Emma moaned again. "Oh, dear God, baby." Gripping Jack's biceps and holding on with all of her might, she thrusted her hips to meet his hard penetration. Feeling his body meet hers, she wrapped her legs around his waist and moved with his smooth rhythm.

His cock glided in and out of her with an easy motion. He kissed her long and deep. Nearing her climax, Emma tightened her grip letting out a scream, "Jack, Jesus, Jackson!"

"Baby, you feel so damn incredible," Jack groaned as his body tensed and he came.

As they laid together afterwards, Emma's phone rang again. She gathered herself and took a few deep breaths to slow her rapid heartbeat.

"Hi, Brandi," Emma said between breaths.

"Why did you send me to voicemail, Em? Y'all can't keep your hands off each other, can you?" Brandi teased.

"Maybe." Emma winked at Jack. "Are you and Ben here?"

"Yes, we're in our room. Has Shea and Rob arrived?"

"I haven't heard from them yet, but they should be here soon. We can meet in the lobby bar. I'll text her and let her know where we'll be."

"Okay, great. See you and Jack soon."

Emma ended her call with Brandi and thumbed to Shea's number. She sent her sister a quick text: **Y'all here?**

In less than a minute, Shea's text arrived. **We're in the elevator now.**

Emma: **Okay, meet us in the lobby bar when you've unpacked.**

Shea: **We will.**

Going back to Brandi's number, she texted her: **On our way downstairs. Shea and Rob are on their way to their room and will join us. See you at the bar.**

Brandi sent a thumbs up emoji.

Freshening up after making love, Emma and Jack left the suite and headed down to the hotel lobby.

***

Down in the hotel lobby's bar, Emma hopped onto the stool next to Jack. He waved toward the bartender while she watched for Brandi, Ben, Shea, and Rob to join them. "A whiskey and a bourbon, neat," Jack told the bartender.

"Jesus Christ. You really are a fucking deadbeat asshole, Jack." Emma grabbed Jack's hand then spun her stool when she heard a familiar woman's voice.

"Kaitlyn, what the hell are you talking about?" Emma asked, sliding off the stool and standing in front of Jack. She felt his hand on the small of her back.

14

"Jack knows exactly what I'm talking about. Ask him. Jenna's better off without you, they all are." Kaitlyn spun and walked away.

"What the fuck, Kait?" Emma called after Kaitlyn, but all she received was a wave of Kaitlyn's hand. Glaring after her, she shook her head quickly at Brandi when she saw her and Ben approaching Kaitlyn. They both nodded at Kaitlyn and kept walking toward Emma.

Looking up at Jack, she saw his eyes blinking rapidly and his mouth open. She grasped his hand again to get his attention. "Jack, what the hell was Kaitlyn talking about?"

His eyes were wide as he watched Kaitlyn leave the hotel lobby.

Yanking on his arm, she reached up and turned his face to her, "Jack!"

Shaking his head and rubbing his neck, he squeezed his eyes shut, then met her glare. "I don't know, Emma. I swear. I don't know."

"We can talk about this later." Emma took a few steps away from Jack as Brandi came toward her. She shook her head from side to side and slammed her eyes shut. Her fear of how Ben would react to Jack left her as she now needed to know why Kaitlyn said what she said to Jack.

Emma reached for Brandi and hugged her tight. Brandi asked, "What was that about?"

She whispered, "I don't know." She held Brandi for several minutes, then let go and smiled at Ben. He stepped in and hugged her, then kissed her cheek.

A bit of awkwardness sat between the four of them, when Ben broke the silence, "Jack." He extended his hand to Jack.

"Ben, good to see you again." Jack shook Ben's hand and nodded.

"Yeah, you too, but I've got one thing to get off my chest," Ben began.

"Ben, not now, please," Brandi begged.

"Yes. Now is the perfect time." Ben stood tall and crossed his arms. "Jack, promise me. No, no. Promise us." He pointed at himself and Brandi. "That you'll take care of this woman." He nodded toward Emma. "She's important to my wife and me. Brandi told me what happened with Jenna and the baby. We're very sorry for your loss." Ben paused, rubbing the back of his neck. "Emma deserves the best. So be the best for her." Ben stared at Jack, waiting for him to respond.

Swallowing hard, Jack pulled in a deep breath, then glanced at Emma. He cleared his throat before saying, "Ben, Brandi, thank you for your kindness toward Emma when things got a little dicey between us. I'm working on getting over the loss of my baby every day. And with this beautiful, loving, supportive woman by my side, I know I'll be fine." Jack drew Emma to him, holding her tightly. "I love Emma with all my soul. I always have, since the first time I saw her. I'll always cherish her and her love for me." He squeezed her tighter and kissed her cheek.

Emma's heart clenched, her breathing intensified while she sucked back the mountain of joyful tears wanting to fall. She knew he loved her, but she couldn't stop thinking about what Kaitlyn had said just moments ago. She smiled weakly at him and pinched his arms that encompassed her.

"Okay, man. You better." Ben held his fist toward Jack, and they fist bumped. Emma smiled at Brandi when she saw her best friend letting out a breath.

Although she felt a sense of relief, Emma still had her sister and brother-in-law to tend with. She knew Shea was fine with her and Jack. But Rob, he'd taken things harder when Shea had told him about Emma and Matt's divorce.

The foursome took seats at the bar, waiting for Shea and Rob to join them. Ben ordered a beer, and Brandi had a Diet Coke.

Emma did her best to push what Kaitlyn had said to the back of her mind. This was the night before she'd marry the man of her dreams. She didn't want anything to ruin their day. But Kaitlyn's words kept repeating over in Emma's mind. She raked her hair and slugged down her whiskey to chase it all away when she felt a hand on her shoulder. She spun to see her sister. "Shea." Emma reached for her. She slid from the stool and embraced her.

Holding Emma tightly, Shea whispered, "I'm sorry the kids couldn't be here."

"No worries. I know they're both busy with school. We'll catch up with them another time." Emma lifted her eyes to Rob. He smiled and hugged her too. "I guess I should introduce you to Jack,

16

Rob." Emma touched Jack's arm. He stood tall beside Emma. "Rob, this is Jack."

"Great to finally meet you." Jack offered his hand to Rob. Without hesitation, Rob took Jack's hand and shook it.

"Good to meet you, too. One thing," Rob said, not releasing his grip on Jack.

"Oh, Rob, not now," Shea pleaded.

"Take care of Emma. Love her. That's it, man. Just love her." Rob released Jack's hand and walked to the empty stool beside Ben, not waiting for Jack to respond.

Turning to face Emma, Jack smiled, his eyes pulling together. She smiled back and took his hand in hers. Squeezing it softly, he brought it to his lips and kissed it.

After finishing their drinks at the bar, the group of six walked to the restaurant. As they neared their table a familiar man's voice called out to Jack. "Hey Dr. Jackson Bryant."

Emma turned along with Jack and saw John Gates, their friend and realtor who'd helped them when they'd needed to move.

"Hey, man. Thanks for coming." Jack shook John's hand as a towering, stunning woman came up from behind John. Leaning toward her, Jack kissed the woman's cheek. "It's great to see you again, Stella." Jack tugged on Emma to bring her closer. "I'd like you to meet my fiancé, Emma. Em, this is Stella Gates, John's wife."

Emma extended her hand to Stella. They shook hands lightly and exchanged a polite cheek kiss.

Turning to the rest of the group, Jack introduced his friends. "Everyone, this is John and Stella Gates."

"Good to meet you. I'm Ben and this is my wife, Brandi. She and Emma are, as they say, besties." Ben smiled and shook John's and Stella's hands before taking a seat next to Brandi.

"Yeah, nice to meet you both. I'm Shea, Emma's sister. This is my husband, Rob." Exchanging handshakes and smiles, everyone took their seats for dinner.

During dinner, Emma, Shea, and Brandi caught up on what had taken place in their lives. Emma glanced Jack's way. He gave her his sweet smile and continued talking with John and Stella.

She placed her hand on his leg; his eyes met hers again. As she leaned toward him, Jack slid his arm around her shoulders and tightened his embrace on her while the conversations continued.

Music began playing, and Emma turned to Jack. "Dance with me." She stood and held out her hand to him. Standing, he clasped her hand with his.

"This is practice for tomorrow, baby." She smiled up at him. She turned to the table and said, "Excuse us, please."

Walking to the cleared area for dancing, Jack brought Emma close to him. "I can't wait until we're dancing as husband and wife. Tomorrow will be perfect, just like you, Emma." Jack led her around the dance floor, holding her as he had before. When the song neared its end, he twirled her around, pulled her into him, and dipped her. He placed a tender kiss on her lips before bringing her back upright.

Applause sounded from the other restaurant patrons. Emma's cheeks heated, and her heart raced. Jack led her back to the table, holding her hand, then placing his arm over her shoulders once they sat back down.

After finishing her second whiskey, Emma leaned toward Jack and whispered, "Let's go back to our room."

Smiling wide, Jack pushed back his chair. "Hate to break up this party, but I'm exhausted." Yawning, he stretched his arms and brought his hands down on Emma's shoulders. She rose from her chair and slipped her arms around his waist, her eyes beaming.

"Sure, Jack. Whatever you say." John winked at Emma and stood next to Jack. "Have a good night." The two men shook hands, then Jack brought John in for a big hug.

Pointing to Shea and Brandi, Emma said, "I'll see y'all early in the morning. Our appointments at the spa are at seven. Don't be late." She touched Stella's shoulder. "Will you join us, Stella? Please?" Emma asked.

"I'd love to. Thank you, Emma." Stella touched Emma's hand and squeezed softly.

"Great. I'll see all of my girls in the morning. Good night, y'all." Emma winked, then turned to Jack and hooked her arm through his. They left the hotel restaurant and walked to the bank of elevators leading to their suite.

In the elevator, Emma backed into the corner and lifted herself onto the railing. Holding on tight with one hand, she curled her index finger at Jack.

He punched the button for the floor where their suite was. The corners of his lips curved upward, his sapphire eyes filled with sin as he slinked toward her. His hands slid around her waist as he lifted her onto his towering firm body.

Her legs wrapped around him, her fingers locked around his neck. Staring into his intoxicating orbs, Emma wet her lips and pinched her legs tighter around him. Their lips smashed together as Jack backed her into the elevator wall. "Oh, God, Jack," she purred, raking her hands through his silky dark-brown hair. Her hands cupped his smooth jaw as she kissed him deeply. Her pussy clenched when he thrusted his body upward jamming her against the elevator wall again. Breathing heavily, she panted, "Jesus, fuck, Jackson." She felt his hard cock through their layers of clothing. She'd thought about abstaining from sex with him until they were married but thought better of it in that moment. She'd never deny him. She wanted him always.

The elevator door dinged and opened. Jack carried Emma on his body to their suite. She reached inside his jacket pocket to retrieve the room key and swiped it quickly to unlock the door. She reached for the door handle and turned it as Jack kicked the door open. Letting it close on its own, Jack walked toward the dining room table and placed Emma on it.

Smiling up at him, she trailed her hands down his white shirt to his slacks. She unbuckled his belt, unbuttoned, and unzipped his slacks. Reaching past the waistband of his boxers, she moaned as her hand found his hard as steel dick, erect and waiting for her. "Oh, baby. Give me one last good ride before I become your bride."

Jack ripped his clothes from his body, then stripped Emma naked. She tossed her head back and braced herself on the edge of the table as he shoved his cock into her wet core. "Hold on, love, hold on tight." Emma caught Jack's sinful grin as he leaned down and covered her mouth with his. Diving his velvety tongue between her lips, they kissed deeply.

Emma grasped Jack's biceps as he banged his dick inside her, making her pussy clench with each penetration. Their bodies met with an intense force she'd never felt from Jack before. She held onto him with all her might as he lifted her from the table. He turned around and leaned on the edge of the table.

Smiling, she placed her tiny feet on the table's edge. With control of their love making, Emma rapidly drove her body up and down on Jack's hard cock. She clasped her hands around his neck

19

again and held his gaze with hers. "Come for me, baby. Tell me, talk to me."

Jack's eyes widened as he jerked his hips up against her. "Dear, God, Em. I want you to come with me. Tell me too, love." His hands came to her face as he cupped her cheeks, pulling her to him. Their lips met, their tongues tangled as their bodies smacked together over and over.

The friction inside of her drove her to scream, "Jack! Jack! Yes, baby, fuck me good, fuck me harder."

Jack turned them around again, placing Emma on the edge of the table. Slapping her hands onto the tabletop, she leaned back as he gripped her hips and pounded her slight body. "Em, I'm coming, Jesus, love." Jack shoved hard into her as she collapsed onto the table.

"Oh…, Christ…, baby," Emma panted as she laid legs spread wide on the table. "Jack!" she screamed when he engulfed her legs with his hands.

"I love you, forever, Emma, forever." Jack covered her mouth with his and kissed her passionately.

CHAPTER 3

The wedding of Dr. Jackson Charles Bryant and Emma Brooke Taylor was all set to take place on February 14, 2023. They chose the luxurious five-star Metropolitan Hotel in New York City. It sat in the middle of Times Square, exactly where she wanted to be to marry the man of her dreams. Emma had planned their stay in one of the suites, as well as their wedding and luncheon in the small banquet hall.

Jack brought his tuxedo; Emma hung the black bag with her ivory-colored mermaid-style wedding dress in the large wardrobe. Hidden under the train of her dress was a red garter belt and ivory heels. She wanted to surprise Jack on their wedding day.

Waking to her 6:00 am alarm blaring, she laid with his arms around her, feeling loved and safe.

He reached across her and smacked her phone to quiet the alarm. His hand slid teasingly across her breasts as his other hand cupped her face. "Good morning, beautiful." His mouth covered hers before she could greet him.

Once their deeply passionate kiss ended, she murmured, "Good morning, gorgeous." Her body tingled all over. Her heart raced faster than a cheetah chasing their dinner. Leaning down to her again, Jack kissed Emma. His tongue pressed between her lips. She moaned, "Mmm, mmm." *Oh my, God! I'm going to marry Jack today. I'm going to marry Dr. Jackson Bryant.* Her mind went wild; her body quivered, knowing she'd wake up with him for the rest of her life.

Bringing her hands to her face, she drew in breath after breath. The reality of the day hit her. Her fantasy was coming true, and she was the luckiest, happiest, most loved woman alive.

"I need to shower and get ready for the spa appointments. Brandi and Shea will wonder where I am if I'm not there." Emma scooted to the side of the bed and slipped on her silk robe. She walked toward the bathroom, turning as she stood in the doorway. "I love you." She blew a kiss to Jack.

Catching it, he blew one back. "I love you too."

***

Jack and Emma showered separately and dressed to meet with their family and friends. Before they left the room, she handed him her gift. "What's this?" Jack asked.

"It's my wedding gift to you. Open it." Emma's heart pounded as he opened the small black box.

Smiling, he held up the teardrop cufflinks. "They're perfect. Thank you, love." He kissed her and walked over to where his tuxedo hung, putting them in the inside coat pocket.

"You're welcome. I have one more surprise for you, but that one's for after we're married." She smiled and walked over to the hotel suite door.

In the elevator, Jack pinned her against the wall. "Last chance," he teased.

Smiling up at him, she placed her hands on his firm chest. Her core blazed for him, but she wanted to wait. "Soon, baby." She brushed his unusually scruffy face, stood on her tip toes, and kissed him.

When the elevator stopped on the lobby floor, Jack and Emma walked to the spa where they met up with Brandi, Ben, Shea, Rob, John, and Stella. The four ladies went together to be pampered and made even more beautiful for the day.

Emma's eyes trailed after Jack as he went off with Ben, Rob, and John. She saw each of them fist bump and pull Jack in for a hug. A tear slipped down her cheek as she let out a sigh of relief, and her racing heart slowed. A thin smile formed, and she waved when Jack turned before he and the guys entered the men's side of the spa.

"Emma." She turned when she heard Shea call her name.

"Coming," she said and caught up with her, Brandi, and Stella. Slipping her arms through Brandi's and Shea's, they walked into the spa with Stella following behind.

Shea leaned close and whispered to Emma, "Don't worry, Em. Rob and I talked last night. He's fine with you marrying Jack. He wants to remain friends with Matt, though. I hope that's okay with you." Shea's eyes came together, and her jaw clenched.

"Of course, it is. I don't want Matt ostracized. I hope he and I can one day be friends again. I don't hate him. I just don't love him anymore. I love Jack." She squeezed Shea's arm and smiled.

"Well, that's good. I told Rob the same. Now let's put all that away and go get gorgeous." At the front desk, they checked in and waited for their appointments to begin.

The four women each had facials, manicures, pedicures, and massages scheduled. They had their hair and makeup done for the ceremony. Emma made sure they were spoiled to the core.

Emma jerked her hand away from the manicurist when she heard someone call out, "Hey, Kaitlyn. Can you get the massage tables ready for the Taylor party?" She spun quickly to try and see if the woman was the same Kaitlyn she knew. Her eyes darted around wildly as she searched the spa. Her heart stopped and she felt lightheaded.

"Emma. Emma," Brandi repeated her name, but she couldn't speak. She sat frozen as she listened for Kaitlyn to answer.

Putting her free hand to her mouth, she choked back tears, remembering what Jenna's friend Kaitlyn had said last night. *No! Stop! I'm marrying Jack today. He loves me. He won't cheat on me.* She shook her head quickly and heard an unfamiliar voice say, "I'm on it." Emma blew out the breath she'd held waiting to hear the Kaitlyn from the spa answer.

Her eyes shot upward, then she closed them for a few seconds. She rubbed her neck to relieve the tension that built up.

"Emma!" Brandi yelled.

She jerked her head up and her eyes shot open. She settled them on Brandi. "What? Oh my. What?"

"Where did you go just then? We've all been calling your name because you looked like you were in a trance. Are you okay?" Brandi asked.

"I'm sorry. I'm fine." She looked at her manicurist and said, "Sorry for pulling my hand away. That name startled me. Can we finish?" She smiled meekly and slid her hand under the partition dividing them.

"Of course. If you're sure you're okay," the young woman said.

Nodding, she looked at Brandi, Shea, and Stella who all stood beside her. "Go and finish your manicures. I'm fine, I promise." She waved her free hand in the air and watched them go back to their nail stations. *Jesus, I need to settle down. There's more than one fucking Kaitlyn in the world.*

After they all finished with the spa, the four ladies walked to the elevator bank. Emma pushed the call button. She took Shea's hand and squeezed it, then reached for Brandi. Stella stood between Brandi and Shea as all four women joined hands. "Em. Do you want any help getting ready?" Shea asked.

"If it's okay with y'all, I'd like to finish getting ready on my own." She glanced at Brandi, then Stella and lastly at Shea.

"Of course, right girls?" Brandi looked at Shea and Stella as they each nodded.

"Thanks for being here with me today. It means the world to me." Emma bowed her head and sniffled.

"Em, where else would we be?" Shea asked as she pulled Emma in for a hug. "I love you," Shea whispered.

Standing back, Emma smiled at Shea, Brandi, and Stella. "I'll meet you all back here, okay?" she asked.

"Yes, see you in a few." Shea hugged Emma again. "Please be happy," Shea said as their embrace ended.

"I am," Emma said. She hugged Brandi, then Stella stepped forward.

"Thank you for including me," Stella said after she hugged Emma.

"You're welcome. I'm so happy to have you and John here with us." The elevator dinged and the doors slid open. Emma stepped inside and waved to her three bridesmaids before the doors closed.

Back in their suite, Emma made her way to the bedroom. She changed into her wedding dress, put on her diamond necklace and bracelet, then slipped into her heels.

Standing in front of the full-length mirror, Emma made sure her dress was on perfectly. She smoothed the dress down her flat stomach and across her round ass. She stepped back, inspecting herself all around, then folded her faux fur coat over her arm and found her small clutch laying on the dresser.

She and Jack had agreed to not see one another once they'd left the suite that morning. She looked around the bedroom and noticed his tuxedo was gone. He'd either had come back and got it or had it sent down to the spa. Breathing deeply and feeling her heart pounding harder, she hugged herself tightly. Emma stopped when she caught her reflection in the dresser mirror. She raised her left hand and admired her engagement ring. She slipped it off and placed it on her right hand for the ceremony. Placing both hands on the dresser, she lifted her tiny frame to the mirror and kissed her reflection. She laughed and said, "Go get that man. He's almost yours."

That's when it all became completely real for Emma. Suddenly her stomach felt like it flipped inside out. A high-pitched laugh escaped her as she stared at Emma Taylor, the artist.

The last time she'd worn a dress like this, she'd married her high school sweetheart, Matt. She'd recalled early in their marriage, when she asked Matt to add a room to their home. She wanted an art studio to work in. He hadn't hesitated for a second. Within the month, he'd had everything put into motion for what she asked for. Several years later he'd put up money for her and Brandi to open BE Unique and never missed an exhibition of theirs. They'd had a long and almost perfect marriage. Many of her paintings held fond memories of their life together. He'd always been in her corner, always there for her. Then when she needed him the most, he wasn't.

She hung her head as she pushed those memories from her mind. *That's all history. Today is about Jack. Not Matt. Matt is my past. Jack, he's my life now. I know I've made the right decision. Jack is the perfect man for me. I'm sure of this.* Today was her wedding day to Dr. Jackson Bryant, her true soulmate.

Lifting her head, she caught her reflection again. Her hands trembled as she wiped the few tears that sat on the brim of her tear ducts. Knowing she still had to talk with Jack about keeping her name, EB Taylor, for her work, she wrapped herself in a tight hug to calm her anxiety. *Not now, dammit.*

She hoped he'd understand once they had the chance to talk when they were back home. She didn't want to bring up anything that could ruin their special day. Especially anything with the name Taylor.

Ready to go back down to the hotel lobby, Emma gave herself another hug as she double checked herself in the standing full-length mirror. *Today's the day I become Jack's wife. The day my dreams come true.*

Breathing deeply and holding each breath for a beat or two, she exhaled. Emma picked up her red and lavender rose bouquet from the table beside the door. She pulled the door to their suite closed then, hearing it lock, walked toward the elevator. She stood tall in her five-inch heels, feeling confident that her decision to marry Jack was the absolute right one for her and their life would be perfect.

CHAPTER 4

Walking with a happy and nervous pep in her step to the elevator, Emma went back down to meet up with Brandi and Shea. When the elevator doors slid open, they were waiting for her. Cupping her mouth, she swallowed down happy tears when she saw them dressed in the beautiful purple floor-length gowns she'd chosen for them. They each held a faux winter white muff with lavender roses adorning them.

Shea and Brandi slipped their arms through Emma's and escorted her to the room where the wedding ceremony was scheduled to take place.

When they arrived at the room, there was a man at the door, waiting for them. "Emma?" he asked.

"Yes, that's me." Her face brightened and she blinked rapidly.

He led them all down a short hallway to a smaller room where they'd wait until it was time to begin the ceremony. A few minutes went by, then Stella entered the room, dressed in the same gown as Brandi and Shea.

Cupping her mouth, Emma looked at Stella and, moving her hands up and down, she asked, "Oh my, gosh. Stella, how?"

"So, Jack had called after he found out what gowns you'd chosen for Brandi and Shea. He told us that he wanted this day to be perfect for you. He gave me the number to Georgia's bridal salon so I could make an appointment to be measured for the exact same gown. He'd taken photos of the muff and flowers you'd chosen when you were out one day and sent them to John. We made sure everything matched. Emma, Jack did this for you because he loves you so very much. You're one lucky woman." Stella held the muff with the lavender flowers on it for Emma to see.

Emma blinked quickly and swiped her hand under her nose. "Oh my, God." She fanned her face and looked around the room for a box of tissues. Seeing her sister near tears, Shea grabbed the tissue box on the small table and handed it to Emma. She yanked several from the box and dabbed her eyes. "Thanks," she said to Shea. Her sister nodded and slipped her arm around Emma's shoulders. Drawing in a deep breath, she looked at Stella again. "It's perfect. Jack thought of everything. I am so very lucky." She reached for Stella, and they hugged.

After catching her breath from Jack's surprise, Emma glanced at the clock on the wall. It read a quarter 'til noon. Her heart raced. Her hands felt clammy. Her insides shook. *It's almost time to marry my dream, my fantasy man, my once secret lover.* Her lips curved upward, and her eyes dazzled like diamonds.

After pacing around the room to let go of some nervous anxiety, she peeked at the clock again. This time it was five minutes until noon. When she began to tremble, Shea embraced Emma to help calm her. She leaned into her sister, then Brandi joined in the group hug.

"Girl, why are you so nervous? This is what you've wanted for so long, right?" Brandi stepped back and placed her hands on her hips.

Standing as tall as her petite frame allowed, Emma brushed her dress and shook her arms. "Yes, it's exactly what I want. Jack is who I want to spend eternity with." Her smile stretched across her face as she pulled in a deep breath.

Startled by a knock on the door, Emma looked at Shea. Shea walked over and answered it.

"Is Emma here?" a woman holding a bouquet of red roses and gardenias asked.

Shea stepped to the side as Emma walked to the door. "I'm Emma."

"These are for you, lucky lady." She handed Emma the bouquet.

"Thank you." Emma opened her arms to receive the flowers. She brought them to her face and inhaled the mixture of soft scents.

"You're welcome and congratulations." The woman smiled and left the room.

"Read the card, Em." Brandi pointed to a small, folded piece of paper tucked inside the bouquet.

Emma laid the flowers on a table and unfolded the card. She read it to herself first, her lungs pulling in a deep breath, her heart beating fiercely. She sucked back all the tears forming in her eyes. *No, not now, dammit.*

Taking another deep breath, Emma read the card aloud. "For my beautiful bride, the love of my life." She stopped and sniffled. She shook her hand in front of her face again trying to dry her eyes. She grabbed more tissues and dabbed her eyes dry, then continued to read the card. "Today, you'll make all my dreams come true. I love you, see you soon." She glanced at her sister and best friend, trying with all she had not to cry, but she couldn't stop the flood of tears tumbling from her eyes.

"Oh, Emma. You're going to ruin your makeup." Shea dabbed Emma's face with a tissue as she blinked swiftly to try and stop her tears.

"I know, fuck!" Emma yelled.

"Take a minute, girl. Take a breath. That man loves you." Brandi pulled Emma in for a tight hug. "I love you, Em. I wish you and Jack the very best of life together."

Another knock on the door sounded again as Brandi released Emma. Shea answered it and another lady came in. Emma smiled when she recognized the woman was the makeup artist from the spa.

"Your fiancée sent me. He said he knew once the flowers were delivered, you'd probably need my help." She set her makeup bag on the table near Emma.

Shaking her head and smiling, Emma said, "Yes, he knows me so well." She glanced at the clock, and it read noon. She sat in a chair to have her makeup touched up and butterflies set free in her stomach as she inhaled breath after breath.

Another knock on the door, and Emma looked over to see a man poking his head through. "Are you ladies ready?"

Brandi, Shea, and Stella looked at Emma, and she nodded. "Yes, sir. Lead the way."

Following the man back to the main room where the wedding was about to begin, Emma hugged Brandi, Shea, and Stella. They

29

lined up, and the man swung the double doors open. The ladies walked in ahead of Emma, Stella went first, followed by Shea. Brandi turned and whispered to her, "I'm so happy for you. You were right. He's perfect for you." She squeezed Emma's hand, then turned and walked on an ivory runner down the aisle.

Standing alone in the doorway, the massive feel of butterflies in her stomach doubled. She saw her bridesmaids and Jack's groomsmen standing in their places. A small ache pinched her heart as she'd wanted his parents to be with them. To celebrate alongside her family and friends. But his dad's stubbornness kept that from happening and only Jack's friends, John and Stella, had come to support him. She sniffled softly and drew in a deep breath. She couldn't change his parents' minds about her, so she blew out that breath and stood tall. She felt her heart drumming to the fastest beat it ever had. Smiling brightly, she began to walk down the aisle when she heard the traditional song of "Here Comes the Bride."

She met Jack's gaze with eyes so wide, her smile wider, and her body quivering inside. The walkway seemed to be miles long as she held Jack's soft blue eyes with hers. She felt like running to him, but she kept pace with the beat of the song. Jack's smile gleamed, his eyes dazzling. He stood at the alter in his black tuxedo with an ivory cummerbund to match her dress.

When Jack came to meet her a little past halfway, he cocked his arm for her. A memory flashed in her mind. At their first encounter, he'd done that same thing, but she hadn't taken his arm that night. She'd insisted he lead the way to the bar, and she'd follow. A tiny giggle escaped her as she slipped her arm through his. At the quizzical look on his face, she blinked long and shook her head from side to side. She'd tell him later about her memory of their first meeting. Jack patted Emma's hand, and they walked the rest of the way to the altar.

Stella, Shea, and Brandi stood on Emma's side in their beautiful purple gowns and winter white muffs. Rob, Ben, and John stood on Jacks' side dressed in tuxedoes with purple cummerbunds to match the women's gowns. Jack had a small rose and gardenia on his lapel, while the other three men wore lavender roses on theirs.

Red and lavender rose bouquets and gardenia bouquets sat on stands covered with ivory-colored tablecloths around the room.

Candelabras with red and ivory ribbons tied in bows, were lit, and placed around the room as well.

Jack and Emma took their places under an archway covered in red and lavender roses and gardenias. Ivory and red lace ribbons with tiny lights intertwined with them dangled all through the arch.

Emma turned and handed her bouquet to Brandi. Turning back to face Jack, she saw his hands open palm up for her. Another soft laugh escaped her when her memory flashed of him doing that exact same motion when they'd been alone in the exam room when he'd still been her doctor. She quivered, then gently placed her hands onto his.

The minister read the traditional wedding ceremony scripture from his book. They'd told him when they'd met with him, that they had their own wedding vows they each wanted to say to the other.

When it was Emma's turn, she looked up into Jack's kind blue hues and said, "I love you. You are my heart, my soul, and my life. I promise to always love you, now and for eternity. I still pinch myself every so often to make sure I'm not dreaming." She paused and lowered her gaze. Her heart pinched for a second. She knew she loved Jack, but a tiny part of her would always care about Matt in some way. She'd find a way to settle those feelings for her ex-husband another day.

Jack squeezed her hands and brought her attention back to him. "Are you okay, love?"

She raised her eyes back to meet his. "Yes, baby. I'm good." She cleared her throat and continued with her vows. "You truly are my fantasy man who came to life. You stole my heart and kept it safe. You protect me from all the hurtful things in this world. You hold me in your loving arms every night. I'll be by your side now to forever, my sweet. I pledge my undying love, respect, and trust to you. I'll love you forever and a day." She blinked long, and when she caught Jack's gaze again, she noticed a tear sliding down his cheek. Her heart warmed and she gave his hand a soft squeeze.

Jack freed one hand and wiped his cheek, then cleared his throat and took Emma's hand in his again. "When I saw you that night at the hotel, a lightning bolt zapped me. When I gazed into your stunning blue eyes that night, I knew something would happen between us, I felt it. I wasn't sure what it was, but I knew I loved you. I can't explain how or why it happened. I held my feelings back

31

because of the situation we were in. It was the most difficult thing I've ever had to do. I loved you from afar for months." Jack stopped and pulled in a deep breath. He blinked, then continued, "I knew you were the one, my forever. I had to figure out how to make us happen. It took several months before I built up the courage to tell you how I felt about you, but when I was ready, I told you. I was so happy you felt the same way. I'll always be by your side. I'll always protect you, respect you, put you first, love you, and hold you all night long. I love you, always only you." He squeezed her hands softly and winked at her.

Emma felt her tears falling and couldn't stop them. Taking his handkerchief from his tuxedo pocket, Jack dabbed her cheeks for her.

Looking at Brandi and John, the minister asked, "May I please have the rings?"

They each placed the gold wedding rings in his booklet. He blessed their rings and handed them to Jack and Emma.

With the saying of the traditional wedding ceremony script of, "Do you take…," to them, Jack held Emma's hand and slid her wedding band on her finger. She took his hand and placed the ring on his. Her heart skipped, pounded, and flipped inside her chest. Her breathing quickened, and she felt a little lightheaded. Pulling in a deep breath to calm herself, she held it in, then let it out slowly.

The minister proudly announced, "With the power vested in me by the state of New York, I pronounce you husband and wife." Looking at Jack, he said, "You may kiss your bride."

Jack's gleaming smile grew brighter than she'd ever seen, it made the sun seem dim. Wrapping his arms around her waist, he drew Emma close, and they kissed deeply for several minutes. His kiss was filled with so much love. His tongue pushed through her lips. She tasted him fully in front of everyone. Now that he was her husband, he tasted much more delicious.

After taking her bouquet back from Brandi, Emma slipped her arm through Jack's as the minister said, "For the first time, I introduce to you, Dr., and Mrs. Jackson Bryant." Emma's body erupted with feelings of blissful explosions. Every nerve ending tingling, her eyes sparkled like a million stars in the night sky. She squeezed Jack's hand as they walked down the aisle toward the door. Turning around to face their family, friends and the few hotel employees in attendance, Jack dipped Emma and planted another passionate kiss on her mouth. Applause from the small group of people filled the room and congratulations were showered upon them.

Emma gazed up at Jack, her mind going in a whirlwind, her heart drumming, her legs weak. He grasped her waist and held her. "Are you okay?"

Smiling at him, she replied, "Yes, my sweet. I'm the happiest woman alive."

He leaned down and kissed her. Her life became perfection on Tuesday, February 14, 2023, at 12:45 p.m. in the Metropolitan Hotel in the heart of Times Square in New York City.

CHAPTER 5

A slew of pictures were taken of Jack and Emma as the newlywed couple, then some of them with Brandi and Ben, Shea and Rob, John, and Stella.

A table for eight sat by the windows overlooking the city. The hotel employees served lunch while their photographer took candid shots of the group. A server opened a bottle of champagne and filled everyone's flutes.

Brandi rose first, tapping her glass and clearing her throat. "Okay, y'all. First, congratulations, Jack, and Emma. The ceremony was beautiful, just like my bestie." She smiled at Emma and Emma blushed. "I'll be the first to admit I was wrong about you Jack. Well, not totally." She shrugged and everyone laughed a little. "But all that's in the past now. Today is about you and Emma beginning anew. Your love for her is more than I ever thought it was. Please take care of her, never hurt her." Brandi looked at Jack, and he nodded her way. "May your marriage be long and happy. Ben, Shea, Rob, and I wish you all the best. We love you. Cheers." Brandi held her flute for all to clank as a group.

John pushed his chair back and stood, putting his hand on Jack's shoulder. "Stella and I don't know all of you very well, but we can see the love you have for Emma and Jack. We wish you both the very best in life. To Jack and Emma."

"To Jack and Emma," everyone said in unison. The group all clanked their champagne flutes once again.

Emma's pulse had quickened during Brandi's and John's speeches. She turned to Jack. Leaning in, she kissed him, then stood

34

and put her hand in his. "To you, my sweet. I love you so damn much. We'll make it through whatever is thrown at us. Whatever comes our way. My darling, Jack. You are my true soulmate." She palmed his cheek and kissed his lips softly.

Standing next to Emma with his arm around her, Jack said, "Guess it's my turn." A light chuckle came from the table. "To my Emma. My beautiful wife." His voice cracking, he bit his lip, then dragged in a deep breath. She tightened her grip on his waist and smiled. Blowing out the breath, Jack continued. "You've made me the happiest man alive. I promise to always be there for you. I'll move oceans to make you happy. You're my number one priority. Nothing comes before you. It's you and I, love. Forever." Jack leaned down as he lifted Emma's chin. Her eyes blinking fast, she touched his flute and kissed him deeply.

A small string quartet set up in the corner of the room while everyone enjoyed lunch. After the plates were cleared, it was time for Jack and Emma's first dance as husband and wife. He went to hold her as he had before, but she took his hands in the proper manner to dance a waltz. The corners of his mouth tugged upward as he took her in his arms. Leaning down, his lips touched her ear. "You took dance lessons, didn't you?"

Smiling, she nodded. "Uh, huh. Surprise." She's always known how to dance, just not the fancy dances. She preferred to dance to fast music where she could throw her hair around and be wild and crazy.

They didn't have a special song to dance to, so they decided to forgo that tradition in the wedding ceremony. Instead, they asked the string quartet to play a standard waltz for them. Emma followed Jack's lead as they glided across the dance floor.

After the waltz ended, the string quartet played a slow song for the entire wedding group of eight to dance to as their photographer snapped more candid photos of everyone. Once the music ended, they all walked over to the cake table. Their cake was a single layer marble flavor with whipped cream frosting. Edible roses and gardenias adorned the cake. Emma had ordered a doctor and artist figurines for the center of their cake, wanting to get away from the traditional bride and groom cake toppers.

As they stood side by side, Jack placed his hand over Emma's on the knife and they cut the first piece of cake before feeding each other.

"Oh, c'mon, Em. Don't be so proper," Brandi said with a grin. A mischievous smile formed on her face as Emma took another piece of cake and slowly brought it to Jack's lips. She placed the cake on his lips and smashed it, dragging her fingers across his smooth jawline.

Bending over, he kissed her. He rubbed cake along her cheek with his tongue. Laughing aloud, she threw back her head as Jack's icing-covered lips drew along her neck and down into her cleavage. She squealed when his velvety tongue licked along her breasts. "Jack!"

Grasping his head, she brought his face back to hers. He wrapped her up in his arms and twirled them around the room.

"I love this woman!" Jack bellowed.

"We can tell, Jack. C'mon and have cake and coffee with us before going off to be alone." Shea winked and patted the seat next to her for Emma to sit.

When everyone finished their cake and coffee, Jack and Emma said their goodbyes and walked hand in hand out of the small ballroom, to the elevators, and up to their suite to be alone.

***

Sweeping Emma off her feet, Jack curled her against his firm chest, and planted a deep kiss on her soft lips. She waved the key card, and he kicked open the hotel suite door. Carrying her over the threshold, he held her as he hung out the 'do not disturb' sign and closed the door. She gripped his broad shoulders tightly as he walked them into the bedroom.

Smiling as bright as the sun on that cold Valentine's Day in New York City, Emma brushed Jack's cheek as he gazed lovingly into her eyes. "I love you more than you'll ever know, Dr. Bryant." She trailed her hands down his arms as he slowly set her on the bed.

Clasping their fingers together, Jack's soft lips grazed her bare shoulder. As he nudged her further onto the bed, his warm breath sent heat to her core as their eyes met. His steel blue gaze mesmerized her, placing her under his trance.

"I love you too, Mrs. Bryant." He crawled onto the bed and laid next to her. His fingers following the delicate curves of her body, arousing her senses to higher levels.

Sucking in several fast breaths, she shivered as the heat chills filled her body. *Oh my, God. I'm Mrs. Bryant.* Her eyes grew wide, and her body shook. She was no longer Emma Taylor. She was Emma Bryant.

Catching Jack's soft blue magnets of pure *fuck me now please,* she placed her hand in his. Bringing it to her breasts, she snuggled into his long, firm body, wanting him to hold her.

"What is it, love?" Jack asked as he kissed her sleek neck.

"We did it," she said. "We're really married, Jack. I…" Emma stopped, sat upright, and faced him. "It feels like a dream. One I never want to wake up from."

"I promise you, it's not a dream." Jack's hand found the zipper on the back of her dress and slowly pulled it down. Shifting himself, he laid behind Emma and kissed her back.

Quivering when Jack's soft lips brushed her skin, Emma turned to face him. Her gown fell from her body, revealing her bare breasts. His hands cupped them as she leaned into him. Taking his time, he circled each of her pebbled nipples with his supple tongue, then nibbled teasingly.

"You'll always be my dream. Take me, Jack. Make me all yours," she purred.

Jack rose from the bed, holding his hand for her to come to him. With her dress hanging at her waist, she wiggled out of it and slipped off her heels as she stood in front of him. The red lace garter belt and ivory panties were all she had on. Tilting her head up to him, she ran her finger along his smooth jawline, the corners of her mouth tugging upward. Her eyes met his, and she instantly drowned in his love.

Smiling sinfully, Jack swiped his hand through her long blonde locks and rested it on the nape of her neck. Holding her tenderly, he trailed his fingers between her ample breasts. He made an infinity symbol across her flat stomach, then glided his long fingers into the lacy waistband of her panties.

Her body trembled at his touch, electric shockwaves shooting through her. "Oh, baby," Emma moaned when his finger slipped into her wet pussy. Her body straightened and wiggled as he finger fucked her. His lips met hers, quieting her moans as another finger went inside her. His velvety tongue plunged into her warm mouth, wrestling with hers.

Pulling back, she squealed as she orgasmed. "Jack, baby. Oh my, God." Peering up at him with a playful grin, she said, "That wasn't fair, my sweet. Come here. I want you naked now." Her eyes widened, and her tongue wet her lips as she reached for his tuxedo jacket.

Pushing his jacket down his arms, she grasped his crisp ivory shirt. She wet her lips again as she held the soft cotton fabric, and with one hard yank, the buttons flew free. Laughing, Emma jumped onto the bed and sat on her knees, wiggling her fingers at him. "Make sweet love to me, Jack. Truly make me your wife."

When he fumbled with his belt, Emma grabbed it and pulled him to her. She quickly unbuckled and unzipped his slacks. Smiling mischievously, she slipped her hand into his boxer briefs, finding her treasure. "Yes, this is what I want. God, how I want you," she moaned.

Jack quickly slid his pants off and crawled onto Emma. He pushed her body down with his. "You're mine, love. I'll make love to you every second of every day. I love you, Emma Bryant. With every ounce of my soul. I love you." Jack's mouth smashed onto hers, diving his tongue in and lapping hers.

Welcoming his passionate kisses, she tasted all of her new husband. Her heart pounded fiercely, her core blazed for him. She cupped his cheeks, gazed deeply into his magnificent sky-blue eyes, and demanded, "Baby, please. Fuck me now."

Her legs fell apart as Jack's firm, fit body glided between them. Pressing his hard shaft into her slick entrance, he let out a moan, "Emma, baby, you're so beautiful. God, you're so wet, so hot."

Pushing deeper into her hole, Jack's hard cock pulsated inside her. She lifted her hips to meet his. Grasping his biceps, she thrusted her body against his. "Baby, I love you," she screamed, feeling her release coming fast. "Oh my, God, Jackson!" Her body shook as she exploded into bliss.

Continuing to make love to her with steady thrusts, Jack's rhythm intensified when he reached his climax. He tightened his grip on her body, cupping her shoulders as his hot semen sprayed inside her. He continued pumping her, and like a well-oiled machine, her young husband fucked her gloriously on their wedding day.

She wrapped her arms and legs around him, kissing him deeply, never wanting him to stop. With one hard thrust, Jack finally collapsed onto Emma. His heated breath on her neck gave her hot chills.

Brushing her dampened hair from her face, Jack asked, "Are you hungry, love?"

With a naughty smile forming, she dragged her hands down his perfect chest, across his sweet ripples, and wrapped her hand around his hard cock. "For you, darling, always for you." As she stroked him, he sighed, then moaned. She nibbled on his ear and whispered, "I'm starving for you, Jack."

"Damn, Em." Jack crawled back on top of her, spreading her legs wide with his body. Kissing her deeply, his tongue twisting with hers. His mouth trailed down her cheek to her neck. "Dinner can wait," he muttered against her shoulder.

"Oh, did you mean hungry for dinner?" She laughed and wrapped herself around him, moving her hips in rhythm with his. His dick glided in and out of her wet pussy, causing incredible friction inside her. Enjoying another ride to her bliss, she dug her fingers into his shoulder blades, holding him tightly to her. Feeling that magnificent man inside her, knowing he was hers for the rest of her life, she ravaged his body, kissing him with all of her passion, all of her love for him. Her walls clenched his heated member when he brought her to incredible orgasms. Ones she'd never reached before.

Bracing himself on his elbows, he cupped her shoulders and thrusted in and out of her for hours. She never stopped coming. One orgasm after the other. She clutched his body hard each time. His kisses were hot, long, and delicious. *Who needs dinner?* She laughed to herself.

Not sure if they'd passed out from fucking endlessly, or if she simply didn't remember falling asleep, she rubbed her eyes. Seeing Jack sleeping with his head on her breast, her heart drummed fast. Softly, she caressed his cheek. Following his smooth jawline to his mouth, her finger trailed along those wonderful lips. "Jack," she squealed when he sucked her finger into his warm mouth. Feeling his velvety tongue curl around her finger, she moaned. Her body humming for him again, she edged herself under him.

Gazing into his soft baby blues, she smiled brightly. No words were needed as Jack's grin revealed all his desires for her. Arching her back as he shoved his stiff rod into her heated core again. She whispered against his shoulder, "All night long, baby. All night long."

"Anything for you, love." Jack's mouth crashed onto hers, his tongue tasting all of her.

Emma had never expected to make love to Jack the entire evening and into the night. But she didn't complain. She never needed anything but him. They'd skipped dinner and enjoyed each other for dessert until their bodies were finally spent.

Kissing him deeply, she held his face in her hands and said, "I love you."

"I love you too." Jack's lips brushed hers softly as they embraced one another, and slumber took them away.

CHAPTER 6

Arriving back in south Florida from their incredibly exhilarating wedding day and night, Jack and Emma had a lot to take care of. First on their to do list was find their forever home.

John recommended Roy Smith to him when Jack and Emma decided to move to south Florida. John had worked with Roy before he and Stella moved to the west coast of Florida. He promised Jack that Roy was the best in south Florida and would find them exactly what they both wanted in their dream home.

On their way home to the rental they were living in, Jack sent Roy a text, letting him know they'd returned and were ready to look at houses immediately. Jack didn't begin working at RG Orthopedic Center for another week, and they wanted to take advantage of his time off to find their dream home.

After unpacking from their New York City trip of a lifetime, Emma ordered them dinner and snuggled on the sofa with Jack waiting for it to arrive. His phone buzzed. He reached across her and picked it off the side table.

"Who is it?" Emma asked.

"It's a text from Roy Smith. He's got us five houses to look at. He sent pictures too." He held his phone for her to see the photos and locations of each of the houses.

Thumbing through each one slowly, she looked at him and said, "I like them all. Don't you?"

"Yeah. I guess we'll have to go to them all and see which one grabs our attention the best. I'll text Roy back and have him set up appointments for them."

Looking up when the doorbell rang, Emma rose from the sofa and answered the door.

"Thanks so much," she said to the delivery person and handed them a tip.

"C'mon, Jack. Dinner's here." She sat the bags of Chinese food on the table and went to the kitchen to get them plates, utensils, and drinks.

With her arms full, she juggled the bottles of whiskey and bourbon, along with the glasses. The tumblers fell from her hands as she neared the table, but Jack caught them and laughed, "You could've asked me to help, love."

"I know but I thought I could handle it all. Thanks for catching the glasses." She leaned into him and grazed his cheek with her lips.

Sitting next to Jack, she picked at her food. She looked at him. "Jack."

"Yes, Emma?" He threw her his sweet, shy smile.

Melting inside, she pushed her desire aside for the moment. "When we get settled in our new home, I want to look for a place to open a new gallery."

"That's a great idea. I can ask Roy if he knows of any open spaces for lease. Or do you want your own building like you had with Brandi?"

"I don't know yet, but I want to keep my options open. If there's a building I really love, then I'll buy it. I have the money from the sale of BE Unique. I want to get back to creating again. Especially my new pieces with my poems. I've written some more. Maybe I'll share them with you," she teased.

"I'll support you in whatever you decide. You don't have to wait until we find our home. Let's talk with Roy tomorrow. I'm sure he can handle finding us a house and you a space for a gallery. John did say Roy's the best here." Jack finished his dinner and drink. As he tipped his glass toward Emma, she nodded. He took her glass and refilled it as she cleaned up the takeout boxes and put the few dishes in the dishwasher.

Retiring to the living room of their small temporary home, Jack flicked on the TV while Emma snuggled against him. The house had two bedrooms and two baths, a small eat-in kitchen, living room and a cement slab out back, which the owner called the lanai. There was a small front porch with enough space for two chairs and a table.

42

When they'd decided to move to south Florida, they hadn't cared what size the rental would be. They'd just wanted to move from west Florida and fast.

After their messy divorces and the loss of Jack's baby with Jenna, they both needed to move away to start fresh. South Florida seemed to be the best place. Emma hoped moving closer to Jack's parents would show them she wanted them in their lives. His dad's resistance and refusal to join them in New York for their wedding caused them both sadness. Emma still held hope Jack's parents would come around. *He can't hate me forever. I'll bring him around. I'll do whatever it takes, for as long as it takes.*

With a new sense of determination, Emma decided she'd figure something out. She wanted Jack's parents in their lives. Jack needed them and she knew what it felt like to not have her parents in her life, especially after her mom died. She never wanted Jack to feel that kind of despair.

***

After walking through three of the five homes Roy had sent them, Emma's hopes of finding their forever home faded. She wasn't happy with any of them. None of them had a pool or lanai. And none of them had a large enough backyard to put a pool in. She hoped to find a house with a pool and large lanai.

Stopping for lunch, Emma, Jack, and Roy sat in a booth of a café. They each ordered sandwiches and waters.

"So, the next two viewings, their locations are better, and the homes are newer." Roy glanced toward Emma.

Peering over her water glass, Emma sat it down and said, "I hope so. I'm anxious to find our house soon. And I want to find a space or building to open my own gallery. I owned one for a while with my best friend. Well, things happened, and she moved out of state, so we sold it. I should have enough cash to buy something outright. Can you help me find something, Roy?"

"Of course, I can. Once we find your home today, I'll send you the list of retail I have available. I'm happy to help you find both." Roy lifted his water glass and tipped it toward Emma and Jack. They did the same back.

Under the table, Emma squeezed Jack's thigh. He placed his hand on hers and smiled.

After paying for lunch, Roy, Jack, and Emma left the café. Driving into the next subdivision, Emma glanced around. Smiling, she felt a warmth come over her. *This feels like home.* She touched Jack's hand as he parked in front of a cream-colored stucco house with beige trim. The landscaping had palm trees and lots of native flowers. She pinched his hand when she noticed the large gardenia bush on the east side of the house and roses on the west.

Stepping out of their car, they joined Roy at the front door as he unlocked it. Walking inside the large foyer, Emma's eyes shot upward to the chandelier above the door. Her hand came to her mouth as she caught her breath. She loved different and beautiful light fixtures. That chandelier looked like a candelabra with at least fifteen candle lights on it. It was a soft gold metal fixture.

"Jack." She tugged on his arm and pointed up. "That's gorgeous."

Nodding, he said, "It is. Let's go see the rest of the house. So far though, I like this one a lot." He placed his arm around her, and they followed Roy into the kitchen to their right.

Her eyes widened as she gazed around the spacious kitchen with an eat-in breakfast nook. The cabinets were light pine with granite countertops in black with specks of gold, browns, and silver. A small square island separated the kitchen and the breakfast nook. A large bay window faced the street. Emma thought they could add a bench to the bay window for a cozy spot she'd enjoy her morning coffee in.

Squeezing his arm and smiling up at Jack, she knew this house was the one. She didn't need to see the rest of the house, but she went through it anyway.

A long bar separated the kitchen from the family room. The dining room was opposite the kitchen and to the left of the foyer. The master suite sat behind the garage, with a large bathroom that held a hidden toilet, a room-long vanity, a Jacuzzi tub, and a separate shower.

The master bedroom was large enough for two king beds, and more. It led out to a lanai with a pool and spa, through French doors. The lanai spanned the entire back of the house. More French doors were in the family room, and a single door from the second guest

44

bathroom led out to the lanai as well. There were three guest bedrooms on the opposite side of the house from the master suite. From the front of the house, the layout ran bedroom, bathroom, bedroom, bedroom, bathroom. Each guest bedroom was fairly decent in sizes and all the same. The bathroom closest to the lanai was smaller than the other guest bath. It only had a toilet, pedestal sink, and a shower stall, whereas the bigger guest bathroom had a toilet, and a full vanity, tub, and shower enclosure.

Tugging harder on Jack's arm, Emma pulled him away from Roy. "Jack, this is the one. Baby, I love it. I don't want to see the last house. I don't care what it looks like. This one *feels* right." She begged him with her eyes to agree.

Jack walked over to Roy. "We want this one, Roy. Emma's in love with this house."

"Okay. I kind of thought she'd be." Roy smiled at Emma. "I can draw up the official offer for the seller when I get back to my office. But let me give them a call since they're my clients too, I should hear back quickly." He turned and walked toward the front of the house, pulling out his phone.

"Oh, Jack," Emma said, turning to him. "I know they'll accept our offer. I can feel it. Everything's falling into place for us." She stretched her arms and wrapped them around his neck when he leaned down, hugging him tightly.

"I hope so, love. Our rental house is kind of small. I want a nice big house to roam around in. One to make love to you in every room. How many rooms does this house have?" Jack scratched his chin and smiled sinfully at her.

"Eleven." She cupped his face and kissed him.

"Don't forget the walk-in closet in the master suite. I count twelve." His grin filled his face.

"I can't wait, baby." Her body trembled all over.

In a few minutes, Roy came back to Emma and Jack with a wide smile. "Congratulations. The Millers have accepted your offer."

Emma grabbed Jack's hands, "Oh my, God. Jack! It's ours." It took all of her strength, but she spun them both around.

"Thanks, Roy. We appreciate your help with this." Jack extended his hand to Roy. They shook hands, then Emma held hers out to him too.

"I'll set up a date for closing. It'll probably be in a few weeks to a month. I'm sorry we can't make it sooner," Roy said.

"That's fine. Most of our things from the west coast are in a POD anyway. When you give us the closing date, we'll schedule the POD to be delivered here," Jack said.

She bounced on her toes and tugged on Jack's arm, her smile filling her face, her eyes dazzling like stars in the nighttime sky.

"I'll call you as soon as the date is set. Congratulations again." Roy walked with them toward the front door.

Emma slipped her hand into Jack's, locking their fingers as she took one last look at the chandelier, then walked to their car.

Ready to burst at the seams with happiness, Emma looked up at Jack and asked, "Where are we going to celebrate?"

"Where do you want to go?"

"I don't know. Stop someplace where we can order champagne to toast our new home."

"Whatever you ask for, I'll give you." Jack brushed her cheek and drove them to a nice restaurant for dinner.

CHAPTER 7

Waking up in Jack's warm embrace a month later, Emma pinched herself for what was the millionth time since getting together with him. She laid in the arms of the man she adored, in their new forever home in south Florida.

They'd moved in and began unpacking over the weekend. She needed to call her sister and best friend to let them know she and Jack were ready for each of them to come and visit. They had plenty of space if they wanted to come at the same time.

Feeling Jack move beside her, she rolled to face him. Knowing he had a busy day at work, she brushed his cheek as he greeted her. "Good morning, beautiful." His lips grazed hers.

"Good morning, gorgeous." She kissed him back, slipping her tongue between his full, soft lips, getting a sweet taste of her favorite flavor. "It feels so wonderful waking up in your arms in our new home, baby." She gazed into his soft baby blues as they smiled at her.

"If we had to, I'd live in a shack, as long as I'm with you." Jack engulfed her with his arms, kissing her lips, her cheek, her neck. "Mmm, I want you so much, but I have to get ready for work," he groaned into her warm shoulder.

"I love you, go and shower. You can make it up to me later." She kissed him softly and trailed her eyes after him as he walked into the bathroom.

Her eyes darted to his phone that laid on the nightstand when it sounded. She scooted on the bed and glanced at the preview. Her heart pinched hard when she saw the text came from a Michelle. She

47

couldn't recall anyone from RG Orthopedic Center named Michelle. Her nerve endings tingled, then chilled. *No, no way Jack would ever cheat on me. He loves me. He knows I love him. No! No! No!*

Emma raked her hands through her hair and slapped her face. She knew Jack loved her and only her. She made a mental note to ask him about Michelle when he finished getting ready for work.

She slipped into her silk robe and went to the kitchen to make coffee and order them a light breakfast. Opening her phone to the food delivery app, she found the closest café and placed her order. Their breakfast arrived just as Jack appeared from their bedroom.

Grabbing his coffee and bagel, he walked to the door. "I love you." He tugged her slight frame against his towering body. She stood on her tip toes, puckering her lips. Sliding his arm up her back to her neck, he held her as he kissed her deeply. "See you soon, love." He slid his hand back down and squeezed her bare ass.

"Oh, hey. That's not fair," she cried as Jack opened the door to leave. "You've got me all worked up now, and you're leaving for the day." Her bottom lip shot out as the edges of her mouth curved down.

"Tonight, I promise." He winked.

"Oh, before I forget. You got a text while you were in the shower."

"I did?" Jack's eyes grew wide.

"Yeah, from a Michelle. Is that a new nurse at the center?"

"Um…," He rubbed his chin and looked down at the pavement. "Oh, yes, she's the newest RN the center hired, and she just started going around with me when I see patients. I have many nurses working with me."

"It's okay, baby. I don't remember every client's name without looking at their contract sometimes." Her heart settled and she let out the nervous breath she'd held. Tilting her head up, she crinkled her lips. He leaned down and met her lips with his. "See you tonight." She turned and went back inside their home. Taking a seat in a chair at the table by the bay window, something nagged at her as she watched Jack drive off. She trusted him with her life, but a chill crawled through her body. To stop her mind from overthinking, she went back to bed and closed her eyes.

***

Bolting up when she heard her phone ringing, Emma felt for it on the bed. Finding it under the sheet, she answered it, "This is Emma."

"Emma, it's Roy. Where are you?"

Smacking her forehead, she scurried off the bed and ran into the bathroom to freshen up. "Sorry, Roy. I fell back asleep after Jack left for work. I'm on my way." She took a second to check herself in the vanity mirror. Ruffling her long blonde locks with her hands, she pulled it all up into a messy bun and threw on some light makeup. She slipped into her jeans and a shirt, then headed to the garage and went to meet with Roy.

Arriving at the first address on the list Roy had sent to her, Emma drew in a breath as she parked her car. She looked at the building and noticed it sat angled on the corners of the two streets, just as BE Unique had. The building before her looked like the twin of her former gallery, and she wondered if she wanted to recreate BE Unique or start with a whole new vision.

Getting out of her car, she scanned the outside of the brick building as she walked to the front doors.

"This one is the more expensive one of the two, Emma," Roy said as he met her there. "So, keep your mind open to the next one." He unlocked the double doors and allowed her to enter before him.

The interior of this potential gallery didn't look anything like BE Unique. It was one large room, with ceramic tile flooring. She walked around the entire room and down a short hallway to the office, a restroom, and one storage room. It was really all she'd need since it would be just her. Even though the outside sat exactly like BE Unique had, the interior was different and smaller, which surprised her. The outside of the building had given the appearance of a larger space.

Rubbing her chin, she turned to Roy. "I need to see the other one, then I'll decide."

"Okay, let's go. It's not far from here and it's on the intercoastal." He led her out of the building and locked the doors.

At the next building, Emma stepped out of her car and met Roy at the entrance. This building faced Coral Street. She panned the outside carefully. A Spanish-style building with two small front windows. "Thanks," she said to Roy as he waved his arm for her to enter ahead of him.

Gasping at the inside of the building, her eyes widened. She spun around. Sucking in several deep breaths, she noticed the wood flooring, and the high ceilings with crown molding. The size of the space was what she loved. Even though there were interior walls that would need to go, she still knew this one was the best of the two. She'd noticed some cracking around the windows and thought she'd need replacements. She walked down the hallway to see the other rooms. She found four rooms, but there was no private bathroom, and the public one desperately needed updated. *I'll need to hire a contractor if I choose this one.* She rummaged through her purse and found a piece of paper and wrote an amount on it, lower than what the sellers were asking. She'd hoped with all the needed repairs they'd come down in price.

"Roy," she called out as she made her way back to where he waited for her.

"Yes?" He turned toward her.

"I love the space here, and the rooms in the back are sufficient to make into my office and storage rooms. There isn't a private bathroom and the one I'd use for a public restroom needs work. I see other things I'll need to hire a contractor to repair, or I may want to gut it all and remodel the entire inside." Emma ran her hand across the back of her neck and squinted. She looked up at Roy. "Ask if they'll take this number." She handed him the folded piece of paper.

"Let me call the seller." He opened his phone and made the call.

Emma walked around the inside again, making a note of the walls she'd hoped could be taken out in the app on her phone. She also wrote down a list of things she would need to be done before she could open for business.

"Emma," Roy called to her.

"Yes." She walked toward him.

A smile forming on his face, he nodded his head. "Congratulations. They've accepted your offer. I'll set up the closing and call you."

Smiling wide, she said, "Great, I need to go to my bank and transfer the cash to my main account. I'm available whenever." She extended her hand to Roy, and he shook it.

"I'll call you later." Roy slid his phone into his briefcase as they walked to the exit.

"Thanks so much for your help. I can't believe I found this place." She walked out ahead of him, then stopped and turned to him. "Oh, do you have a list of contractors you're familiar with? I'm definitely going to need one before I can open to the public."

"Of course. I'll email you the list the company has on file. They're all exceptional, and have been thoroughly vetted, so you won't need to worry."

At her car, Roy held the door for her. "That's a relief. Thanks again, Roy. You've been a big help to Jack and me." Emma slid into her car as Roy closed the car door for her and nodded. She waved to him and drove home.

***

When Jack arrived home, Emma had the dining room table set with candles, their dinner and drinks waiting for him.

"Whoa, what's this for?" he asked as he wrapped his arms around her and kissed her cheek.

Turning while in his arms, she cupped his face and kissed him. "I have a surprise to tell you." Her smile filled her face and her eyes danced. "Sit." She sat in his lap after he sat in the chair.

"Emma, what's going on?"

She held up her phone with the picture of the future home of her new gallery. "This, Jack. I bought it," she squealed and hugged him around his neck.

"That's fantastic news. I knew Roy would help you find your new place. Where is it and when can I see it?" Jack took her phone in his hand and thumbed through the few pictures Emma had taken.

"It's on the intercoastal, in a fabulous location. It needs to be renovated though. So, it'll be a little bit before I can have my first exhibition." She lifted Jack's face to hers.

"The space looks perfect for you. I know it will become yours once the renovations are complete." Jack laid her phone on the table and embraced her dainty body. She leaned against his firm chest and laid her head on his shoulder.

"I'm so excited for this new adventure, baby." She went to kiss his cheek when Jack turned his face to hers. She gazed into his baby blue eyes and smiled.

"This is just the beginning of it all, love." His lips covered hers and he kissed her deeply.

CHAPTER 8

Emma had set up several easels in the spare bedroom she'd turned into her home art studio, and each day that week, she'd spent her time painting her poems.

Dragging out the bag of pencils, she laid it open on the long dresser. She stacked the canvases on each easel, then opened her journal where all her poetry waited for her to paint. Thumbing through the titles, she settled on her first poem.

She thought for a few seconds, conjuring an image that best fit the poem she'd written. *Hot, that's what this painting needs to be. Flames, and sparks.* She painted the canvas black, then let it dry. Next, she carefully drew the outlines of those images, beginning with the hot fire. Like bursts with the flames on the canvas, then she used a thin paintbrush to write her poem in the center with orange paint:

OH BABY

Oh baby,
My heart belongs to you.
I watch you sleep,
My beautiful lover.
In your arms,
My body is ablaze for you.
Once only a dream to me,
Oh baby,

You've made my reality
Simply perfection.

Stepping back, she tapped the end of the paintbrush to her lips. Happy with her piece, she woke her phone again and chose the poem titled, 'Your Eyes' to be her next piece.

Drawing a caricature-like image of Jack, she picked a medium paintbrush and mixed the blue paint until it matched his eyes. Smiling, she felt his love all around her as she painted. The focus of this painting and poem were his eyes. Jack's mesmerizing, gorgeous blue hues of pure love. She finished painting his dark brown hair, then sipped on her coffee while deciding the shade of blue she'd use for her poem.

Using the blue she'd used for Jack's eye color, she began to pen the poem with a thin paintbrush. She stepped up to the easel and began to write her poem:

YOUR EYES

I drowned in your soft blue eyes that first time we met.
Your gaze held mine for much too long.
I knew then you were trouble.
Good trouble that I wanted to be in.

Your eyes spoke to my soul.
We made a deep connection that will never be broken.
Baby, your fuck me eyes trapped me
The instant they caught mine.
Oh, your eyes.

Stepping back again, she felt this one was complete. She tapped the paintbrush handle to her lower lip and bit down on the end. Nodding to herself, she looked at the list of poems remaining and painted two more.

With all four of her canvasses finished, Emma plopped a small blob of black paint onto the palette and picked up a thin paintbrush. She signed each piece, *EB Taylor.*

"That's stunning…"

"Jack, you startled me." Turning quickly toward him, her heart skipped a beat. She slid to her right just a bit to shield Jack's view of her signed name. She hadn't painted in a while, and she hadn't had the chance to talk with him about her keeping Taylor as her professional name. Looking up at him standing in the doorway, she wrinkled her brow and bit her lip. She jammed her hands into the pockets of her painting smock.

Holding the doorframe above his head, he said, "I'm sorry, love. I didn't mean to interrupt." He walked into the make-shift art studio and took a closer look at each of her paintings.

She swallowed hard as her gaze danced around the room. She asked him, "What are you doing home so early? Did your patients cancel? Why didn't you call or text me you were on your way home? Jack." Emma grabbed his arm and tugged.

Ignoring her questions, he rubbed his chin, then pointed to her signature and sighed heavily. "What's this? You're not changing your name?"

Taking a few seconds to get her thoughts in order, she removed her smock and stood next to him. "Oh, Jack. That's my professional name only. I'm known as EB Taylor in the art world. All my previous work is signed that way." She placed the palette and paintbrush on the dresser and reached for him. Jack took a step back and shoved his hands in the pockets of his scrubs. Her eyebrows furrowed as she stepped closer to him. "Jack, please, baby. I need you to understand this." She pointed to her signature. "It's only for my art." Tugging his hand from his pocket she placed it on her heart. "In here, I'm EB Bryant. Where it matters most. And EB, while it's Emma Brooke, is also Emma Bryant. And will be for the rest of my life." She looked up at Jack when he pulled his hand free from hers.

"I do understand, but I don't like it at all. I don't want you to be known as anything Taylor. That's not who you are anymore. You're Emma Brooke Bryant. Why can't you drop the Taylor part and sign your art going forward as EB?" Jack placed his hands on his hips and stood his ground.

"No, you don't understand. I can't drop the Taylor part, Jack. Dammit. You're a professional, I'm sure you have colleagues who've kept their maiden names…,"

"None of them are my wife and Taylor isn't your maiden name, Emma." Jack's eyes turned dark. His jaw tightened, his lips a thin line.

Her head fell to her chest, her eyes filled with tears. "Jack, please. I don't want to argue with you about how I sign my art." Stepping toward him, she slipped her arms around his waist. She pressed her cheek to his chest and listened to his slow heartbeat. "I love you. But please don't ask me to do this," she whimpered and hugged him tightly.

"I love you too, Em. I won't force you to do anything, but I want you to know I don't like it. Not one bit." His arms rested on her shoulders.

Her heart clenched as she sensed his reluctance to hold her the same as she'd held him. She squeezed him again, then tilted her head up to him. Noticing his hard glare and dark eyes, she released her embrace and stepped back from him.

She needed space, and air. Her throat tightened as she hung her head. "I need some air." Emma spun and walked away from Jack. Once out of his sight, she ran out onto the lanai and sat on the rim of the Jacuzzi, her head in her hands. Her body shook. She couldn't believe their first argument since being married was about her professional name. *Why doesn't he understand? It's just a signature. It's not who I am. Fuck!*

While out on the lanai alone, Emma thought of ways to convince Jack that using Taylor for her art was just the way things were. She needed to find a way to soften him to being okay with it. Then an idea came to her. *The gallery. I'll name my gallery, EB's.*

Hoping that'd be a compromise he'd accept, she brushed her hands through her hair and went to stand when she felt his hand on her shoulder.

"Emma, I...," Jack began and sat beside her.

Putting her finger to his lips, she said, "It's okay. I have an idea. I want to name my gallery EB's Gallery. Do you like it? I won't use EB Taylor for the gallery's name, only for my artwork. And maybe over time, I can begin to sign my pieces EB. But not right now, Jack." She took his hand in hers and squeezed it.

"I do like the name. Emma Bryant's Gallery, and I do understand, love. It hurt to see Matt's last name. You're my wife now. And I know changing your name isn't something you can do

56

immediately. You're an established artist known as EB Taylor. So, while I don't like it. I love you and will support you in everything." His arms engulfed her.

She leaned into his embrace and slipped her arms around him, squeezing him tightly. She felt his arms tighten around her. Tilting her head up to him, her heart warmed, her body tingled. "Thank you, baby. Your love and support is all I need."

Jack leaned down and kissed Emma deeply. Placing his hand on her cheek, he brushed his thumb gently across it. "You'll always have me, Emma. Always."

CHAPTER 9

With Jack unable to accompany her at the meetings with the project managers, Emma paced around the future space of her new gallery. She looked out the small windows as she passed by them. She definitely wanted these two front windows replaced with picture windows. She wanted passerby's to be able to see inside in hopes they'd come in and become paying customers.

She spent the day meeting with the contractor company's project managers. She watched each of them take notes of what she wanted done, and the necessary repairs and upgrades she'd made a list of.

Nearing the end of her day, she waited at the makeshift counter for her last appointment to show up. She looked up when the front door opened and a man with a striking resemblance to Matt, her ex-husband, entered. He had the same messy hair, but a little lighter in color. He appeared to be the same six foot tall as Matt was. She blinked quickly to clear her head and hopped off the stool.

Meeting him in front of the counter, Emma said, "Hi, I'm Emma Bryant. It's nice to meet you."

"Hello, I'm Doug Barry with B&T Construction. Nice to meet you too, Emma." Doug looked around the room and opened a leather notebook. "So, tell me what you need from us?"

Staring at Doug, she couldn't move her eyes from him. He had the same big brown eyes as Matt. He was fit like Matt, he even sounded a little like Matt.

Not wanting to ask a personal question of someone she'd just met, she handed him the folder. "Here's my list of what's needed to be repaired, replaced and what I hope can be removed."

"Let me take a look at this." Placing Emma's folder on the counter, Doug flipped it open and carefully scanned each item listed.

Emma went back behind the counter and hopped onto the stool. She twisted her wedding rings as she watched him read her list of what she needed and wanted done for her gallery. She glanced at her watch when she saw him rub his neck and made a note in his folder. She needed to settle herself. After a day of doing the same thing with three other project managers, her nerves were about shot.

"Okay." Emma jumped when Doug finally spoke to her. "This all looks good, Emma. Let me take this back to the office and I'll send our estimate to you tomorrow."

Hopping off the stool, she walked toward him and extended her hand to him. "Thanks, Doug. I'll make my decision by the end of the week on which company I'll go with. Either way, you'll hear from me."

Shaking Emma's hand, Doug said, "Great. I promise we'll do the best job if you pick us."

She smiled and stared again at Doug. "Are you sure you're okay, Emma?"

"I'm sorry. I just can't get over how much you look like my Matt…," Her hand came to her mouth, "I mean my ex-husband, Matt." She dragged her hand through her hair and blew out a breath as she walked with Doug to the door. "We'll talk soon. Have a great night."

"Thank you, Emma." He pushed the door open and left her standing in the doorway.

Emma couldn't move her eyes from Doug as he walked to his car. She noticed his stride matched Matt's.

Turning, Emma retrieved her purse from the counter, then turned off the lights and locked the door. She went to her car and drove home.

***

Emma waited for Jack to come home and share all of her news from the day. She knew he'd be as excited for her as she was. Lying across their bed, she closed her eyes.

Feeling his hand on her shoulder, she jumped. "Oh, shit. I must've fallen asleep." Rubbing her eyes awake, she stretched as Jack sat next to her. "How was your day?" She petted his arm and snuggled close to him.

"Busy. Let's order pizza." Jacks phone chirped and he pulled it from his pocket. Glancing at it, he laid it face down onto the nightstand.

"Who was that?"

"Michelle again. I'm sorry. She's so new, she has a lot of questions." His eyes raised.

"I trust you." Emma rose from the bed and went to the bathroom to splash some water on her face. She couldn't shake the chill that ran through her. Hoping Jack wasn't lying to her, she let it go.

When she came out of the bathroom, Jack wasn't in their bedroom and his phone wasn't on the nightstand. She walked out of their room and found him on the sofa, with his phone in hand.

"Jack," she said as she stood beside him.

He placed his phone face down again and looked up at her. His lips were in a thin line and his eyes came together. "I ordered dinner. It should be here in a few minutes." His gaze dropped to the floor, and he raked his hand through his hair.

"Thanks, baby." She sat next to him and slid her arms around him. "I saw the four men from the construction companies today. All four companies would do the renovations, but one of the companies seemed to be the perfect fit. So, I've made my decision." She looked at him when the doorbell rang.

Rising from the sofa, Jack went to answer the door. Emma went to the kitchen and grabbed plates. She placed them on the bar, then got glasses and poured them each a drink. Jack thanked the delivery person and joined Emma in the kitchen. They sat at the bar and enjoyed dinner.

"Which company did you decide on, Em?"

"I'm going with B&T. There was something about Doug, the project manager, he made me feel comfortable and confident that B&T is the company to do the renovations I need done." Emma knew what it was about Doug that made her feel that way, but she didn't see any reason to tell Jack.

The new gallery was all hers. When Jack and Emma married, they decided to keep their monies separate. She insisted on this because of his parents. She didn't want them to accuse her of marrying Jack for his money. They each had checking accounts of their own and a joint account for household expenses that they contributed to equally. She knew she could take care of herself if she had to. While she always respected Jack's opinions, she made all the decisions about her gallery on her own.

"It's your gallery, love. I'll be by your side and support every decision you make. I can't wait for your grand opening and your first solo exhibition."

"Thanks, baby. I can't wait either. I need to call Shea and Brandi with my news." She took his hand in hers just as his phone chirped again. "Jack, really? I mean why does she text you? Why not Dr. Ruben or Dr. Grayson?" Dropping his hand, Emma slid off the stool.

"Because she's my nurse, Em. I'll let her know tomorrow that the after-center hours texts should stop." He reached for her hand again.

Letting him hold it this time, she tried to smile, but her anxiety rose. She pulled her hand free and crossed her arms. *He's not cheating on me. I know he's not.*

"Emma."

She turned her back to him and wiped her eyes. "Em, I'll talk to her tomorrow." Jack came around to face her. Tilting her chin up, he leaned down and kissed her tenderly. "I promise."

Seeing what she'd hoped was his complete honesty in his sky-blue eyes, she leaned into him and wrapped her arms around him. Wanting to trust him fully, she gave in again and decided to let Jack take care of his work issues.

CHAPTER 10

On her way to the gallery, Emma stopped by her favorite coffee shop, the Coffee Castle. She'd found it soon after she'd closed on her building and made a point to stop in each morning when she came to her future gallery.

Looking at her phone as she entered the coffee shop, she bumped into the body exiting. "Oh, excuse me...," Emma began.

"No worries, Em." He grasped her arm as she stepped back from him. Jerking her head upward, her eyes wide as she stared at her ex-husband.

"Matt, what the...." She stiffened her stance and pulled her arm free of Matt's grasp. "What are you doing in south Florida?" she asked, her voice rose an octave as she stepped inside, doing her best to stay composed.

"It's nice to see you too, Emma." Matt followed her as she walked toward the counter.

Stopping mid-stride, she turned to face him. "Yeah, sure. Nice to see you too, but what are you doing here?" Her hands on her hips as she stared at him.

"I have a big job down here I want to stay on top of. It's important to me it gets done exactly as my client has asked." He stepped toward her. "You know I've always been a hands-on guy." He smiled.

"I didn't know Marcus had clients in south Florida." Emma smiled back. She didn't see the harm in being polite to him. They were divorced and she'd hoped they could be friends again, but she didn't expect to see him so soon. Pulling her sweater together, she nodded toward the counter. "I need to get my coffee and go to my gallery. Oh, you don't know." She met his big brown eyes and recognized his familiar warmth.

"Okay. What don't I know?" He shrugged and placed his hand on her shoulder to move her out of the line forming behind them.

Smiling up at him as he held a stool for her, she hopped onto it. Still the gentleman he always was. He took a stool beside her at the long bar.

"I bought a building. I own my own gallery." She smiled brightly.

"Congratulations. I'm sure it will be fantastic. When is your grand opening? I'd like to come. If it's okay." He raised his eyes to her and touched her hand laying on the bar.

Looking at Matt's hand covering hers, she knew she should pull it back, but she'd caused him so much pain, so she left her hand there. "It's going to be a while. My building needs renovated, and I've hired a company, B&T. Have you heard of them?" she asked as she glanced at her watch when the reminder to meet Doug vibrated.

"I have. They're good, Emma. They'll give you exactly what you want." Matt pinched her hand and smiled.

"That's good to hear. I need to order my coffee and get going. I'm meeting my project manager there this morning." She slid from the stool and looked up at Matt. "It's really good to see you. I hope your project goes well."

"Thanks, Em. I know it will." He leaned down to her.

"Matt." She pushed on his shoulder. "I need to go." Her cheeks felt hot as she shook her head from side to side.

Matt raised his hands, then stepped back from Emma. He waved his arm for her to pass. "Good luck with everything. I hope to see you again soon," he called after her.

At the counter, she turned quickly and nodded to him. She waved, then turned back to the barista and ordered her coffee.

***

Seeing Doug Barry standing outside of her gallery, Emma picked up her pace. When she got close enough, she said, "Sorry for the delay. I ran into someone I knew at the Coffee Castle."

"Oh, no problem. I just got here a minute ago"

"Okay, let's go inside. I have somethings to add to my list of renovations." She squinted as she looked at him. She hoped B&T Construction would work with her extra ideas without too much trouble.

Placing her coffee cup on the counter, she handed Doug her list. "This won't be a problem, will it? I don't care what it costs. I can pull out a loan. I want this place absolutely perfect for when I open." She squeezed her right eye shut and looked at him with the other.

After running into Matt, she still couldn't get over Doug's resemblance to him, even though Matt's appearance had changed since their divorce. His disheveled hair was cut closer to his head. He was grayer. Matt had been more of a casual, t-shirt and jeans guy when they were married. This morning, he wore jeans, a white button-down shirt, and a dark blazer. She took note of how handsome he still looked.

Emma sipped on her coffee while Doug read over her list. He glanced up when he finished. "No. This won't be a problem at all. It may add a few weeks, but we can handle it. You're my first priority as far as all my projects go. I'll need to let my boss know of your added items. I'm sure he'll sign off on them. And I need to be sure with the engineers these renovations can be done. Can I call you later tonight?" He asked as he placed the list in his briefcase.

"Yes. My ex-husband worked as a project manager, so I do know a little about it. I'm pretty sure what I'm asking for can be done. But if not, we can work something out." Emma came from behind the counter and led Doug to the table and two chairs she had set up for them.

"We definitely can. Now let me show you the plans we have drawn up for what you gave me. I explained to the architect what you said to me, and I showed him your art. I wanted him to get the feel of exactly what you wanted." He rolled open the plans over the square table sitting between them.

Cupping her mouth, she blinked rapidly as she looked over the drawings. Her heart raced, and she wanted to wrap Doug up into a hug but refrained from doing so. She knew that was highly inappropriate.

"Oh my, God. I... I... this is..." she stammered.

"Emma? Are you happy with these drawings?"

"Yes, oh my, gosh. I have a vision of what I want my gallery to be, these drawings enhanced all of my thoughts." Taking a moment, she thought about her new gallery, her new home with Jack, keeping hope Jack's parents would one day accept her. Everything was falling into place. Her life's trajectory was going in the right direction for Emma to have her happily ever after with Jack. She took several deep breaths, trying to calm her excitement. "Have you submitted these for permitting yet? Or do we have to wait on the engineer's drawings?" She raised her eyes to Doug.

"We have to wait." He smiled and showed Emma the rest of the plans. "But I can let you know later approximately how long before the plans will be done and submitted for approval. And a start date for us to get in here and demolish what needs to be. Then a timeline for you so you can plan your opening." After rolling the plans and sliding them into a tube, Doug asked, "Is there anything else you'll need from us?"

Scratching her forehead, she looked at him. "I don't think so. I know it'll take a bit longer than first thought, but that's okay." Emma knew she had plenty to do to keep her busy. She had to sort through her older pieces and decide which ones she'd use for her grand opening. A heaviness came over her as she sighed when she realized most of her inventory revolved around her life with Matt. She sat quietly as she folded her hands in her lap while she remembered her sunrise painting she'd done the morning before she fell and injured her shoulder. She had many paintings that reminded her of Matt and their happy life. But now she wanted to feature her poem paintings. All of them centered around Jack and her love for him.

"Emma, Emma," Doug said.

"Oh, sorry. My mind wandered away for a bit." She patted her cheeks and rose from her chair. "I'll have a key made for you today and meet you back here in the morning, okay?"

"That's fine. The sooner we get started, the sooner you can have your grand opening." Doug followed her to the front door.

"I won't be in every day, but maybe once or twice a week to check on the progress. If it's okay."

"Of course. You'll have to wear a hard hat during the demolition. I'll have an extra one for you when you stop in." He reached for the door handle and pulled it open.

"Thanks so much. I'll see you in the morning."

"Sounds good. Have a good day." He waved and left.

Closing and locking the door, Emma walked around her future gallery. She had a list of color themes in her mind to use for the chairs she'd need. She loved burgundy with cream or brown, but also purples and reds and two-tone blues. Regardless of the coloring scheme, she would require an interior designer, so she dug in her purse and pulled out her phone.

Glancing at her notes, she saw caterer at the top of it. She shuddered when she thought about hiring one. Jack's ex-wife had been her's and Brandi's caterer at their events at BE Unique. And while Jenna and her girls did a wonderful job for them, hiring a caterer would be stressful. She knew Jenna didn't live locally so the chance of running into her was slim. She wondered how Jenna was doing since the loss of her baby. Jack still had bad days when they'd be out together, and a young family walked by or sat near them at a restaurant. She hoped one day none of that would affect him, but only time would tell. Deciding to keep an open mind in the process of looking for a caterer, she'd interview as many as she could to find the right one for her big night. She added interior designer to the list and remembered she needed to call her sister, Shea.

Thumbing to Shea's number, she sat behind the counter and touched Shea's name.

"Hi, Emma," Shea answered.

"Hi, Shea. How's everyone?" Emma asked.

"We're all great. Busy. You caught me on a break, good timing. How's Jack?"

"He's good. He got the position he wanted with the private orthopedic center. He's dealing with the Jenna and baby thing. It's a process."

"That's good to hear. Give him time and love. Losing a child is tough. I know you know that. So, how are you?"

Her heart pinched when she'd remembered all the failed attempts she and Matt went through to try to have a family. She'd had one successful fertility attempt take, but she miscarried before her second trimester. After that, she told Matt she couldn't try again, it was much too emotionally draining. His answer surprised her, and she clenched at her heart when she heard his voice in her memory say, "You're all I need to be a family."

"Emma, you still there?" Shea asked.

"Yes, I am, sorry." She shook her head to clear her thoughts. "I have good news to share. I bought a building and I'm going to make it my new gallery."

"Holy crap, Em. That's fantastic news. Where? Have you named it? When's your opening? I want to be there," Shea said.

"It's on the intercoastal. I'm going to name it, 'EB's Gallery.'"

"I love it. It fits perfectly since it'll only be your stunning art. So, when's the grand opening, please tell me. I need to make our flight reservations."

"I will, I promise. The building needs renovated and that'll take a while. But as soon as I can, I'll let you and Brandi know. I want you both here with me and Jack."

"Okay, Emma. Hey, I need to go, I'm being summoned to the floor. I'll call you soon. Love you."

"I love you too, Shea. Bye." Emma touched the red phone icon and stuffed the phone into her purse.

Taking one more walk around the nearly empty building, Emma envisioned how her opening night would look. She'd feature her poem paintings and her newer pieces since she and Jack had married. She'd been able to keep the artist and writer's block at bay. Her journal app kept all her poems safe for when she was ready to paint them onto canvas.

She left her gallery and called Brandi on her way home, filling her in with everything she told Shea. Emma couldn't wait for opening night and having Jack by her side as she welcomed everyone to her very own gallery.

CHAPTER 11

It'd been six glorious months since they'd married. Their lives had become busier between Jack's work at the center and being on call every third weekend at the hospital.

Emma spent her days creating new works of art in her home studio, getting ready for her grand opening exhibition.

The renovations on her gallery moved along at a steady pace. She went in twice a week to have Doug walk her around and show her the progress that'd been made. Her vision was coming to life before her very eyes.

With the busyness of their professional lives, their home and sex life became less active. Emma missed the closeness they'd shared during the tumultuous time before they married and the few months right after. She always tried to be home when he should've been, but she felt Jack pulling away from her and getting more involved with his work and less with her.

One Sunday morning, the bright sunshine woke Emma as she and Jack enjoyed a quiet weekend relaxing at home.

His arms tightened around her as she rolled over to greet him. Feeling his erection as she turned, her body quivered all over. He buried his face into her warm neck and kissed it softly. His tongue trailed along her cheek. When his lips met hers, she tasted her favorite flavor.

"Good morning, beautiful." Jack's baby blues smiled at her.

"Good morning, gorgeous, I've missed this." Her hand slid between them as she curled her fingers around his hard cock.

"Mmm. I've missed you, love." Spreading her legs, she welcomed him as he moved his body between them. His hands gliding along her body, he caressed her soft skin. Kissing her stiff nipple, he circled his tongue around it, causing her to tremble beneath him.

"Oh, Jack," she moaned as she lifted her hips to him, inviting him to penetrate her. She needed him inside her. It'd been much too long since they'd made love.

With one swift move, his hard dick glided between her slick folds and plunged into her hot aching pussy.

"Baby, go slow. I want to savor you for a while," she purred against his cheek.

"You feel so incredible, Em. Jesus!"

His cock rubbed her core perfectly. The heat rising inside her body made her orgasms intense. She wrapped her legs around his waist and dug her heels into his ass, pushing him deeper into her center. They rocked to a smooth rhythm as their bodies smacked together over and over. His velvety tongue danced with hers. His hands cupped her shoulders as he braced himself on his forearms.

Catching his loving gaze, Emma brushed his cheek and smiled. "You're my everything, Jack. No matter what." She blinked quickly as he kissed her lips softly.

"I won't ever hurt you, Emma. Please don't doubt me," his voice cracked as he kissed her.

He slowly pushed his hard shaft into her again, and her back arched as she moaned with pleasure. His lips sucked on her neck, then her collarbone. Grazing his soft lips across her skin, he took her breast into his mouth. He nibbled tenderly on her pebbled nipple as she moaned again.

"Please don't stop, baby. Oh, dear God. Don't stop," she begged him.

Wanting to fulfill Emma completely, Jack thrusted into her slower as her center walls clenched around his throbbing dick. Her dainty body jerked hard as her arms and legs tightened around his long firm body.

She cried out, "Jack, Jack, take me higher." She cupped his cheeks and grabbed his gaze. "Make me come like never before, baby." She pulled his face to hers and smashed their lips together. Her tongue darted into his warm mouth and wrestled with his.

69

"Goddamn, love." Jack slid his arms under her and rolled them over, yanking her onto his groin.

Splaying her hands on his tight chest, she rode him. She bounced on him, throwing her head back and squeezing her thighs against his. Jack's fingers rubbed her swollen clit when she leaned back from him. Circling her clit as she quickened her gyrations on him, he groaned and thrusted upward into her wet pussy. "You're driving me crazy, Emma. I can't hold on. Oh, Christ." His hands gripped her hips as he flipped them over, so he was on top of her.

With Emma under him again, Jack buried his cock into her as deep as their bodies allowed. Her body felt shockwaves as she dissolved into pleasure when Jack came, and she hit her release.

"Baby, you're amazing. I love you so much." Emma traced her finger around his ear and kissed his salty lips.

Lying to her side, Jack covered her flat mid-section with his hand. "I love you too."

After a few minutes of cuddling, Emma sat up and faced Jack. She folded her legs, leaned down and grazed her lips across his. "Jack," she began.

"Yes, love." He placed his hand on her knee.

"I've been thinking." She slammed her eyes closed and scrunched her nose.

"About what?"

Opening her eyes, she said, "I want to invite your parents to my gallery's grand opening. It's still a while off, and maybe a more public setting would help. Your dad could mingle and not feel trapped. That way he wouldn't be forced to talk to me if he doesn't want to. What do you think?" She took his hand in hers and intertwined their fingers.

"We can invite them, but Em. Please don't get your hopes up. I know my dad and he's the most stubborn man ever born. Knowing him, he'll take Mom on a vacation just so they'll have an excuse to not attend your gallery's big night." Jack's mouth turned down and his eyes came together. He sighed.

Letting go of his hand, she folded her hands in her lap. Her lips pressed slightly, and her eyebrows came together. Her head fell to her chest as she sighed heavily. She didn't know what else she could do or offer to have his parents accept her, or simply meet her. Her shoulders slumped.

Jack lifted her face and said, "Hey, I'll text Mom in a few days. Maybe if we invite them now, they'll at least consider it. But I don't want you to be hurt by them again. I love both of my parents, despite their flaws. My dad, he's a good, caring man. He's just having trouble with me divorcing Jenna. He'd rather blame you for my marriage failing then listen to me tell him what actually happened. They both know the truth. I chased you; I wanted you." He tugged her to him and embraced her lovingly. "Mom knows the entire story. She understands why it all happened as it did, and she's fine with it. She said she just wants me… us to be happy. She knows you make me the happiest man alive." He squeezed her tightly.

"I know if your dad would just give me a chance, I can win him over. I know he'll like me once he meets me, or at least he may not hate me. I know it, Jack." She pushed herself up from his embrace and held his gaze. "I'm excited to meet them. I want us to spend holidays with them as a family." She sighed. "But I'll be patient and give him all the time he needs." She fell onto him and buried her head in his shoulder, kissing his neck, then his lips. "The next time you see or text your mom, tell her I understand, and one day we'll meet and talk. Oh, and tell her you're my world."

CHAPTER 12

A few weeks later, Emma sat on the bench in the bay window of their kitchen enjoying her morning coffee. Jack had left early for a full day of surgeries and told her he'd be late, and to not expect him for dinner. She knew working at RG Orthopedic Center was Jack's dream job, but she never expected him to be working so much. With his on-call weekends, they barely had time alone anymore.

Her gallery renovations were on schedule. She'd been painting new landscapes while Jack was busy and writing new poems to paint onto canvas as well.

She glanced out the window when she saw a delivery car drive into their driveway. Standing, she went toward the front door to meet the woman walking up the sidewalk.

"Good morning," Emma said to the stout older woman holding a bouquet of roses and gardenias.

"Mrs. Bryant?" The woman looked at Emma after she read the iPad she'd held in her free hand.

"Yes, that's me." Emma's smile filled her face.

"These are for you." The woman held out the beautiful bouquet and Emma laid out her arms to receive it.

"Thank you. Please wait here." She turned and went to the kitchen. Laying the flowers on the table she dug in her purse for a tip. Back at the front door she handed the woman a ten and said, "For you. Have a great day."

"Thanks. You too." She turned and walked back toward her car.

Emma returned to the kitchen and brought the bouquet to her nose. Drawing in the soft scents of the roses and gardenias, her heart warmed. She moved the flowers to find the card. The small envelope read, *Mrs. Emma Bryant.* Feeling Jack's love all around her, she opened the envelope and read the card. *Emma, my love. Our lives have been so busy, but never doubt my love for you. You'll always be my priority. I love you, forever and a day. Jack.*

A tear landed on the notecard, causing the ink to smear. "No, no. Fuck." She reached for a paper towel and tried to dab the card dry. Barely able to read the card, she laid it on the table and went to find a vase for her flowers. Finding a decent size vase in the pantry, she filled it with water and cut each stem, then arranged the flowers in the vase.

Walking into the family room, she placed the flower vase on the coffee table next to one of their wedding photos. She stepped back and embraced herself. Pulling her phone from her pocket, she sent Jack a text: **Thank you, baby. See you tonight**.

Not expecting Jack to respond, she went and showered, then dressed in jeans and a tank top. A full day of painting in her home studio was on her agenda.

As Emma propped open an easel, her phone rang. Seeing it was Doug, she answered it.

"Hi Doug. What's up?"

"Hi, Emma. There's a bit of an emergency here. We had the crew working over the weekend to help speed up the timeframe." He sighed. "Then this morning one of the plumbers remodeling the public bathroom found a lot of mold when he tore out the existing drywall."

Knowing a little about this from her marriage to Matt, she didn't panic. "Um, okay. When my ex-husband came across mold on a job site, he'd call a mold removal specialist. That's probably what you should do."

"Sure, we can. This delay may upset your timeframe though," he said.

"I hope not but let me know as soon as you can." Emma knew if Matt's company had been her contractor, he'd have taken care of this without a call. And maybe his crew would've found the mold sooner. He'd never worry her with something like this. He'd make his crew work double time to keep the timeframe they'd agreed on.

73

She knew Matt would've taken care of her and her gallery above and beyond any other contracting company. *Maybe I should've looked at Marcus as well as I did the other four. Too late now. Hmmph.*

"Actually, Doug. I want to see how bad it is. I'll be there in a few minutes." Emma left the guest bedroom and grabbed her purse from the kitchen table. Sliding into her car, she turned it on and drove to the gallery.

As she drove past the Coffee Castle, she caught sight of who she thought was Jack sitting inside with a woman. She slowed down and wondered why he was there. He'd told her he had a full day of surgeries and would be late. She sat at the red light and stared into the coffee shop.

Her heart pinched as she watched him talk with the woman. Emma could see him showing her something on his phone. They weren't sitting close like she and Jack always did, they sat across from one another. *Stop overthinking, stop it now.* She chastised herself.

Startled by a horn blaring when the light turned green and Emma didn't go, she shook her head and drove to her gallery. She'd ask Jack about his meeting with the woman when he got home later.

Parking her car near the front of the gallery, she glanced back toward the coffee shop. *No, I trust Jack with my life. It must be work related, probably Michelle, his nurse.*

Before entering the gallery, Emma shook out her hands. She reached for the door handle and pulled it open.

Forcing her best smile as she entered, she dropped her purse on the small table by the door. "Doug," she called out.

Glancing around she saw her vision of her future gallery almost completed. Everything she'd ask for was being done. She made a mental note to be sure to thank not only Doug, her project manager, but also his boss and the owners of B&T. After all, they approved everything for her.

"Hey, Emma." Doug came up to her from the hallway where the public restroom was. Handing her a mask, he said, "You need to wear this. The mold is really bad."

Sliding the mask on and securing it around her ears, she said, "Thanks. Now let me see just how bad it is." She waved Doug to go ahead of her.

While waiting for Jack to come home, Emma painted. She opened her phone to her photos and chose one from their time in New York City. The towering buildings appeared to touch the sky. The cottony, white puffy clouds dotted the deep blue sky. It all made her want to go back. Take Jack and go back to the place where they became husband and wife.

Startled by Jack's hand on her shoulder, she spun and swiped the paintbrush across his green scrubs. "Oh, shit. I'm sorry." She placed the paintbrush on the easel and reached for his top. "Take this off, I should soak it in warm water."

Lifting it as far as she could, her eyes caught sight of his perfect physique. She sighed. Emma needed to talk with Jack about seeing him earlier. She needed to wait to have sex with him. No matter how badly she wanted him.

He leaned down for her to pull his top over his head, then swooped her up in his arms. "Jack, put me down." She wiggled in his arms.

"Why, Em? I missed you today." He drew her dainty body closer as he curled his arms.

"I need to get this in warm water." She held up his green scrub top and waved it around.

"Don't worry about that one top, I have plenty." He grabbed it from her and tossed it aside.

"Okay, but please put me down." She pushed on his shoulders and wiggled herself to try and get free.

Frowning, Jack placed her down. "What's wrong, love? You used to enjoy it when I swooped you off your feet." He combed her long locks with his fingers, then twisted them around.

Emma paused and blew out a breath. Touching his forearm, she glanced upward to meet his baby blues. Seeing his love for her, she dropped the idea of asking about his meeting at the coffee shop. She trusted him completely.

"Doug called. The plumber found mold." Her eyes fell to the floor.

"Shit, Em. How bad is it? What are they doing about it?" Jack touched her chin and tilted her face up to him.

"He has to call a mold removal service." She sighed. "Maybe I should've called Marcus Construction."

Jack stepped back from her and folded his arms across his chest. "Wait, why? Why Matt's company? What would they have done differently, Emma?" His glare piercing her.

Running her hand over her neck, she said, "I don't know, but I know how Matt works. He's very good at his job. Maybe Doug is too new at this." She shrugged and turned away from him.

"I don't see how hiring Matt's company would've made a difference. They would've found the mold too and called you." Jack's hands fell to his hips.

"Maybe." She shrugged, then her phone rang, and she pulled it from her pocket. "It's Doug." She walked toward the kitchen and answered it.

"Hey Doug, tell me some good news."

"Hi, Emma. I do have good news. I spoke with my boss about the mold situation, and he took care of it. The mold removal company is on site now. I don't think there will be much of a delay if any at all."

"Oh my, God. That's great news. Thank you and please, when you speak with your boss again, tell them I said thank you." She walked back into the family room and noticed Jack texting on his phone.

"You'll be able to tell him yourself soon. I think he's coming in this week to have a look around," Doug said.

"I look forward to meeting him. Let me know what day and I'll be sure to come in." Emma watched Jack closely as he continued to text while she was on her phone.

"I don't know the exact day. He likes to pop in and inspect things. But I can give you a quick call or text when he arrives."

"No worries, Doug. I'll see you later this week. And thanks for the good news. I needed some." Emma ended the call and walked over to the sofa where Jack sat, still texting.

Plopping beside him, she leaned on his arm. He quickly closed his phone and pocketed it. Smiling at her, he leaned down and kissed her nose.

"What did Doug have to say?" he asked.

"Oh, the mold is being taken care of now. He said when he called his boss and told him about the mold, his boss took control of the situation." Her eyes shined.

76

"That's good news. See, you didn't need to worry at all. Doug handled it. You made the right decision when you chose B&T. They're making your gallery perfect." Jack slid his arm around Emma and hugged her tenderly.

"I guess I did." She trailed her hand across his tight ripples. "How was your day?"

"Surgery all day. I'm exhausted. How about we go to bed?"

"So, you were stuck at the hospital all day?" Her curiosity wouldn't let go of the fact that he'd just lied to her.

"Yeah. I had a few minutes for a lunch break with my PA and the nurses, but that was it. It's been a long day." He nudged her forward and moved to the edge of the sofa.

Standing, Emma thought for a second to let his lie go, but instead, she placed her hands on his arm when he stood next to her. "Jack." She tilted her head up and looked into his heavy eyes.

"Yes, love." He caressed her back and laid his hand on her shoulder.

"Are you sure you only had a few minutes for lunch today?" she asked.

"Yes. Why?" Jack asked, removing his hand from her.

"I went into the gallery after Doug called about the mold because I wanted to see for myself how bad it was. On my way, I drove by the Coffee Castle, and I saw you there with a woman. Jack, please…." She pinched his forearm.

"Emma…." He raked his hand through his hair and looked away from her.

"No, Jack. I saw you." Emma stepped back from him.

Drawing in a breath, he scratched his face and rubbed his neck. An uncomfortable silence rose between them.

"Jack, who is she?" Emma asked, her heart pinching.

"She's a nurse that works with me. We had a surgery cancelled and we both needed to get out of the hospital for a break. That's all it was. Just lunch." Jack took a step toward Emma. Reaching for her, he took her hand in his. "I would never hurt you." He gently tugged for her to come closer.

She glanced up at him. Catching his sky-blue eyes, she recognized his sincerity. "Then why not just tell me when I asked about your day?" She pulled her hand free.

"I didn't think it was a big deal. It was just lunch with a co-worker. I'm sorry." Jack offered his hand to her.

Looking at it, then up into his soft baby blues, Emma sighed. She knew deep inside her heart Jack would never hurt her. She knew his love for her was true. But a chill remained, and she didn't know why. Dropping her gaze to his waiting hand, she said, "It becomes a big deal when you try to pass it off and not tell me the truth. Jack, please don't…,"

Engulfing her with his arms, he held her tight. "Emma, I will never cheat on you. I swear to God. Never."

With her arms at her sides, she lifted her hands and placed them to his ribcage. She felt his heart as it drummed against her ear. "I believe you," she whispered and slid her arms around him.

His grip tightened as he kissed her hair, then released her and stepped back. Cupping her face, he brushed her cheeks with his thumbs and leaned down. He kissed her softly. Taking her hand, he led her into their bedroom. He lifted her onto their bed and began removing her clothes. Sitting on her knees in her bra and panties, she smiled, tugging him closer.

Trailing her hands slowly down his flawless physique, she leaned into him, kissing each of his firm pecs as her hand slipped into his scrubs. She curled her hand around his stiff cock and began stroking him. She'd much rather make love to him than have doubts about his love for her.

"Emma, my God." Jack laid his head on her shoulder as she stroked his shaft faster. Feeling him throb, she yanked his scrubs down and replaced her hand with her mouth. "Jesus." Jack fisted her hair and gently moved her head up and down his length. Taking him deep, Emma sucked hard on him, wanting to taste his sweet cum. Feeling him stiffen then throb, she knew he was close to his release. She grabbed his tight ass with her hands and held it, not wanting a drop of him to escape her mouth. His hips thrusting against her as she moved up and down. Jack let out a loud growl, "Oh, love. I can't hold on, I can't. Emma!" Then he came.

Enjoying every drop of him, she slowly released his cock from her mouth, kissing the tip softly. Glancing upward, her grin full of sin, she said, "Baby, you are so luscious." She licked her lips as he lifted her up to him. Standing on the bed, she cupped his face and looked down into his irresistible ice blue eyes. "Fuck me, Jack. Fuck me all night long." She hopped onto his tall body, wrapping her arms and legs around him.

Falling onto the bed, his warm breath wisped across her neck, his soft lips arousing her body even more as he ducked under the sheet. After kissing her breasts and licking her nipples, he poked his head from underneath the covers and smiled playfully at her. Cupping his mildly scruffy jawline, she sat forward and met his lips with hers. She tasted his sweet mouth fully, driving her tongue across every inch of his delectable mouth.

Moaning and writhing beneath him, Emma fisted Jack's dark brown hair, threading her fingers through it, then pushed him down to her clit. Spreading her legs wide, giving him the access he wanted, she placed her feet on his shoulders and lifted her hips as his tongue edged its way into her pussy. "Jesus, fuck, Jack!" Emma shouted when he sucked on her clit. Sliding his long fingers into her, he bent them at just the right angle to find her G-spot.

She bucked her hips to make his fingers go deeper; her eyes rolled back. She smacked the sheets with her hands and yanked them hard when he made her come. His tongue never stopping, his fingers pushed inside her as deep as he could go. Lifting the sheet to catch his eyes, Emma grinned wide when she watched him trail his tongue across her inner thigh to her clit. He slunk his way up her tiny frame. *Oh, God, how I love this man!*

He kissed her navel, her flat stomach, her ribs. Taking in a mouthful of her perfectly round breasts, his tongue worked to harden her nipple. "Mmm, mmm. You taste so delicious, love," he said, then kissed her passionately, plunging his tongue into her mouth and burying his hard cock into her wet core.

With an intense and rapid pace to his lovemaking, Jack's hands slid under her when his body jerked hard. "Jesus Christ, Emma." Another slam against her and he collapsed onto her, sliding from her body, resting his arm across her midriff. His head laid on one breast. Breathing heavily, his lips caressed the side of her other breast.

She laid breathless, holding him, feathering her fingers through his silky hair, thanking God they'd found one another. Her body tingled from the blissfulness of being with him. Slipping her hand to her ass, she pinched herself. *Jesus, I am awake. I am married to this fabulously magnificent man.*

Jack's hand slowly crept between her thighs again.

"Oh, baby," she purred. "Please don't stop."

Massaging her tenderly, his fingers slid in and out of her. Her body ignited again as he brought her to a level of climax she didn't know existed. Kissing him deeply, her tongue trailing along just inside his lips, she tasted her favorite flavor, Dr. Jackson Bryant, her young and viral husband. Pinching her legs together as she reached the edge of the universe, she squealed, "Oh my fucking, God! Jackson, oh, Jack!" Her chest heaving, she clutched his arms. "Jack, yes, oh fuck, yes!"

Lying side by side, their bodies drenched in sweat, Emma stared at the ceiling, a tear sliding down her face. *How could I have ever doubted this perfect man? He's mine and I'm his.*

She clutched her chest while Jack's hand petted her curves. "I love your smooth soft skin. I could lie here forever caressing you, kissing you, making love to you." Jack's warm breath sent her body escalating again.

"I'd love to stay in bed with you for the rest of our life together." Emma caressed his cheek and snuggled even closer to him.

Catching his seductive blue globes, they yanked her into his sexual aura as he leaned closer to her lips. Her eyes grew wide as he slithered between her legs. His mouth crashed onto hers. Slipping his tongue inside, sliding it around, he tasted her again and again.

"Oh my, God," Emma moaned, calling out his name as he fucked her again. His stamina lasted a while longer, her orgasms taking her to the outer edges of reality. Her body quivered, jolted, trembled, and shook. She moaned, squealed, and cried out with ecstasy. Her hands groped his body; she came more times than she could ever count.

While she never wanted to doubt Jack or argue with him ever again, she thoroughly enjoyed their incredible make up sex that lasted hours upon hours.

Lying facing one another, Emma palmed Jack's cheek and gazed deeply into his mesmerizing eyes. "I love you, baby." She leaned closer and kissed him.

"I love you, Emma." Jack's arms slid all around her, pulling her dainty body into him and holding her tight as night came and they fell asleep.

CHAPTER 13

Emma spent the morning and early afternoon packing her home art studio away. She'd planned on moving most of her things into her new gallery when it was finished.

She kept one easel and a box of paints and pencils in the closet, along with a few blank canvases. The rest she placed neatly by the door to the garage in the kitchen. She'd ask Jack to help her move it all to her car when the time came to take it to the gallery.

Before she finished organizing her things, her phone rang. She brought it out of her pocket and laid it on the counter. "Hi, Shea," Emma answered and placed it on speaker, then went to fill her coffee mug.

"Hi, Emma. How are you and Jack? I haven't heard from you in a while," Shea said.

"I'm sorry. I've been preoccupied with the gallery renovations and painting new pieces for the grand opening. But we're doing well. Jack's super busy at the center. And..." Emma paused.

"And, what, Em. Spill it," Shea insisted.

Unsure if she wanted to tell her sister of Jack's reaction to her keeping the name EB Taylor for her art, she paused again.

"Emma, are you there?" Shea asked.

She knew Shea would know something wasn't perfect between her and Jack. So, she told her sister. "Yes, I'm here." She blew out a breath, then continued, "Okay, but it's been settled."

"I don't care, tell me what happened."

"We had an argument a while back. Our first since being married." Emma sighed as she remembered how upset Jack had been.

"About what?"

"My signature on my paintings."

"Oh, let me guess, you're still signing them EB Taylor, right?" Shea asked.

"Well, yeah. Shea, you know that's my professional name. It's how I've always signed my work. He got upset, but I came up with a compromise that he's good with."

"And what's that?"

"I named my gallery, EB's Gallery. I dropped the Taylor."

"Jack was okay with that?"

"He said he was. And I said I would consider dropping the Taylor from my signature in the future, but I can't right now," Emma said as she refilled her coffee.

"He's a proud man, Em. Honestly, I'm not surprised by his behavior at all. But I also know how much he loves you. He'll find a way to swallow his pride and be by your side whatever name you use as your signature or professionally. He'll internalize his pain, so keep an eye out for any change in his behavior. Be aware, Emma," Shea warned.

"I will, thanks Shea. But that's not what's concerning me at the moment."

"Why? What else is wrong?"

"The crew found mold and instead of just taking care of it like Matt would've done, Doug called me. Of course, I got worried and went into the gallery to see for myself how bad it is." She huffed out a breath.

"Wait. What does Matt have to do with your gallery?"

"Nothing, but I know he would've handled it."

"So, you're telling me the project manager called you before he called in a professional to take care of the mold? What could you do about it? Do they need your permission to remove it?" Shea asked.

"No, they don't need my permission to fix it. I remember when the crew found mold on a few of Matt's jobs. He just hired the pros and once the mold was taken care of, he'd let the owners know.

gallery is to me."

"You keep bringing up Matt. Are you sure you and Jack are good?"

"Shea!" Emma yelled. "Yes. We're fine. I'm just saying Matt wouldn't have bothered me with this. He would've had it cleaned up, then informed me. Since I know about it, I'm a bit worried. That's all."

"Okay, Em. How does this affect your date for the grand opening?"

"Not much really. I want to miss the hustle and bustle of the holiday season, so the grand opening will be the end of January. And consider this yours, Rob's, and the kid's invitation to my grand opening. Please come early, please. I miss you." Emma sat on the barstool and sighed.

"Of course, Em. But I doubt the kids will be with us. RJ has school and that's close to when they start workouts for baseball season out here. And I'll check with Amelia, but I'm sure she has clinical she shouldn't miss. I hope you're not too upset if they don't make it."

"Oh my, no. It's okay. I'd hoped to see them though. But we both understand. Jack and I will be sure to visit them soon."

"Sounds good, Em. And I'll put in for the week before so Rob and I can be there to help with anything."

"You're the best sister. But don't worry, I'll hire a crew to help me hang the gallery. You can help with the fun stuff."

"Hey, isn't Jack's birthday in January?" Shea asked.

"It is, but he doesn't want to overshadow my big night. We can have a celebration at the house. You, Rob, Brandi, Ben, and us. I'll order food and a cake for one evening." Emma put a note on her phone to remind her.

"No, don't order any food. I'll make dinner for everyone. Order a cake and have some decorations we can put up for Jack's birthday party. It'll be fun."

"You'd do that for him? That's so sweet of you and thanks. I know he loves your cooking. I've put a reminder note on my phone to take care of it after the New Year. I can't wait to see y'all."

"Us too, Em. It was great catching up with you. I should get back on the floor. Call me soon. I love you."

"I will Shea. Love you too. Bye." Emma tapped the red phone icon and hopped off the barstool. She went back to her studio and finished her chore she'd began before Shea called.

CHAPTER 14

Stopping at the Coffee Castle on her way into her gallery, Emma waited for her order when she saw Matt entering the café. She turned, hoping he wouldn't notice her. The barista exposed her when she called her name, "Emma."

Keeping her attention toward the counter, she stepped forward and picked up her cup. Nodding at the young girl, she felt a hand engulf her shoulder.

"Good morning, Em. It's nice to see you again." Matt's hand lingered on her shoulder.

Ducking out from his hold and stepping back from him, she felt a chill travel through her. "Good morning, Matt." She smiled politely. "I'm sorry, I can't stay and chat. I have a meeting at my gallery with the project manager and his boss this morning." She scrunched her face and began to walk toward the exit.

"No problem, Emma. I'll see you soon. Take care." Matt waved when she turned and looked at him before leaving the coffee shop.

As she walked to her car, Emma sent Jack a quick text: **I love you. See you tonight.** She slipped her phone into her purse.

She arrived at her gallery, ready for Doug to show her the progress and to meet his boss. Mainly to thank them for taking care of the mold situation quickly.

Seeing Doug waiting for her by the front door, she parked her car and walked toward him. "Good morning. How does my gallery look?" she asked smiling brightly.

"Good morning, Emma. We're getting there. Thanks to Mr. Taylor…"

Holding up her hand, she interrupted him, "Wait, who?"

"My boss, Mr. Taylor. He's the owner. Well, one of the owners." Doug pulled out a company business card and handed it to her. The one he'd initially given her was only his business card listing him as a project manager with B&T.

Taking the card in hand, she read it. Slapping her hand to her mouth, she shook her head and blinked slowly. *Fuck me. How did I miss this? When did Matt leave Marcus? How will I tell Jack? Oh. My. God.*

"Is there something wrong?" Doug asked.

"No, nothing at all," she said quickly. Breathing deeply to calm herself, she slipped the card into her pocket.

"Okay, great. We can wait for Mr. Taylor inside." He opened the door and stood to the side.

Entering her gallery, Emma slowly spun around to take in everything the crew had finished. Her vision of what she'd wanted was coming to completion. She walked the length of the showroom area, then back to Doug. Waving her arm around, she said, "This is so exciting to see. I'm pleased with it all so far. I can't wait for the loft to be completed. That may be my…" she stopped talking when she caught sight of Matt entering the gallery. She sucked in a breath and put on her sweet smile. "Hi, Matt," she said.

Doug turned toward the entrance and said, "Oh, hi, Mr. Taylor." He looked at Emma, then at Matt and back to Emma. Scratching his head, he bit on his pen.

"Hi, Emma. It's nice to see you again." Matt walked toward her and Doug. "I see the confusion on your face, Doug. Emma and I are old friends."

"Yeah, we're old friends." Emma agreed and smiled.

"Okay, well then, I don't need to introduce you to one another." Doug let out a breath. "Alright, let me take you both around and show you the progress. Emma, I'm sure you'll be happy when you see the roominess of your office and your private bathroom. Follow me." Doug waved his arm and led Emma and Matt down the hallway.

He pushed the door to Emma's office open. She entered her office, looked around and inspected the private bathroom. Each room still needed painting, but everything was what she'd asked for. Rejoining Doug and Matt in the hallway, she said, "It all looks great. I'd like to see the storage rooms and public restroom."

"Sure. Follow me." Doug turned and led her and Matt through the other rooms.

After the tour of her almost completed gallery, she sat at the small square table with the folding chairs. She wanted a whiskey, but only had her coffee with her. Sipping on it, she watched as Matt spoke with Doug. Matt pointed to the loft area and Doug nodded in the affirmative.

A few minutes passed by when she saw Doug head back down the hallway and Matt rambled over toward her. She took in several deep breaths and sat forward. Clasping her hands on the table, she said, "So, Matt. Why didn't you tell me my gallery was your big project when I ran into you a few months ago?"

Pulling the folding chair out, he sat next to her and covered her hands with his. "Because you would've fired B&T. Don't deny it." He caught her stare and held it.

Sliding her hands out from under his, she rested them in her lap. "Maybe. But I wish you would've told me back then."

"I'm sorry, Em. I'll be honest with you. When I saw your name on the proposal for this place, I told Doug to do whatever it took to get this job." He scooted his chair closer to her and touched her arm.

Looking at Matt, her mood softened. "So, you're telling me you would've done this job no matter what I asked for?"

With a firm voice, he smiled and said, "Absolutely."

Her heart warmed knowing he'd done anything to make her dreams come true. "Well, thank you. I will admit I'm beyond happy with the progress so far. I'm most excited to see the loft when it's finished."

"I just told Doug to get the guys on that area immediately."

Looking up to where her loft will be, she relaxed back in her chair, crossing her legs. "That area will be my studio. I wanted it out front so I can have the gallery open while I draw and paint."

"I love that idea, Em."

A bit of awkward silence sat between them. Emma was grateful to Matt for all his company had done for her, but she knew she had to tell Jack. She couldn't keep this from him. She'd figure out how to make Jack understand it was all business with Matt. Nothing more.

Rubbing her neck, she looked at Matt and said, "Um, I guess I owe you a personal thank you for taking care of the mold issue so quickly."

"You're welcome, and I'm happy you're happy with the work my company has done. I'm sure you'll love your gallery when it's completed."

Taking a sip of her coffee, she asked, "So, tell me, Matt, when did you leave Marcus? And after all those years, why would you leave there?"

"I had an irresistible offer come my way and I needed a change." Releasing a heavy sigh, his shoulders slumped.

"Really? An irresistible offer made you leave the company you nearly helped build. There must be another reason." She didn't believe an offer of any amount of money would make Matt leave Marcus Construction.

He covered his face with both hands, then looked at Emma directly, catching her gaze. "You're right, Em. It wasn't just the offer. I left Marcus Construction because the demands they made on me cost me you." His eyes came together, and his smile left his face.

Emma's mouth fell open as she began to respond, but her words caught in her throat. Her heart clenched. She blinked rapidly, trying to stop her tears from falling. *Oh my God. Oh my God. Oh. My. God.* Her breathing hitched. "Matt, I…." Her head fell to her chest. She crossed her arms over her body and grabbed her shoulders, hugging herself while trying to figure out how to answer him. Her head swayed as she sat silently.

"Emma." She raised her glassy eyes to him, and he said, "I own half of B&T with a silent partner. They called me shortly after I signed the divorce papers. I have total control over the company. When I asked to be part of ownership, they agreed. My partners asked very little of me money wise as my buy in. They said they needed someone with my experience to run their company." Matt touched her elbow, giving it a soft squeeze. "I needed a new beginning after the divorce. And this is what dropped into my lap. I'm going to make B&T the best construction company in the southeast. Maybe the whole east coast."

Falling back in her chair, she blinked slowly. Her heart slowed as she looked at Matt. He'd reminded her of the pain she caused him and no matter how happy Jack made her, she'd always carry some guilt with her. "I don't know what to say, Matt." She ran her hand through her hair and sighed.

"I didn't tell you all that to bring up anything hurtful. You asked me why I left Marcus. I told you the truth. You don't need to worry about me. I keep busy with B&T." He sat back, placing one leg over the other.

"I'm so proud of you and happy for you." She swallowed hard. "And grateful to you for taking care of this." She swung her arm in the air. "You made a dream of mine come true again." She leaned forward and offered him her hand.

Taking it in his, he squeezed it gently. "It's been my honor to help you reach your dream again. I remember when you and Brandi wanted to open a gallery back home. That's what this felt like again. It took me back to the time of our foursome." He smiled at her.

"Oh my, gosh. I remember like it was yesterday." Her mouth formed a slow smile. "Brandi and I always wanted to own a gallery together since we were kids. And you made it happen." A few minutes of silence hovered between them. Emma dropped her gaze to her lap. She drew in several deep breaths, then her eyes met his.

"Emma, we had a good run and much more than just our thirty-two years of marriage together. We had high school and after graduation. I don't regret any second of it. Not one. I hope you don't either."

Staring at Matt, Emma cupped her cheeks and wiped the tears that dampened her face. "No, Matt. I don't regret it at all. We were happy for a long time. You'll always be my first love. No one can take that from you." Tilting her head, she smiled. She wiped her cheeks again with her palms and reached for her purse. Opening it, she pulled out a few tissues and dabbed her eyes and wiped her nose.

Covering his face with his hands, Matt rubbed them over his cheeks, then dragged them through his hair. Several minutes passed, then Matt asked, "Will your exhibition be all of your new pieces?"

"No, I have a lot of paintings from our time together. A lot of sunsets from our beach vacations. A few landscapes from our mountain trips. But my featured work will be my new poem paintings. I won't sell any of those. They're too personal to sell."

90

"We did have a lot of getaways that gave you your inspiration. I'm happy you're still going to display them. They're great memories." He scratched his chin and said, "Maybe I should buy one from you. For old times' sake. I can hang it in my office."

Smiling at him, she said, "You've done so much for me. I'll be sure to have one delivered to your office back home."

"Thanks, Em. I'd love to have one of your paintings for my office." He rose from the chair and stepped toward hers, holding the back of her chair as she stood.

Smiling at him, she walked toward the front door with him. "I should get home."

Before leaving, Matt said, "I'll check in again when the work gets closer to being finished. Take care of yourself, Emma." He touched her arm and smiled.

"Thank you, Matt. For making BE Unique and this gallery a reality." She extended her hand to him.

Taking her hand in his, he tugged on her gently, pulling her into him. She hugged him and patted his back. She drew in a deep breath when he kissed the side of her head. He stepped back trailing his hands down her arms, then clasping her hands. "You're welcome. I'll always be in your corner."

She blinked slowly, and gently pulled her hands from his. "I need to go…." She covered her mouth. Pushing past Matt, Emma bolted from her gallery, hurrying to her car.

Sitting in her car, she glanced at her teary-eyed reflection in the rearview mirror. She knew she loved Jack completely. He was her world. But after seeing Matt again, and after he'd made sure her dream would come true, she knew she'd always have a special place in her heart for him. They'd spent too much time together for her to not have any feelings for him. But she knew the love for him wasn't what it used to be. It wasn't that deep in love feeling anymore. She cared for Matt and always would. She was deeply in love with Jack. Her decision to marry him and be with him was the right one for her. She had no regrets, despite the tears streaming down her face as she drove home to Jack.

CHAPTER 15

Emma had dinner delivered and set out on the dining room table, complete with candles and his favorite bourbon, neat. Sitting on the bench seat in the bay window of their kitchen, staring out at nothing, she jumped when Jack came in from the garage and kissed her cheek.

"Hey, love. What's got you so anxious?" he asked.

"You surprised me, that's all, baby." She smiled at him. "Dinner's ready in the dining room. Wash your hands and join me there." She stood and nudged him to the sink.

Meeting her there, Jack surveyed the table. "Emma. What's up?" He pulled her into him and embraced her.

Tilting her head up to him, she smiled. "Later, let's have a nice dinner and relax first. Please." Her eyes came together as she freed herself from his arms and sat in her chair.

Jack sat next to Emma at the head of the long table. He placed his hand palm up on the table. Their eyes met. Smiling her sweet smile, she walked her hand into his. Jack engulfed it with his and tugged her closer to him. "Whatever is bothering you. Know that I love you." He kissed her lips softly, then raised her hand and kissed her knuckles.

"I know. And I love you." She nodded toward his plate and said, "Let's eat, then we can talk about my day." She stabbed her fork into her salad and began eating.

They had a lot to talk about. She knew that news wouldn't go over well, but she had to be honest with Jack.

After cleaning up when they finished dinner, Emma and Jack retired to the family room. Sitting on the sofa together, she faced him and took his hands in hers. She breathed deeply, then cleared her throat. "Jack. I met one of the owners of B&T today." She looked into his soft baby blues and tried to smile.

"How were they? I hope they met your expectations."

"Baby, there's no other way to say this, so here goes." She bowed her head, then raised it back to look him in his eyes. "It's Matt," she blurted out and slammed her eyes shut.

Silence hovered between them for several minutes. Her face scrunched and she held her breath. She felt her heart pounding in her throat. Her ears heated as she waited for Jack to say something.

Letting go of her hands, he raked his hands through his hair and scratched his face. "Matt, as in your ex-husband, Matt Taylor?" he asked.

Closing her eyes again, she nodded her head up and down. "Jack, it's a… It's nothing I can't handle."

"I'm not sure what to say." He huffed out a breath and rubbed his hand across his neck.

"You don't have to say anything. I wanted to be completely honest with you." She scooted closer to him. "I found out today when I met with Doug. I swear to you I had no idea Matt was the T in B&T." She palmed his cheek and turned his face toward her. His soft blue eyes drew together, his jaw leaning heavy in her hand. "Matt said he has a silent partner. And he left Marcus because the partners made him an offer he couldn't refuse. Jack, I believe him." She decided not to tell Jack why Matt really left Marcus.

Sitting up straight, he took her hands and held them. "I don't trust him. He's up to something." His stare bore into her.

"Oh, Jack. I don't think so." Emma sighed. "I've known Matt for a long time. I'd know if he were lying to me. That's not who he is." She shook her head slowly, realizing she'd have to keep Matt's real reason to herself forever. She'd never tell a soul.

"Emma, I don't know how I feel about Matt showing up out of nowhere. How did he find out about your gallery? Is he keeping tabs on you?"

Thinking for a second, she shook her head. "He didn't show up out of nowhere. I hired B&T. They didn't solicit me. I should've done my own research, but I trusted Roy's list. He said they were all

93

vetted and were all good solid companies." She huffed out a breath. "And there's no way for Roy to have known about my divorce." She paused and looked down at his hands holding hers. "I've already told Matt he should've told me his big job was mine when I ran into him at the coffee shop before any major demo was done."

"And what was his excuse for not telling you?" Jack asked.

"He said he knew I'd fire them immediately. He said he wanted to help make my dreams come true again." Emma threaded her fingers with Jacks. "Baby, you are the one that makes *all* my dreams come true. Matt helped with my gallery, that's it. Yes, it's important to me, but in the grand scheme of things, it's a building." She brought his hand to her lips and kissed it. "You are my everything. You make my life worth living. Just you, Jack." She scooted onto her knees and placed her hands on his shoulders. Leaning into him, she kissed him.

Wrapping his arms around her, he kissed her back. His tongue pushing through her soft lips. She slid her arms around his neck and straddled his body. When their kisses ended, she held his face in her hands. "Let's go away for the weekend. Anywhere away from here."

"I like that idea. Where should we go?" Jack reached for his phone that laid on the side table. Waking it, he typed in the travel website.

Emma leaned on his warm shoulder and watched as Jack thumbed through several weekend getaway options.

When a secluded mountain cabin popped up, she touched his phone screen. "There. Let's go to the mountains. It'll be nice and chilly at night, and you can keep me snuggly warm." She brushed his cheek and grinned sinfully.

"Sounds perfect, love. I'll make the reservations for the cabin. Find us the flights for Friday night and a rental SUV."

She glanced around for her phone and realized she'd left it in her purse. Walking to the kitchen, she retrieved her purse and brought out her phone. Finding their flights and rental SUV, she plopped onto the sofa next to Jack and said, "All set, baby."

CHAPTER 16

Arriving at the secluded cabin with darkness surrounding them, Emma touched the flashlight on her phone to help light the way. She shined it onto the keypad and pressed the code to unlock the door.

Inside, she found a lamp to light the room, then located the thermostat. Being in the mountains, and very secluded, Emma shivered as she turned on the heat to sixty degrees, keeping the cabin on the cooler side so Jack could keep her warm.

The cabin had a spacious living room with a stone fireplace and a big, brown furry rug lying in front of it. She shivered again when he came in with the luggage, the cold air following him in. "Oh sorry, love." Jack kicked the solid wood door closed.

She walked toward the door and locked it. Following him into the master suite, which sat beyond the living room, she noticed another large furry black rug in front of the fireplace in the bedroom. Smiling, Emma enjoyed a mental image of making love to Jack on both rugs, many times. After unpacking, she went to the kitchen and made them each a hot chocolate. She jumped when Jack's arms wrapped her up from behind. "Hey, baby." She turned in his embrace and tilted her face up to his.

Leaning down, he kissed her. "What are you making?"

"Hot chocolate to help warm us up a little. You can finish heating me up later." She winked and handed him his mug.

Walking into the living room, they sat on the sofa and sipped on their cocoa. She didn't want to ruin the mood, but Emma knew she needed to be sure Jack understood this thing with her ex-husband was only business.

She sat her mug on the side table, turning to face him, she took his hand in hers and snuggled it between her breasts.

"What's this for, Emma?" Jack turned his hand and held hers in it.

"Jack, we need to finish talking about the Matt thing."

"Em, right now?" Letting go of her hand, his eyes fell to his lap.

"I want to be sure you understand it's strictly a business arrangement. And I need you to please trust me. There's no competition here. None. Matt is the owner of the company I hired to renovate my gallery." She took his hand in hers again and tugged on it to make him look at her. "Baby, you're my world. No one will ever take your place." She raised her eyebrows and scooted closer to him.

"I still don't trust him." A low growl came from his throat as he gripped her hands tighter. "But I do trust you, completely. Please keep your guard up whenever Matt stops in at the gallery." Jack drew her into him and engulfed her body. Wrapping her in his arms, he leaned down and kissed her. "I don't want to talk about this anymore." Jack took her hand and pulled her up from the sofa, then led her into the bedroom.

Smiling inside along with electric pulses traveling from her head to her toes, Emma said, "I don't either. I want to enjoy you all weekend long. Just us."

She hopped onto the bed and sat up on her knees. Curling her fingers over and over, she bit her lip as he lifted his cotton sweater over his head. Her eyes wide as she enjoyed the view of her extremely sensual husband. With a fire pooling in her core, she extended her hand to him. "Give me your hand, baby."

Jack stepped toward her, his hand reaching for hers. He watched her as she edged herself closer to the end of the bed. Sliding his hand up her skirt, she purred, "I'm wet for you. Take me, Jack. Fuck me all night long."

She grasped his shoulders when he glided his fingers through her drenched folds. "You feel amazing, love." He placed his other hand on the small of her back, holding her tightly to him.

She jerked upward when his finger shoved into her. "Oh, God," she moaned. Cupping his square jaw, she drew him to her and melded her lips to his. His tongue shot into her warm mouth, tangling with hers.

Yanking her clothes from her, he smiled then lifted Emma from the bed and carried her to the fluffy black rug on the floor. He laid her down gently, then stripped his clothes off. "Come to me, baby. You're exquisite to look at, but I want you inside me," she said as she wiggled her fingers at him.

He knelt beside her, his full arousal waiting for her. Curling her fingers around his hard cock, she slowly stroked him. His head fell back as a deep groan came from him.

Positioning herself on her side, she licked his tip and trailed her tongue down his long shaft. "Oh, Emma," he moaned and fisted her hair.

Sliding her tongue back on his length, to his tip, she took him into her warm mouth. His hands moved her head up and down on him as he fucked her mouth. She opened her throat to take him deep. "Christ, Em. Slow down." His shaft pulsated as she sucked him off.

She enjoyed making him feel his bliss before her and she knew he could come more than once. Repositioning herself, she squatted on her knees for a better angle to massage his dick in her mouth. Splaying her hands on his solid thighs, she moved her head up and down slowly as she listened to Jack moan and groan. His body straightened and his grip on her head tightened.

Quickening her pace, she sucked harder and took him deeper. "Oh, damn, Emma!" Jack moaned and thrust his hips against her face. His sweet, warm cum sprayed down her throat.

Licking her lips as she laid back on the fluffy rug, she smiled sinfully up at Jack. "Mmm, baby. You will always be my favorite flavor."

Lying beside her, he propped himself on his elbow and cupped her cheek with his other hand. "I love you, beautiful." He leaned down and claimed her mouth with his. She wrapped her arms around his neck and yanked him onto her, opening her legs wide for him to lie between them.

Resting his elbows on either side of her head, he gazed deep into her soul. "I love you with every ounce of my existence." She brushed his cheek then slid her hand to the nape of his neck and drew him to her. Kissing him deeply, she felt his cock harden against her body. She quivered beneath him in anticipation of him fucking her to the point of no return. She wanted him to make her reach the pinnacle of her bliss over and over. To make her orgasms feel like she rocketed to the edge of forever.

Jack glided his hard cock into her wet pussy, thrusting in deep. He kissed her neck, her cheek, her lips. Their tongues twisting passionately, while his hips met with hers over and over. "Jesus, Jack. Oh, God, baby," she moaned.

Groping his firm body, she locked her legs and arms around him. His arms engulfed her dainty body, pulling her up with him as he sat back on his legs.

Sitting on his lap, his long length deep inside her, she gazed into his mesmerizingly gorgeous blue orbs. Emma held Jack's cheeks in her hands. Leaning in she kissed him tenderly. His cock throbbed inside her. "Emma, you're driving me crazy. I love how you feel. Tight, warm, and so damn wet. Goddamn, I'll make love to you all night long. Hold on tight, love." His hand slid up her back, drawing her to him as their lips melded together. Their kisses were full of passion.

She bounced on him, ran her hands through his soft brown hair, dug her fingernails into his broad shoulders with each orgasm she reached. Not wanting their love making to end, she measured her pace and rocked slowly on him. "Fuck me forever and a day, baby. Please don't stop," she panted against his neck.

Lifting Emma from his lap, he rose from the floor and swooped her off her feet. He carried her to the bathroom and placed her on the edge of the jacuzzi tub. "Bath or shower?" His grin was filled with sin and pleasure.

Tapping her cheek, she raised an eyebrow and said, "Shower now, bath later." Her eyes danced and she bit her lip.

Jack turned on the shower. Checking the water temperature, he smiled and opened the glass door wider for Emma to enter the stall.

They stood under the shower head as the water cascaded down their bodies. Tilting her head up, she reached for him. Drawing him down to her, she kissed him. His arms slipped around her waist, lifting her onto him. She wrapped herself around his firm body, laying her head on his shoulder. His hard erection touched her clit, and she moaned, slowly lowering her body onto his cock.

Locking her fingers together around his neck, her body leaned back as he thrusted his hips upward into her. "God, Jack. You feel so good inside me."

He backed them up against the shower wall. She squealed when her back touched the cooler tiles. It wasn't long before those cool tiles were warm from the friction of her body moving up and down with Jack's fast rhythm. His hands cupped her shoulders, his mouth covered hers, his tongue plunged between her lips and tangled with hers. Gliding his tongue down her neck, across her collarbone, he licked hcr nipples.

"Emma, God, Emma," he growled with a mouthful of her ample breasts.

"Jack! Jack!" she screamed as her body released her bliss and her center walls clenched his throbbing cock.

His legs weakened and he leaned against the tile wall, sliding to the shower floor with her landing on his lap. They laid in the corner while the hot water rained down on them.

After their hot shower, Jack and Emma slipped into the white plush robes and went to bed. He drew her close to him, kissed her tenderly and wrapped his arms around her.

CHAPTER 17

Walking into the almost finished gallery, Emma smiled as she looked around and saw her vision taking shape.

The loft was perfect, the new flooring exactly as she hoped. The walls still needed the fresh coat of paints, but the new picture windows were in and looked amazing. She had an appointment with her interior designer to finalize the fabric colors for the drapes. She'd put it off until she knew the completion date.

Checking her new office and private bathroom, the storage rooms, and the public restroom, Emma felt a warmth of pride in all she saw. Her dream was almost complete. She fumbled through her purse and brought out her phone, snapping some pictures to send to Shea and Brandi.

After taking the photos, she heard the front door open. Seeing Doug and Matt enter, she walked toward them. Extending her hand to Matt, she smiled. "Good morning, gentlemen."

He took her hand in his and gripped it gently. "Good morning, Emma." He held onto her hand longer than she expected as she tugged it free. She turned to Doug and shook his hand quickly.

Walking along with Doug and Matt, Emma listened as everything she'd asked to be done was nearly completed. There was still a month of work left, but most of it was cosmetic. The basic heavy work had been finished just this week.

With Christmas and New Year's fast approaching, the crew would be off over that timeframe. She knew it added to the delay, but in the end, everything looked exactly as she wanted.

"So, Mr. Taylor, as you can see, we have less than twenty-five percent of the job left to do." Doug turned toward Emma. "And Emma, do you notice anything we need to fix, or is it up to your expectations?"

"Everything looks really great. I can't wait for it to be finished." Emma smiled.

"Yes, Doug. You and your team have done a fine job for Mrs. Bryant." Matt blinked hard when he said Emma's married name. He turned to her. She nodded and smiled politely.

"Thank you, sir. And, Emma, I'm happy that you're happy with the progress. I need to check on something with the foreman. Will you both excuse me?" Doug glanced from Emma to Matt. They each nodded and watched him walk away.

Matt stepped closer to Emma and placed his hand on her shoulder. Feeling a familiar yet distant warmth in her heart, she peered up into his big brown eyes. Her heart tightened as she remembered how they'd been such good friends before they'd ever dated. She wished it were that simple. She wished they could go back to that simple time and get a redo. She rested her hand on top of Matt's that lingered on her shoulder.

Smiling, she said, "Thank you for making sure things went as I wanted them, Matt. But…" She gently lifted his hand from her shoulder. Feeling him squeeze it, she went on. "But this is where it ends." She broke their gaze and hung her head. A heavy sigh escaped from her.

Not releasing her hand, he tugged on her arm to get her to look at him. She raised her eyes to him. "Oh, come on, Em. I won't get an invitation to your grand opening?"

She yanked her hand from his and said, "Do you know how awkward that would be?"

"What does it matter? We're divorced. You married the guy. Is he that insecure?" Matt pried.

"No, Jack isn't insecure at all. I just… I don't know, Matt. Let me think about it. Okay?" She smiled softly.

"That's good enough for me. You can text me the invite. I have the same number. Unless you deleted me and need it again." Matt shrugged.

"No. I didn't delete you." She sighed as a pinch of pain came and went. Realizing she never told Jack she'd kept Matt's phone number, she made a mental note to let him know. She never wanted to keep anything from Jack. She met Matt's gaze again. "We may have had a messy divorce, but I don't hate you. I never did. I want the best for you too."

"Thanks, Em. That means a lot to me. I may be going out on a limb here, but can I buy you a coffee?" He looked at her with raised eyes and a toothy smile.

"Um… I don't think that's a good idea. Maybe another day. I need to go home."

"Okay. Another day then. Take care, Emma." Matt placed his hand on her shoulder, then trailed it down her arm as he walked past her and over to Doug.

Watching Matt talk with Doug, she felt that same familiar warmth again. The same feeling she'd always had during the happier times in their marriage. She went toward the door. Turning, she saw Matt watching her. She waved and smiled; he did the same back. Ducking her head, she exited the gallery and walked to her car.

Before getting into her car, she turned and looked at the gallery. Her very own gallery.

Smiling as she slid behind the wheel, she knew she and Matt would always have some kind of bond. They'd spent too many years together to never speak again. And he'd taken care of himself rather well. He looked sharp in his tan khakis and navy-blue polo shirt. He'd kept his hair short, and his face held a five o'clock shadow rather nicely.

CHAPTER 18

After the holidays came and went with no time spent with Jack's parents, Emma asked him one morning, "Do you want a party for your birthday? We can invite your aunt Cheryl and your friends."

"No. We can celebrate with a quiet dinner, just you and me. You're all I need." He took her hand in his and brought it to his lips, kissing it softly.

"Okay, if that's what you want."

"It is." Letting out a long sigh, his shoulders slumped, and he rubbed his neck. Jack had shown Emma the text he'd sent his mom, asking them to have dinner with him and Emma for his birthday, but his mom had politely declined. She'd said they were packing for a month-long trip to France. Since that text, Jack's moods had been quiet and somber. Emma worried more about how his dad's refusal to meet her was hurting Jack than how it was hurting her. After nearly a year of marriage, him still refusing to meet her, she figured his dad would never agree to see her.

She'd already made plans with Shea for a birthday dinner for Jack, but she wanted to be sure he'd be okay with it. "You know Brandi, Ben, Shea, and Rob will be here soon for the gallery's grand opening. We could wait and have a birthday dinner with them. It's up to you, baby." She lifted his chin.

"Sure, Em. That sounds good. I need to get into the center. What are your plans for today?"

"I have my final walk-through with Doug." She glanced at Jack.

"Just Doug?" he asked, wrinkling his brow.

"I think so. But I can't stop Matt from showing up." She touched his arm.

His eyes raised. "I don't trust him."

"I know you don't. But please trust me." She tilted her head to the side. "I'm happy with everything so far and they finished a week early. I'm so excited to see the completed work." She stood and walked to the door with him. "If you want, I can ask Doug to do the walk-through when you're done with work tonight?" She grasped his hand in hers.

"I may have a long day. You do what you need to do. You can walk me through the gallery over the weekend."

"Okay, It's a date." She bounced on her toes.

Smiling, he leaned down and kissed her. He slid his arm around her and pulled her close to him. His passionate kiss sent her body reeling and wanting him. "You'll get more of me later. I love you." Jack kissed her again, then their hands fell apart as he walked to his car in the garage. She pushed the button for the garage to open and waved as he backed out and drove off.

***

While waiting for Doug to meet her out front of her new gallery, she panned through her phone and stopped on Matt's number. The ID card had a photo of him from years ago when he'd worn his hair longer and had a beard and mustache. Smiling at the photo, she'd realized she'd always hold Matt tucked away in a corner of her heart. She hated what happened and what she'd done to their marriage, but she also knew it hadn't all been her fault. They'd both made mistakes, although hers had been the worst. Shaking her head to erase the negative thoughts, she decided to put it all behind her. If Matt stopped in her gallery, or showed up at the grand opening, she'd deal with it then. She planned on sending an invitation to the company in general.

"Good morning, Emma." She jumped at Doug's voice. "I'm sorry. I didn't mean to startle you." He smiled at her.

"Oh, good morning. It's okay. I was off in thought."

"Um...." He rubbed his chin and glanced around.

"What is it? Is something not finished?"

104

"Oh, no. Everything is one hundred percent finished." He looked around again. "Mr. Taylor is on his way. He called me as I parked my car. I hope that's okay."

Realizing she couldn't avoid Matt forever, she'd be grateful to him, but she'd keep it all professional. She'd keep her distance but try not to seem ungrateful. She worried Jack's mistrust of Matt had merit. She'd be sure to let him know how the walk through went later.

Matt's flirty behavior with her at the coffee shop took her by surprise. She didn't want to be rude to him, but she felt taken aback when he leaned down to her like he was going to kiss her. Shaking her head to clear her worries, she decided to make it clear to Matt they could be friends only.

"It's fine, Doug. No worries. Matt and I have settled everything from our past. We may even become friends again." Emma smiled and silently prayed what she said aloud could one day be true.

Letting go of his breath, he said, "Great. Now let's go inside. Mr. Taylor will be arriving soon." Doug unlocked the door and pulled it open for Emma to walk in before him.

As she walked inside her brand-new gallery, her heart pounded, and her eyes filled with tears of elation. She gasped as she looked around at the final design that had come to life thanks to Matt's construction company. He'd managed to be a part of this gallery, unbeknownst to her in the beginning. He'd found a way to take care of her. Was it his way of saying he was sorry for letting her down when she'd needed him the most? Maybe one day they'd share a drink and a conversation about it all, but for now, she was simply grateful for the work.

Within a few minutes of entering her gallery, Matt came in behind them. She jumped when he touched her. "Sorry, Emma. I didn't mean to scare you." He let his hand drag down her arm.

"It's fine, Matt. I was off dreaming of my grand opening." Emma smiled and took a step away from him.

"Well, what do you think? Is everything done as you asked?" Matt waved his arm around the gallery showroom.

After looking all around her, she turned back to Matt and Doug. "It's perfect. Thank you both for making this happen exactly how I wanted." She walked over to one of the picture windows and gazed outside. Tilting her head up to her left, she saw the gallery's sign hanging over the front door. "EB's Gallery." She hugged herself as her hands tingled. She knew her grand opening would be the best night of her life since she'd married Jack.

She'd chosen blue drapes with a sheer liner that hung perfectly against the cream-painted walls. The crown molding gave the ceiling a completed look. For the flooring, she'd chosen a cherry vinyl. The elevated loft area and stairs sat off to the right when entering the gallery. The stairs matched the floors. The railing up the stairs and around the loft matched the walls.

Emma's gallery was ready for her to hang her artwork. She'd purchased all the backlighting needed and had hired an electrician to help her. Chandeliers hung from the ceilings of the showroom and down the hallway. There were eight in total. All a soft brushed brass with eight lights.

She headed for her office, in which sat a large mahogany desk and a reddish leather high-back chair. Shelves covered two walls, and she had a tall cherry wood filing cabinet for her business papers. The two windows in her office were normal sized and had dark wooden blinds, no drapes. She also had two multi-colored cushioned chairs sitting opposite her chair.

"What's this?" Matt asked, picking up her nameplate that sat on her desk. It read, **EB Taylor.**

"What, Matt?" She walked into the private bathroom.

"Why didn't you change your name when you married him?" Matt asked.

"I did," she answered from the bathroom. "You know I'm known as EB Taylor in the art world. I'm not changing it. Not right now." She came back to her desk and took the nameplate from Matt, placing it back down. "Jack and I already talked about it. It's not a big deal, Matt. Don't read anything into it." She caught him smiling and needed to be sure he understood Jack was fine with it, even though she knew he wasn't.

"Okay, Em. You know..., people will talk when they see your 'professional' name is the same as mine."

"Yeah, so what. Jack will be here when I have exhibitions. And a lot of people use professional names other than their married name." She looked at Matt, and seeing his grin, shook her head, but let him think want he wanted. She was and always would be with Jack now.

Emma walked out of her office and to the two storage rooms in the back of the building. She inspected each one thoroughly, and then the public restroom, which didn't resemble a public restroom at all. She'd asked for a comfortable home-like design, and she'd gotten exactly what she'd asked for. A large unisex one-person restroom with a long walnut vanity, a chrome sink, and fixtures. The oversized oval mirror had chrome sconces on either side. The toilet sat in a water closet for extra privacy. Emma planned to hang a couple of her small paintings that weren't for sale on the restroom walls to make it feel even more like a home. She left the restroom and returned to the showroom.

Walking over to Doug and Matt, she said, "Well, gentlemen, your company did a fantastic job. Thank you so much. I absolutely love it." She extended her hand to Doug first, and he shook it quickly.

"I'm so glad you're pleased," Doug said.

Taking Emma's hand in his, Matt covered it with his other and shook it gently. Holding her hand, he squeezed it. "Yes, Doug is right. We're all very happy it came out how you wanted, Emma."

Freeing her hand, she threw Matt a thin smile and held his gaze. "I guess I owe you the final payment." Turning to Doug, she said, "Let's go back to my office, and I'll initiate the bank transfer for you."

The two men followed Emma to her office. She sat behind her desk and pulled her laptop from the computer bag she'd brought with her. She punched in her password, then opened her bank app. Going to the transfer page for her bank, she sent the last of the monies she owed B&T for the work they'd done for her.

Looking up from her laptop, she said, "All done." She rose from her chair and walked from behind her desk.

Emma led the two men back to the front of her gallery. She leaned on the counter and looked at Doug. "Thank you again. You did a great job overseeing everything. I'll be sure to let you know when my grand opening is."

Digging in his pocket, he brought out the key to the gallery that Emma had given him. "Here you go. Please do, my wife and I would love to come. It was a pleasure working for you and helping bring your dream to life. I wish you the best." He turned and walked out of the gallery.

Emma watched Doug leave and waited for Matt to follow him.

"How about that coffee, Em?" Matt asked.

Looking at him, she hesitated for more than a beat or three. She'd love to have a friendship with him, but how would Jack be with it? She'd never betray Jack. He was her world. Her eyes fell to the floor, and she sighed.

"I'm sorry, Matt. But I can't." She turned and walked toward her office. Feeling his eyes on her, she kept walking down the hallway. Hearing the front door open, then close, she released the breath she'd held. Her heart pinched knowing she'd hurt Matt yet again, but Jack's feelings mattered more than having coffee with her ex-husband.

CHAPTER 19

Unlocking the front door of EB's Gallery, Emma turned to Jack and said, "Take my hand. Now, close your eyes." She grabbed his hand and led him inside.

With a million sparks flying through her body, she bounced on her toes. "Okay, Jack. You may open your eyes." Her smile filled her face as she watched for his reaction to her new gallery.

"Wow, Emma. This is…." Jack turned all the way around and inspected the showroom completely. He scooped her up by her waist and twirled them around.

She wrapped her arms around his neck. Staring into his dazzling blue eyes, she met his lips with hers. "So, what do you think?"

Placing her back down on the floor, Jack glanced up to the loft. "This is incredible. I absolutely love it. This loft area for you to work in is perfect. The showroom is open and free flowing." He leaned down to whisper in her ear, and she felt his breath and shivered. "Where is the storage room?" He smiled and squeezed her softly.

"Follow me, baby." Her tongue slipped out and wet her lips as she blinked slowly and took his hand in hers. Leading him down the hallway, she stopped in front of the public restroom and opened the door. "First, this is the restroom for my guests." He peeked inside. She led him to her office next. "And this is my office."

They walked into the large room. Jack panned around, moving closer to her, and placing his hands on her slight shoulders. "Want to start here?"

Peering up at him, she grinned sinfully and bit her lip. Nodding slowly, she backed them to her desk. Jack hoisted Emma onto the wood, then his hands resting on her knees, gently parted her legs as he walked between them. Dragging his hands up her thighs, he leaned down and kissed her neck.

Cupping his soft, square jaw, she pulled him closer, melding their lips together. Her tongue found his as she wrapped her legs around his waist and forced him against her. She moaned when she felt his erection.

Wanting him to fuck her, she pushed back and yanked on his scrubs. She pulled his top off. Her hands tumbled down his perfectly hard body, landing on his tip. He let out a moan as he reached for Emma's top and stripped it from her.

Unhooking her bra, he slid it down her arms. Taking her left breast in his mouth, he nibbled on her stiff nipple. Her body erupting into heat beyond anything she'd ever felt, she breathed, "Fuck me, Jack. Now!"

And with that, the rest of their clothes were removed and tossed aside. Sitting naked on her desk, she took a second to admire him. Breathing heavily and aching for him to be inside her, she opened her arms for him.

He walked back between her legs, lifted them around his body and thrusted his cock into her hot, wet pussy as his body leveled hers onto her desk. Their mouths crashed onto one another's, and their tongues twisted together. His body slapped against hers over and over. Harder and harder he went, holding her body around her waist to go deep inside of her. She moaned with sheer ecstasy from each penetration into her. "Dear, God, baby. Yes, yes, goddamn."

She gripped him tightly with her legs as she came close to her bliss. Wanting to hold off until he came too, she held her breath. She felt her walls clenching his cock. She felt him throb and knew he was close to exploding. His body became rigid and his pounding of her more rapid.

"Damn, Emma," he groaned, his body moving in fast thrusts, slapping hers loudly. He reached under her and scooped her up with his hand on her round ass. Catching his intense stare, she kissed him hard and long.

She kept kissing him as he walked with her. The cold wall touched her back when he thrusted her against it. She cupped his cheeks and gazed deep into those damn scintillating eyes. "You're so fucking perfect, Jackson. Don't stop, please." Her lips met his, and her tongue traced around the inside of his lips before plunging into his sweet mouth.

Jack continued fucking Emma against her office wall, shoving her petite body with his. She slapped the wall, grasping for something to hold on to. When she found nothing within reach, she wrapped her arms around his neck and held on for the ultimate ride of her life.

Her body erupting into orgasm after orgasm, she squeezed him as each one came and went. She enjoyed her young, viral husband with every second of the lovemaking, christening her office. With one long, hard thrust, Jack moaned loudly, "Oh, God, Em!" His body straightened as she felt his dick release his cum inside her.

She squeezed her legs around him, laid her head on his shoulder, and whispered, "Baby, you're incredible. I love you." She kissed his shoulder, his neck, his cheek, then his soft lips.

Holding her on him, he walked to her desk and placed her onto it. With their bodies glistening, she ran her hand across his firm pecs. He tucked her long blonde hair behind her ear and leaned down. Kissing her softly, he said, "I love you, always."

She smiled at him and hopped from her desk. They gathered their clothes and dressed. Walking to the door, she turned to him. "I'll show you the storage room, but we can save christening it for another day." She winked and took his hand in hers.

"I think that's a good idea." He kissed her hand and followed her to the storage room, then they walked back to the showroom and up onto the loft.

Emma made the loft a comfortable working space complete with two easels and a shelving unit for her paints, brushes, and pencils. She'd bought crates to hold several different sizes of canvases. Her rolls of white sketch paper leaned against the corner walls. She'd ordered a futon, a cushion chair, and a lamp to sit between them. Each of her easels also had lights attached to the tops. A large cream oval rug with swirls of blues, laid in front of the futon.

Plopping onto the futon, she patted the seat beside her. Jack sat next to her. He embraced her tenderly, kissing the top of her head as she laid against his firm chest. Tilting her head up, she smiled again and said, "It really is all mine. Another dream came true." She squeezed him. "I can't wait for the grand opening. It's going to be fabulous."

"I'm so proud of you, love. You made this happen." His embrace tightened. "The grand opening will be perfect." Lifting her chin up, he touched her lips with his.

CHAPTER 20

With three weeks until the grand opening of EB's Gallery, Emma packed her pieces into her car and drove there. She had scheduled a crew to help her hang the artwork and an electrician for the backlighting placements.

Carrying her coffee and purse, she unlocked the front door and entered the gallery. She walked up the stairs onto the loft and put her items on the table between the easels.

"Mrs. Bryant?"

Emma quickly turned when she heard her name called. "Up here." She waved and began to descend to the showroom floor.

Raking her long blonde locks, she pulled it up into a messy bun, ready to direct the crew of two, a young man and a woman. Extending her hand, she said, "Please call me, Emma."

"Hi, Emma. I'm Chuck. It's nice to meet you. This place looks great." Chuck looked around the gallery.

"Hi, I'm Chrissy. Happy to meet you, Emma." Chrissy took Emma's hand and shook it softly.

"I've been told y'all have experience with hanging galleries." Emma looked between them.

"Yes, we used to work at one back home in Michigan," Chrissy said.

Tapping her chin, Emma asked, "Are y'all related?"

"We're twins. We worked for our uncle and aunt who owned the gallery," Chuck said.

"That's cool. Are we ready to begin?" Emma asked.

"Yes," Chuck and Chrissy answered in unison.

The bell above the front door clanged and Emma turned to see who it was. Expecting the electrician, she drew in a quick breath. Her eyes stared wide at Matt.

"Excuse me, please. I won't be long." Emma walked toward her ex-husband.

Huffing out a breath she'd held, she put her hands on her hips and asked, "What are you doing here?"

"Good morning to you too, Em." Matt smiled and glanced around the showroom.

"Matt, what are you doing here?" she asked again with a firmer voice.

"I was in the neighborhood. Here." He handed her a large cup. "I know you work better after a few coffees. Since you wouldn't go with me for coffee, I stopped and got this for you."

"I have coffee. It's up there." She pointed to the loft. "But thanks." She took the cup in hand and took a sip. "You still haven't answered me, Matt." She looked at him, still standing with her hand on her hip.

"Okay, I confess. I'm heading home today, and I wanted to see you before I left. I want you to know I'll always be here for you. For anything. If something isn't right here, please call me directly. You can count on B&T Construction to make things right. And you can always count on me." He caught her stare. "As a friend. To be there for you." Matt brushed her arm softly.

Taking a step back, Emma said, "Thank you, Matt. That's sweet of you. But I'm good. Really. I'm happy for you. You've gotten to the top with B&T. I'm proud of you." She smiled and looked over at Chuck and Chrissy. "But I need to get to work. We're hanging the gallery today and I have an electrician coming soon too."

"Thanks, Emma. I'm proud of you too. Your gallery will be a huge success. If it's okay, I'd like to come by after it's open. Doug and his wife will be at the grand opening. I'll leave you to get to work." Matt offered his hand to her.

Placing her hand in his, she felt the familiarity again in his touch. "Sure, Matt. As a friend. Good luck to you." Emma went to pull her hand free. Matt's grip tightened as he drew her to him and embraced her. Not wanting to cause a scene, she let him hug her for a few seconds. She patted his back as she'd done before. A goodbye hug for her ex-husband.

"Bye, Emma," Matt said.

"Bye, Matt," Emma said and waited as he exited her gallery, then turned and walked toward her helpers. "I'm sorry about the interruption. Let's get this gallery done." She led them to her car to bring in all of her pieces.

After setting each piece against the walls, Emma stood back. Tapping her chin, she looked at each one and moved several around. Standing back again, she nodded. "Okay, this is the way I want them placed." Looking at her watch, she said, "We can start. The electrician should be here any second."

And just then, the bell over the front door clanged again. "There he is." She walked toward the lanky older man. "Hey, Stan."

"Hi, Mrs. Bryant," Stan said, laying his toolbox on the floor and wiping his hands down his gray work suit.

"Call me Emma, Stan. Follow me. We've started to hang the pieces over here." She pointed to the far-left corner of the gallery and led him that way.

Spending the entire day and into the evening hanging her artwork for the grand opening exhibition, Emma stood back and walked around the entire showroom. She wanted every piece to be properly lit and exactly where it belonged. Liking what she saw, she met Stan, Chuck, and Chrissy at the front counter and paid them for their hard day's work, along with a tip to each.

Driving home, she thought about Matt's visit and what he'd said. All of his heartfelt kindness seemed sincere. She'd trusted him for over thirty years while married to him and before that as high school classmates and friends. There was no reason to doubt him when he wished her well and said he was proud of her. She'd always remember the happy memories of their years together. Especially the day she and Brandi opened BE Unique. She, Matt, Brandi, and Ben were all dressed to the nines. The community came out and supported them in droves. She and Matt celebrated the successful opening with a wild passionate night of sex that went on for hours. She smiled when she remembered how in love they were. But Matt was her past. Her future belonged to Jack.

Emma hoped Jack would understand her and Matt's connection and not be jealous. She had to think of what she'd tell him to ease his worries if he voiced any. Jack had nothing to worry about. She chose to be with him. She made the decision to marry him and live a life with him for better or for worse. Jack and only Jack held her heart in his.

Exhausted from her day of preparing the gallery with Stan, Chuck and Chrissy, Emma fell asleep on the sofa while waiting for Jack to come home. She jumped at his touch, her eyes shooting open as she grabbed his forearm tightly.

"Jesus, Jack. You scared me." She released his arm and sat upright. Dragging her hand through her hair, she tried to tuck her wild mane behind each ear.

"I'm sorry, love." He sat next to her and massaged her shoulders gently. "Did you finish putting up your artwork?"

"We did, and...." She glanced up at him, hesitating a beat. "Promise you won't get mad, but I need to tell you something. It's nothing bad. I want to be completely honest with you all the time." She gripped his hands and pulled them to her.

"Okay, I promise. What is it?" he asked.

"Matt came..."

"When? Why? What more does he want with you, Em?" Jack interrupted her.

"He stopped in to say goodbye. That's all." She lowered her head and pulled in a deep breath. Thinking of the right words, she paused. "Jack, Matt is going back home. He wanted to stop in and see the gallery and wish me well. He wasn't there long at all." She caught his furrowed brow. "You've got nothing to worry about." She tugged on his hands and brought them around her. She embraced him tightly and laid her head against his warm chest.

Kissing the top of her head, Jack tilted Emma's face upward. "I know. I just don't trust the man. If he didn't have ulterior motives, he would've kept his distance like any other job." Jack rubbed his face and said, "He still loves you, Emma." He tightened his embrace and caressed her tenderly.

"It doesn't matter anymore." Emma pushed herself off Jack and turned to cup his face. "I love you. That's what matters. You and me." She moved her finger between the two of them. She stood and stepped between his legs. Leaning down, she kissed his pillowy full lips, then jumped into his lap, straddling him. "This is all I ever wanted. Us, baby. Just us." Wrapping her arms around Jack's neck,

Emma crossed her arms and held her elbows. She nestled her face into his soft brown mane, breathing in his incredibly enticing scent. Even after a full day of work, she loved how he smelled. She loved every last thing about him.

CHAPTER 21

The next two weeks flew by. Shea and Rob arrived and settled into one of the guest rooms. The next morning, Emma got up to have breakfast delivered before her sister woke, but when she opened her bedroom door, the aroma of bacon filled her nostrils. Walking toward the kitchen, she stopped and placed her hands on her hips.

"Dammit, Shea. I wanted to have breakfast here for you and Rob." She dragged her fingers through her hair and went over to her sister by the stove. Hugging Shea from behind, she said, "Thank you."

Shea turned and hugged Emma. "You're welcome. I knew you'd want to try and beat me to the punch, but you know I love to cook."

"If you insist. But we are going out for dinner, my treat when Brandi and Ben get here later this week. Okay?" Emma leaned over the stove and smiled at her sister.

"Okay. One dinner out. Now go make coffee for us." Shea hip bumped Emma and she walked away from her sister to the coffee pot.

"Good morning, ladies. What smells so good?" Jack asked when he entered the kitchen dressed in his green scrubs, ready for work.

Emma finished readying the coffee maker and walked over to him. Slipping her arms around his waist, she hugged him tight. Looking up at him, she puckered her lips. Jack leaned down and kissed her. After their kiss he said, "Good morning, beautiful."

"Good morning, gorgeous." She stood beside him with her arm still around his waist.

"I see y'all are still at it," Rob's voice came from behind. He patted Jack on the back and sat on a barstool.

"Can you blame me?" Jack fist bumped Rob and sat on the barstool next to him.

"Not if she's anything like her sister…"

"Robert!" Shea yelled and tossed a dishcloth at him. Laughter filled the room.

Emma walked over to her sister and gave her a quick pat. "I knew it," she whispered to Shea.

Smiling, Shea winked at Emma. Emma leaned against the counter and watched Jack and Rob share a brotherly conversation. Warmth filled her heart and body. A sweet grin filled her face as they joked, nudged, and did another fist bump. Her eyes glassed over with tears of pure joy seeing Rob and Jack like this. She'd always worried how Rob would adjust to Matt being gone and Jack being his brother-in-law. But it seemed her worries had all been for naught. The two men got along well. She hugged herself and kept watching them until she heard Shea's voice.

"Earth to Emma."

"Oh, yeah, what?" She shook her head to clear it.

"Will you get some plates and silverware for us?" Shea asked.

"Sure. Do you want to eat here or in the dining room?"

"Here is fine. The guys are comfortable. So why move?"

"Okay. Jack, Rob. Coffee?" Emma asked.

"Yes," they both said.

Pouring everyone a cup full of coffee, Emma placed them on the bar and retrieved the half-n-half from the refrigerator and got the canister of sugar as well. Hopping onto the stool on the other side of Jack, she tugged on his arm. He leaned over to her and brushed his lips across hers. Her eyes smiled brightly as she caught his gaze.

"Breakfast is served. Dig in," Shea announced as she placed the plates filled with eggs and bacon before Rob, Jack, and Emma.

"Looks and smells delicious. Thanks, Shea," Jack said and jabbed a forkful of eggs.

"Yeah, my wife makes the best food." Rob leaned closer to her and kissed her cheek.

"Thank you, guys. It's nothing, really. I could teach Emma a few things while we're here." Shea smiled at Emma.

Rolling her eyes and shaking her head from side to side, Emma waved her fork in the air. "There's a really nice local deli we love to support and keep in business, right, Jack?" She nudged him.

"Oh, ah… yeah. They make really good food. Um… not nearly as good as this though." He raised his coffee cup and took a quick sip.

"Nice save there, bro." Rob offered his fist to Jack, and he bumped it with his.

Seeing the brotherly connection deepening between Jack and Rob before her very eyes made Emma's heart happy. The joy it brought to her life couldn't be described.

After breakfast, Jack left for the center. Emma, Shea, and Rob all dressed and headed into the gallery.

Parking her car, Emma looked at her sister and said, "Are y'all ready to see my new gallery?"

"Yes, we are. Let's go inside." Shea unhooked her seatbelt and stepped out of the car, onto the sidewalk.

Joining Rob and Shea, Emma watched as they looked around the outside of the gallery. Shea looked up at the sign above the door. "I love the name. It fits perfectly."

"Thank you. C'mon, let me show you inside." Emma brought out the keys from her purse, unlocked the door and pulled it open. Letting Shea and Rob enter first, she followed and locked the door when they were all inside. "Well?" she asked, twirling around the open showroom.

With her hand covering her mouth, Shea blinked quickly as she panned the showroom, and glanced upward toward the loft area. "Oh my, God. Emma! This is amazing. Come here." Shea opened her arms and walked toward Emma. Hugging her, Shea said, "Mom would be so damn proud of you. I'm so damn proud of you." Still hugging Emma, Shea breathed deep, "I… I… wow. Emma. Not just the design of the gallery, but your art is stunning." Letting go of Emma, Shea walked over to a piece. She pointed at it. "Is this your new creation?"

Nodding, Emma walked over to Shea. "Yes. These are my poem paintings. I had a time when I couldn't draw or paint. So, I

120

wrote my feelings in a journal, and this is what became of them."
She waved her arm before several pieces.

"You never mentioned you had artist's block. Why?" Shea
walked along the wall and read each of the poems, touching the
frames of some, then covering her mouth. When she turned back to
Emma, her cheeks were wet with tear streaks. Emma opened her
purse and handed Shea a tissue.

"Here, I keep these handy." Emma smiled as Shea took the
tissues from her.

Wiping her face, Shea embraced Emma. "I wish you'd told me
about this. When did all this happen?"

"It began the night Matt agreed to sign the divorce papers.
You'd think I would've been able to paint with that news, but I
couldn't. Jack had told me to text him as soon as I was done meeting
with Matt. He hated that I was meeting Matt alone. So, I texted him.
He didn't respond. He'd promised he would. He'd insisted he'd be
able to take a break from the counseling session and answer me, but
he didn't. Something felt terrible, just awful. My mind blocked all
my ability to draw and paint. I found a journal app and started to
write. And here we are." Emma waved her arm across her poem
paintings.

Shea's eyes closed, and she dabbed her face with the damp
tissue. Embracing Emma again, she held her tightly. "I know you
were in a lot of pain during all of that but look at the beauty you've
created. This, all of these poems, they're your silver lining in that
darkness. These are so emotional, so beautifully painted." Shea
rubbed Emma's arms over and over.

Blushing, Emma held Shea's hand and squeezed gently.
"Thank you. I know you're right. It was a difficult time. It's over
now, and Jack and I are married. He's still healing from the loss of
his baby, but we're happy. Everything is good."

Feeling Rob's hand on her shoulder, she turned to face him.
"What do you think?"

"It's fantastic. Whoever you hired to design this and renovate
this, they deserve a gold star and a hell of a review."

"Oh, geez...." Emma swallowed hard. "I guess I forgot to tell
you." Her mouth twisted.

"Okay, Em. What did you forget? Who did you hire?" Shea
asked.

"Let's go up on the loft and I'll explain." She led Shea and Rob up the stairs and pointed to the futon for them to take seats. Sitting in the cushion chair, Emma clasped her hands in her lap. So, I hired B&T Construction," she stated.

"Oh, good. You didn't hire the company Matt worked for. So why the hesitation?"

"Well, that's just it. B&T is Matt."

"Wait, what?" Shea sat forward. Robs eyes opened wide. "What do you mean, Matt *is* B&T?"

"Yeah, Matt is the T in B&T…"

"Hold on," Shea interrupted Emma. "What the hell happened at Marcus that caused Matt to leave? He's worked there since college."

"Matt said he had an offer made he couldn't refuse. He has complete control."

"Who is the B?" Rob asked.

"I don't know. Matt said he has silent partners. They wanted someone like him to run the company and didn't require him to pay in half. So, he took the offer and left Marcus." Emma shrugged.

"And what did Jack say?" Shea asked.

"He's not happy, but I reassured him Matt isn't up to anything. Matt took this job on with honest intentions." Emma looked at her sister and brother-in-law as they looked at each other.

"Hmm." Shea rubbed her chin. "The Matt Taylor I know would never hurt you. He still loves you. So be careful when he's around. Men's feelings are tricky."

"I thought Matt was up to something in the beginning, but we talked, and he was honest with me. I was upset at first and worried about Jack's reaction, but it's been worked out, best as it can be. Jack will always have suspicions where Matt is concerned. All I can do is reassure him it's him I chose to spend my life with." Emma drew in a deep breath and pulled her long hair up into a messy bun, sliding a pencil through it. "And I know Matt and I have a lifetime bond, but only as friends. I've made it very clear to him."

Rob stood and paced the small floor area of the loft. He leaned against the railing and said, "Please don't get upset, Emma, or you, Shea." He looked at his wife and then Emma.

"Robert," Shea began. "Do you know something we don't?"

He huffed out a breath and scratched his face. "Well, kind of." He squinted and pinched the bridge of his nose.

"Spill it," Shea demanded

"Okay, okay. It's not terrible," Rob said, glancing again at Emma.

"Whatever it is, just tell me." Emma rose from her chair and walked toward him.

"I knew Matt was coming down here. We talk a lot." He paused. "I know you told Shea you didn't want Matt ostracized and we've been friends, brothers since before I married Shea." He sighed, his shoulders slumped. "I should've said something to you, honey." Rob looked at Shea. "I'm sorry."

Placing her hand on Rob's arm, Emma said, "No reason to be sorry. Did Matt tell you what he was coming down here for? Did you know about him leaving Marcus?" she asked.

"I didn't know. He told me he'd be seeing you a lot. And he'd hoped you'd be happy to see him. I told him not to be stupid. That you and Jack were happy and to leave y'all alone." Rob's eyes came together. "I'm really sorry, Emma, if he made you feel uncomfortable at all. I know he still loves you. He always will."

Waving her arm in the air, she then laid it on Rob's shoulder. "No worries. When I first ran into Matt at the coffee shop, it was awkward. Eventually when I found out he was B&T, we worked through it. I can't be mad at him. Look at this place. He made another dream of mine come true. I'm grateful to him and his company."

Shea joined them by the railing and glanced around the gallery. "I guess you're right, Emma. After everything y'all went through, he still made this happen for you." Shea turned and faced Emma. "Are you sure Jack is okay with Matt having his hands in this?"

"No, but Jack knows I love him and won't ever betray him. We're solid and nothing will break us. I'm positive of that." Emma took Shea's hand and squeezed it.

CHAPTER 22

Brandi and Ben arrived three days before the grand opening of EB's Gallery. Emma asked Brandi to do a boudoir photoshoot for her. She wanted to give the photos to Jack for their first anniversary. Brandi was more than happy to help with everything she asked.

They went to the gallery in the afternoon. Emma had her negligees, heels, and boots in her bag, along with some props. The photoshoot took three hours with all the clothing changes and the makeup artist Emma had hired to do her makeup for her. Once Brandi finished taking Emma's photos, she showed Emma on her computer where she'd hidden them in a password protected file.

"I'll work on these when we go home and have the special anniversary album sent here, so Jack won't accidentally get it," Brandi said.

"Great idea. Thanks for doing this. I hope he likes this." Emma clasped her hands together.

"He's a man. He'll love it, Em. Stop worrying." Brandi closed her computer and slid it in her bag. "Okay, now let me photograph your gallery."

While Brandi took the photographs, Emma paced back and forth. Rubbing the back of her neck, she shook out her hands and bounced on her feet, trying to settle her anxiety. She didn't know why she felt so nervous. She'd had plenty of exhibitions before at BE Unique. *But never one by myself. Ahh!*

After watching Brandi take many photos, she caught up with her by her poem paintings. "Hey, do you remember when we first opened BE Unique?"

Looking at Emma, Brandi blinked rapidly. "Seriously, Em? Of course, I do. That was the second-best night of my life." She placed her camera on one of the tables. "What's got you so sentimental?" She rubbed Emma's arm and squeezed her elbow.

"I don't know. It's sort of déjà vu for me. You're here with me, taking pictures of the gallery. You did the same thing before we opened BE Unique." Emma brushed her hand below her nose. "Sometimes I miss it. Do you?" she asked as she walked toward one of her paintings that had hung in their gallery years ago.

"I miss it. But mostly because it was ours. I miss working with you." Brandi joined Emma by the painting of the beach they'd all went to for a weekend getaway. The foursome: her, Matt, Brandi, and Ben all stayed in side-by-side beach cottages. She'd painted the beach during the daytime and then a sunset scene from that weekend. "Emma." She felt Brandi tug on her arm.

"Oh, sorry. This painting. Do you remember when I painted it?" Emma asked.

"I do. That was a fun weekend." Brandi smiled. She walked back to the table where her camera sat and picked it up. "Em, I should finish so we can get back to your house."

"Yes. Okay. I'll wait at the counter." Emma smiled at Brandi and walked over to the front counter. She hopped onto the stool and watched her best friend finish photographing her gallery.

Thirty minutes later, Brandi joined Emma at the front counter. "Are you ready?"

"I am." She looked at her best friend. "I need to call the caterer, and make sure he's ready for Saturday night. I should check with Mark from the PR firm. Oh, shit, Brandi." Emma felt her heart beating too fast. She gripped the counter.

"Emma, talk to me. Why are you so nervous? You've got this. Your grand opening exhibition is going to wow this town. Everyone will know who you are. Give me your hands." Brandi came around and placing her hands in Brandi's, Emma gripped hers tightly.

Breathing deep breaths to calm herself, she looked at her best friend. "I don't know. My anxiety has been on overdrive. This is my first solo exhibition. We always did these together." She hung her head.

"No, you're not doing this alone. Jack's here. I'm here. Shea, Rob, and Ben are here. We've got you and you've got this. C'mon, let's take one more walk around the showroom and make sure this is the look you want." Brandi tugged on Emma's arms.

"Yeah, and I'm so happy y'all are here. But…." she rubbed her neck and raised her eyes to Brandi.

"But what, Em?"

"Jack's parents declined our invitation." Her eyes came together as she fought back her tears.

"Hey, that's their loss. You and Jack asked them to come. Y'all did all you could. I know it hurts you both, the way his parents are acting toward you, but you know Jack loves you. That's what matters. Not his parents." Brandi cupped Emma's arm.

"I know. I hate to see Jack in any pain and his parents being so stubborn is making it worse. I wish I could make it all go away." She sighed.

"You can't change them, so stop trying to. Let Jack handle his parents." Brandi tugged on Emma's arm.

Looking at her best friend, she nodded. "You're probably right. I still hate it. I want everyone to be happy. Like how Jack makes me the happiest woman alive."

"Then focus on him and your gallery," Brandi said.

Letting out a breath, Emma said, "I will. Thanks." Emma slipped her arm through Brandi's, and they made one last trip around her gallery. They ended in the middle of the showroom. "It's exactly how I envisioned it." She pinched Brandi's arm.

"It's going to be a fabulous night." Brandi patted her hand as they walked toward the front door.

"Oh my, God. I'm so nervous and excited."

"It's like riding a bike, Em. Once you've learned how to, you'll always know. Your artwork is who you are. Be proud of all of this." Brandi swung her arm in a big motion toward the gallery's showroom. Then she turned back to Emma. "And that you did this on your own."

Emma blinked rapidly and brought her hand to her mouth. Tears sat on the brim of her eyes as she glanced all around her gallery. Nodding, she said, "You're right. I am proud of myself. And not in an ego boosting way. This" she twirled around with her arms wide, "This is all my own. Everything here is from me." She reached for Brandi, and they hugged.

"Girl, I'm so happy for you." Brandi squeezed Emma tight before releasing her.

"C'mon, we need to stop at the bakery and pick up Jack's cake. I did remember to order one for him." Emma smiled.

As Emma flicked off the lights, she took one more look at *her* gallery. A warmth filled her soul. She pulled the door closed and locked it. Clasping her hand with Brandi's, she tugged on her arm and pointed up to the gallery's sign. "That's all mine, Brandi."

CHAPTER 23

Walking into the kitchen from the garage, Emma smelled the dinner Shea had made for the group. She went to the oven and peeked inside.

"Close that," Shea barked at her.

Emma jumped and let the oven door slam shut. "What? I can't look into my own oven?"

"You've never used the damn thing." Shea walked over to Emma and stood between her and the stove. "Did you and Brandi get everything sorted?"

"Oh, we did. The gallery looks so good." Emma clasped her hands between her breasts and grinned wide. "Brandi helped me figure it all out, and she took a bunch of photos. I really miss working with her." Emma sighed.

"That's what will make your big night extra special. Having Brandi there with you to celebrate. I'm so happy we're all here with you and Jack. It's going to be amazing. Oh, did you get the cake for him?" Shea asked.

"I did. It's in the fridge."

"Good. Dinner is almost ready. Will you set the table for me?"

"Sure, let me go and wash my hands and splash some water on my face. I'll be right back." Emma walked toward her bedroom. She looked out the French doors that led to the lanai and saw Jack with Ben, and Rob relaxing out there.

After refreshing herself, she returned to the kitchen and retrieved the plates needed for dinner. "Hey, Brandi, will you grab the silverware?" Emma asked.

"Got it," Brandi said.

They set the table, then Emma went to the lanai and called for the guys to join them. Leading them to the dining room, she turned to Jack. Looking up at him, she embraced him. "I missed you, baby."

"I missed you too, love. Is your gallery ready for Saturday? Are you?" Jack asked.

"It's as ready as it's ever going to be, but I need to make a couple of calls after dinner to double check some things." Emma sat in her chair as Jack helped slide it under her.

Sitting at the head of the table, with Emma to his right, Jack said, "Thank you for making dinner, Shea. It smells delicious." Jack tipped his glass to Shea.

"You're welcome, Jack. And happy birthday," Shea said.

"Thanks. Having y'all here to celebrate with me is what's made it a happy one." Jack sipped on his drink.

Emma looked closely into Jack's eyes. She knew he hid his pain from everyone. His parent's being absent from all the big events in his life was taking a toll on him. She felt it each time she'd ask if he heard from his mom, and when she'd ask him to reach out to them again. Each time their answer was the same.

She slid her hand onto his leg underneath the table. Turning his head to her, he smiled weakly, then patted her hand.

After dinner, everyone retreated to the family room. Emma cleared her throat and caught Brandi's attention. Cocking her head to the side, she stood and went to the kitchen with Brandi in tow. "Will you help me light these candles?" Emma asked.

"Sure, but why didn't you just buy the number candles?" Brandi asked.

"Because this is more fun." Emma stuck out her tongue and dumped the box of candles onto the counter. She brought the cake out of the refrigerator and sat it next to the pile of candles. She counted the number of candles she needed and began to place them into the cake. Brandi followed with a lighter and lit all thirty-nine of them.

It took a few minutes to get all of the candles lit, and when they did, Emma walked slowly back into the family room with Brandi in front of her.

Emma began singing the birthday song as she walked closer to Jack. Brandi, Shea, Rob, and Ben all joined in and sang along.

Staring directly at Emma, Jack's face blushed, his eyes sparkling. He blew a kiss to her and touched his heart. She sat the well-lit cake on the coffee table.

When the singing ended, Jack said, "Thank you all. Emma, I love you so much." With one arm, he embraced her gently, then waved the other arm around. "And y'all. Man, I love y'all too."

"Happy birthday, Jack," everyone said in unison.

Bending over the cake, Jack drew in a deep breath. He blew it out hard, and every candle went out. Emma squeezed his shoulder as she stood beside him. "Did you make a wish, baby?"

"Of course, love." He drew her into him and kissed her deeply. She wrapped her arms around his neck and kissed him back with every ounce of passion she could.

Picking up the cake, Shea asked, "Does everyone want cake and ice cream?"

"Yes," came from the group.

"Brandi, will you help me?" Shea asked.

"Yep." Brandi jumped up from the chair she'd been sitting in and followed Shea to the kitchen.

"Tell us, Jack. What did Emma get you for your birthday?" Rob asked.

Speaking before Jack could, Emma looked at her brother-in-law. "Well." Emma smiled sinfully. "Sorry but that's none of your damn business, Robert." She winked and snuggled even closer to Jack.

Brandi and Shea came back into the family room with cake and ice cream for everyone.

"Here, Jack. A little something from me and Rob." Shea handed him a gift bag.

"What?" Jack took the bag and looked inside. "Thanks, but this wasn't necessary." He pulled out a bottle of his favorite bourbon.

Emma glanced at her sister with a smile and said, "Thank you both."

"You're welcome. It's an easy gift and we know you'll enjoy it, Jack," Shea said.

Clearing his throat, Ben handed Jack a bag the same size as Shea had. "Enjoy, man."

Looking inside, Jack laughed and pulled out another bottle of the same bourbon. "Thanks. Did y'all shop together?" Jack pointed his finger toward Shea, Rob, Brandi, and Ben.

"Ha, ha. No, but I guess we think along the same lines," Shea said.

"Well, thanks to all of you. Anyone want a glass?" Jack asked as he got up from the sofa.

"Sure," Rob chimed in.

"No, thanks. I'll stick with beer." Ben held his bottle and tilted it toward Jack.

"Any other takers?" Jack glanced around at Emma, Shea, and Brandi.

"No thanks," the three women all answered.

Watching Jack walk into the kitchen with Rob following him, Emma's heart filled with happiness as she watched Rob and Jack form a brotherly bond. Her eyes sparkled as Jack and Rob came back into the family room, laughing and fist bumping.

After a while Shea, Brandi, and Emma cleaned up the cake, ice cream, and plates from the birthday celebration. Glancing at her watch, Emma said, "I don't know about you two, but I'm ready for bed."

Shea smiled and nudged Emma. "Yeah, sure you're going to go to bed and sleep." Shea winked and threw her arm around Emma.

"Eventually we will." Emma hugged Shea and kissed her cheek. Taking hers and Brandi's hands, Emma led them back into the family room. "Alright, y'all can do whatever you want." Letting go of Brandi's and Shea's hands, Emma walked over to Jack and grasped his. "Time for bed, baby." She tugged on his arm, and he stood next to her, placing his arm across her shoulders. Smiling, she said, "Goodnight y'all." Emma and Jack went to their bedroom.

While he was in the bathroom, she slipped into a sheer black negligee. Lying across the bed, she waited for him to return to her.

Knowing her night would be extraordinary, her body filled with heat. Her thoughts of him made her body hum for him. Closing her eyes, she saw his perfectly toned body above her. She sighed as her mini dream went on. She rolled to her side, watching the bathroom door, wanting to see him come to her.

As the bathroom door opened, her body quivered. She licked her lips as Jack appeared. Lifting her arms, she wiggled her fingers,

131

inviting him to her. Her eyes scanned him from head to toe. She salivated when her eyes focused on his hard cock, standing at full attention. She crawled to the side of the bed and met him there.

Kissing his firm pecs, she caressed his exquisite towering body. She folded her fingers around his hard-as-steel dick and began stroking him. He fisted her long blonde locks, holding her head as she kissed his tip and licked the pre-cum that trickled out.

"Mmm, you are so fucking delicious." Sitting on the side of the bed, she took him into her warm mouth. With her hands on his sweet peach of an ass, she squeezed his plump cheeks as she sucked on him, bringing him deep into her mouth. She licked him as he stood before her. Holding her shoulders when his knees buckled, he let out his breath and drew in another.

"Oh, God. Emma," he moaned over and over. His hands moved from her shoulders to her head. Fucking her mouth, he thrusted faster against her.

Moaning as she sucked on him, she wanted him to reach his highest bliss. She caressed his plump ass cheeks with one hand and his ball sack with the other. His tight body moved in rhythm with her head bobs. Taking his incredibly hard shaft in and out of her mouth, she kissed the tip, stroked the shaft, and nibbled on the base when she took him deep.

"Em!' He gripped her shoulders tight. "Love!" He thrusted his hips as she plunged down on his cock. "Jesus Christ!" And one last, "Oh my, God. Emma!"

She held his ass as he came inside her sweet mouth. Looking up at him, she licked a drop of cum from her lips. Her eyebrows bounced, and a sinful smile formed.

Yanking him with all her might, she dragged his long body between her toned legs. His dick still hard, he spread her wide. Her back arched as he penetrated deep into her hot wet pussy. Gliding smoothly in and out of her, he moved their bodies in a sensual rhythm.

Jack's soft lips crashed onto hers, his velvety tongue tracing the inside of her mouth. Her body became engulfed by his erotic moans each time their hips met with a soft slapping sound. She yearned for him more and more. Never wanting the night to end, Emma gripped him hard when her orgasm erupted and sent her to the edge of the universe.

"Don't stop, baby. More, please. Make love to me again and again," she panted breathlessly as he laid beside her. Tracing her body with his fingers, he kissed her soft skin.

Rising beside her, he slipped his arm under her petite body. He sat on his knees, flipped her onto her stomach, and lifted her onto her knees. Heat rose again when Jack's lips met her ass. His soft hands gently squeezed her bum. His lips kissed her back. His fingers slid into her pussy. One, then two. "Oh, baby," Emma cried out when he hit her G-spot. "Oh God."

Jack's long fingers reached deep inside her. Moving in and out. One and two, then a third, and she grabbed a pillow to stifle the incredible release she wanted to scream so loud. Her body shook while he plunged over and over inside her with his fingers. When he stopped, she twisted her body to look at him. With his gaze so full of sin, her breathing quickened when she watched him lick each of his fingers. "You are delicious too, love."

Her chest rose and fell as she stared at Jack, her perfect husband of not quite a year. "Baby, I love you so fucking much." She laid her head on the pillow and reached for his hand.

Grasping it, Jack tugged softly. "One more?" he teased.

"Yes, please. Oh God, yes!" Her heart drumming at a pace she'd never felt before, her body shaking in anticipation of fucking him again. "It's your birthday, baby."

"Mmm, so I can have what I want?" he asked.

"Anything at all." Emma raised her head and caught Jack's wicked smile.

Feeling him move to his side of the bed, she kept looking behind her. He leaned his body against hers and held a bottle. "We haven't done this in a while." His smile became even more wicked.

"Just be gentle, and you can do whatever you want, my sweet." She blinked slowly.

Hearing the bottle top open, she relaxed her entire body. She'd welcome him inside her no matter where he entered her. Jerking slightly when she felt the coldness of the gel running down her ass, she sucked in a breath and gripped the sheets.

"You're amazing, love," Jack said as he placed his cock between her ass cheeks. Going slowly as she'd asked of him, he slid down her crack, then touched his tip to her. As he pushed in gently, she tightened her grip on the sheets. He backed out, then went in deeper. Finding his rhythm, Jack moved in and out of her ass slowly and steadily. Her body reacted with each plunge. She slid her hand under her body. Finding her clit, she massaged herself while Jack ass fucked her. "Jesus, Em. You're so smooth, so tight, oh God."

Emma twisted her body again to watch Jack reach his bliss. Seeing him orgasm would make her release that much more erotic. She rubbed herself faster and faster as Jack's rhythm increased. Feeling the soft smacks of his body against hers, she saw him bite his lip. His body moved back and forth. How he had this kind of stamina amazed her. Her toes curled as his body straightened. And with one final thrust into her, he let out, "Em, Em, Em. Goddamn!"

Her body soared to infinity when his cum sprayed into her ass, and her orgasm let loose. "Jackson!" she squealed as his firm body collapsed onto her. Covering her completely, he kissed her shoulders. He slid her hair aside and kissed her damp neck, his breath upon her body sending hot chills to her core.

Jack slid to her side as she rolled to face him. Cupping his face, she kissed his full lips, sliding her tongue inside his warm delectable mouth. She held his face in her hands and stared deep into his mesmerizing blue eyes. "I love you. I can't ever imagine not loving you. My heart beats only for you, Jack. Only you."

"You've made me the happiest man in all of creation. Without you, nothing matters. This was the best birthday I've ever had. And that's because we're together. I love you, Emma Bryant. Forever." Jack brushed her cheek and kissed her deeply.

Smiling at him, she wrapped her arms around him and melded her body with his. Kissing his neck, then his lips, she said, "Happy birthday, baby."

CHAPTER 24

"Oh my, God. Jack." Emma's chest rose and fell quickly. She gripped his arm, her hand not coming close to closing around his bicep. "Tonight's the night. I can't believe my very own gallery's grand opening exhibition is about to take place. Why am I so damn nervous?" She flicked her fingers, then fanned herself as Jack managed to park the car.

"Everything will go perfectly, please stop worrying. You've checked with Richard, and he said he and his crew had all the food ready. I saw all the fliers posted around town, and your RSVP list is quite long." He turned to her. "Emma, breathe."

Her eyes came together as she drew in breath after breath and held his hands. "Okay. I think I'm ready. Let's go inside." She picked up her small black purse, which matched her sparkling black body-hugging mid-thigh dress and five-inch heels.

Waiting for Jack to open the car door, she checked her makeup in the visor mirror one last time.

"You're stunning, love. C'mon." Jack held his hand out for her.

As she placed her hand in his, she scanned her ravishingly handsome husband. Jack wore a black suit with a crisp white shirt, no tie. His shirt laid open as it had when they'd first encountered one another. Her memory instantly went back to that moment. Her body quivered as he drew her out of the car. She placed her hand on his firm chest and let out a sigh. Peering up and catching his heavenly blue orbs, she said, "I cannot wait to get you home."

Smiling, he brought her hand to his soft lips. He kissed her knuckles, then leaned down and met her lips with his. "I can't wait either," he whispered into her ear, sending a bolt of electricity through her already excited body.

Emma slipped her arm through Jack's. She straightened her spine as she walked toward the front entrance of her gallery. Looking up, she noticed the sign sparkling bright. Her eyes danced as she squeezed his bicep.

Opening the door, Jack stood to the side to allow Emma to enter first. Her hand immediately came to her mouth when she saw Richard and his staff standing before her dressed in their blue and white serving uniforms.

After inspecting all the food and walking her gallery before officially opening it, she and Jack met Shea, Rob, Brandi, and Ben in the center of the showroom.

"Your gallery is exquisite, Em. I'm so proud of you." Shea walked toward her with her arms open. The sisters embraced for a few seconds.

"Yeah, girl. You outdid yourself. Congratulations." Brandi gave Emma a quick hug.

Blushing, Emma glanced at Jack. His grin filled his face. He stretched his arms outward, and she took his hands in hers. Twirling them around, Jack wrapped her in his arms. "This is your night, love. Enjoy it." He leaned down and kissed her.

Bowing her head, Emma cleared her throat. "Thank you all for being here. I never thought I'd be able to do this on my own. After we sold BE Unique, I wasn't sure if I even wanted to own another gallery. But here I am, here we are." Emma stepped back and embraced Jack. "This isn't possible without my charming husband. His unwavering support pushed me to do this. His undying love gave me the confidence to persevere." Emma tugged on Jack's arm. She met his gaze. "I love you so damn much, Jackson. So fucking much." She wrapped her arms around his waist and squeezed as hard as she could.

"I love you too, Emma." Jack kissed her cheek. "I think it's time." He pointed to his watch.

"Oh, Jesus." Emma's eyes grew to the size of the moon. She brushed her hands down her dress and walked toward the front door. Shaking her arms, she glanced back at her family standing and waiting for her to open her new gallery. She smiled and touched her hair. Blowing out a deeply held breath, Emma reached for the handle and swung open the front door.

Standing in the doorway, she said, "Welcome to EB's Gallery. Please come in and enjoy." She stood to the side and greeted everyone as they entered. She noticed Jack had met up with Dr. Grayson and his wife after she'd greeted them. He looked comfortable chatting away with his colleague.

Emma continued welcoming those coming in a steady stream. "Doug, oh thank you for coming." Emma shook his hand.

"Of course, Emma. This is my wife, Connie," he said.

"Nice to meet you," Emma said and softly shook Connie's hand.

"You too, Emma. Your gallery is beautiful." Connie scanned the showroom.

"Thank you. I owe it all to your husband and B&T. They made my dream come true." Emma smiled at Doug.

"Glad it all came out how you wanted." He nodded.

"Please enjoy the evening," Emma said. He and Connie walked by her and into the showroom.

After greeting many more patrons, Emma needed to find Jack. She walked around, then went to the bar for a water. There, she heard a much too familiar voice. Looking toward the end of the bar, she gasped. Her heart leapt into her throat.

What is he doing here? And when did he come in? I just walked away from the entrance a few seconds ago.

"Hi, Emma, what can I get you?" Richard asked.

"Just a water, thanks." Her gaze fixated on Matt standing at the end of the bar talking with someone she didn't know.

"Emma? Emma?" She jumped when Richard touched her arm. "Here you go." Richard handed her a glass filled with water.

"Oh, geez. Sorry. Thanks for the water. Have you seen Jack?"

"Yeah, he was over there." Richard pointed to the other side of the room by her poem paintings.

Emma looked that way and noticed Jack talking with Dr. Ruben. She began to walk toward him when she felt a hand on her arm. Looking up, she saw Matt standing beside her. His cheeky grin filled his face.

"Hi, Matt." Emma looked Jack's way, worried he'd see them and get the wrong idea. Wrinkling her brow, she stole a glance at Jack again. His back was to her, but her throat tightened as she grabbed her arm, rubbing her elbow.

"Congratulations, Emma. This place is as elegant as you are." His hand lingered on her arm.

"Thank you, but I thought you went home." Swaying back and forth, she kept her eye on Jack.

"I did." Matt stepped toward her and touched her shoulder. "Em, why are you so nervous?"

Her eyes darting to meet Matt's, she said quickly, "I'm not nervous."

"Okay. If you say so." Matt squeezed her shoulder.

Stepping back so his arm fell from her shoulder, Emma twisted a loose strand of hair. "Matt. Why did you drive all the way back down here?"

"When Doug told me the date of your grand opening, I put it on my calendar. I wouldn't have missed this for anything. I told you, I'm always going to be in your corner, that's what friends are for, right?" His grin turned sinful. He winked as he took a long pull on his beer.

Drawing in a deep breath, Emma looked around the showroom. Seeing Jack walking toward her, she pressed her elbows close to her body. She held her breath and slammed her eyes shut as she wanted to make Matt disappear. Not knowing how Jack would react to seeing Matt, she felt dizzy. Remembering to breathe, she blew out her breath and steadied herself.

"Hi, Matt. Good to see you," Jack said. She turned to find him standing next to her, holding his hand out for Matt to shake. "I want to thank you and your company. You helped make my wife's dream come true." They shook hands quickly, then Jack brought Emma close to him, slipping his arm over her shoulders. She slid her arm around his waist, holding onto him tightly as she looked up at him.

"Jack." Matt politely nodded toward Jack. "You're both welcome. These were all Emma's ideas, though. We just brought them to life." Matt scratched his almost clean-shaven face. "Congrats again, Em. I'm happy for you." Matt walked by her, lightly bumping her hand with his as he passed.

Pulling her hand away, she stared as Matt walked over to Doug and his wife.

She turned to Jack. "I'm sorry, baby. I didn't think he was coming."

"No need to apologize, love. I had a feeling he'd show up. He owns the construction company that renovated this magnificent gallery for you. It would've been really shitty to try anything tonight. I won't ever disappoint you, let you down, or put you second." Jack held Emma's hands tight. "You are my forever." Letting go of her, he slipped a hand around to the nape of her neck. He leaned down and covered her mouth with his, kissing her deeply. After their kiss, he pulled back. "Now, go. Mingle with your guests. I love you." He turned her around so she could see everyone and gave her a soft shove.

Taking two steps, she looked back over her shoulder at Jack. She blew him a kiss and walked toward a group of couples by her sunset paintings.

Approaching the two couples, Emma cleared her throat. "Good evening and thanks for coming. I'm Emma, or EB if you like." She extended her hand to each of them.

The woman took her hand, the rings on her fingers flashing under the light. "Hi, I'm June and this is my husband, Ray, my daughter, Julie, and son, James." Releasing her hand, Emma waved at June's dark-haired family. "We love this sunset one here and the sunrise one over there. Do you recall where you were when you painted them?" June pointed to ones from years ago when Emma and Matt had gone up to the beaches in Georgia for a vacation.

Her heart clenched when she'd remembered that weekend. It had been an anniversary trip. She couldn't recall which one though. Matt had made all the arrangements and whisked her away. He even packed the car with her art supplies. Dropping her gaze, she wiped a tear that escaped. *It's a fond memory, I have a lot of them. I'll make tons of new ones with Jack.*

Emma straightened her spine and waved her hand over the sunset painting they all stood in front of. "This piece holds a lot of happy memories for me. It was a surprise vacation to celebrate an anniversary. I woke up in the morning and drew that sunrise painting over there." She pointed to a painting across the room. "And this sunset on the same day. I'd never done that before. They are the only two pieces like that on display tonight."

"We came here tonight wanting to buy a painting for our family room. But now…" June turned toward Ray. "Honey, I think I want both." Emma watched as Ray smiled at June and nodded. "Will you sell them as a set, Emma?" June asked.

"Of course, I will. Thank you so much. I'll get my husband to help wrap them when the exhibition ends. In the meantime, I'll mark them sold for you." Emma brought out a packet of small sold stickers from her purse and placed one red sticker on the frame of each painting.

"These will look great hanging side by side in our family room." June clasped her hands together and smiled at Emma. "I've read your poem paintings, Emma. They are beautiful. Such raw emotion pouring from the canvas."

"Why thank you. I appreciate your kind words. The poems are a new creation for me. They're very personal, but I wanted to include them in my grand opening," Emma said. "Enjoy the rest of your evening, and I'll get with you later, okay?" Her eyes raised as she looked at June.

"Thank you again, Emma." June slipped her arm through Ray's and turned to walk away.

Walking toward a young couple standing by her painting of a pumpkin patch, she smiled wide. "Hi, welcome to EB's. I'm Emma."

"Hi, Emma, I'm Katy. This is my wife, Louise." Each woman shook Emma's hand. Pointing to the painting, Katy said, "Where was this painted? The location looks familiar."

"This painting is from the west coast of Florida. North of the Tampa area. More in the country local. I went driving one day and found it." Emma smiled as sensual pulses travelled to her toes. She remembered when she found this pumpkin patch. It'd been after one of her appointments with Jack. Once he'd cleared her to draw and paint again, she scouted locations. When she came upon the pumpkin patch in the painting, she pulled over. With her sketch pad and pencil in hand, she drew and daydreamed about lying with him on the soft bed of hay where the pumpkins sat stacked.

Many of her works of art that were on display tonight came from her married life with Matt, and technically, the pumpkin patch did as well. She was still married to Matt when she'd drawn and painted it, but her attraction to Jack had overcome her. Matt's absence in her life made a space for Jack to lay claim. And he did just that.

Looking at each other, Katy and Louise both said, "We want it."

"Of course. Let me place this sold sticker on the frame, and when the exhibition is over, Jack will help you take it to your car. I hope you ladies enjoy the rest of the evening and thank you." Emma shook both of their hands.

Turning to look for Jack, she saw Brandi and Ben talking with Matt. A pang went through her heart as she watched them. It looked like nothing had ever happened. They laughed. Matt and Ben fist bumped several times. Brandi hugged Matt. *Our foursome, I miss it. We had such fun for a long time. Dinners, vacations, BE Unique exhibitions.* Emma clenched her chest as she stood silently wondering if she'd ever have a new foursome with Jack in place of Matt. Would Brandi and Ben be as playful and joking around with Jack as they always were with Matt? Did she ultimately make the right decision?

Sighing, Emma then nodded as she realized the relief, she felt seeing the three of them talking. A warmth settled inside her.

"Hey, love." Emma jumped when she heard Jack's sweet voice.

"Hi, baby." She slipped her arm around his waist and hugged him tightly.

"Are you okay? You seemed lost in thought."

"Oh, yes. I'm good. Hey, I'll need your help when the exhibition ends. Okay?" Emma looked up into Jack's soft blues and smiled.

"Of course. Whatever you need. I'm here for you." He leaned down and kissed her lips. He glanced at his watch and asked, "What time does it end?"

"At ten." She looked at her watch and saw it was already nine-thirty. "Oh, geez. I guess I should make an announcement soon."

Walking toward the stairs of the loft area, Emma asked Richard to get everyone's attention. He nodded and grabbed a glass and a knife. Clanging them together over and over, he said to the room, "Could I have everyone's attention, please? Emma would like to say a few words."

With all eyes on her, she swallowed hard, shaking as she stood on the fourth stair from the floor. She grabbed the railing and shook her free hand. Catching Jack's gaze, she did her best to mentally tell him to come to her. Her breathing calmed when she saw him heading her way. Standing on the floor beside the railing, he held her hand as she readied her thoughts.

With a gleam in her eye and her shoulders back, she cleared her throat. *You've got this!* Her inner voice assured her. She glanced around the gallery as her heart pounded. Pulling in a deep breath, she put on her best smile and began. "Thank you for being here tonight. I'm humbled by seeing all of you here supporting me and my art." She paused, pulling in another deep breath as Jack lovingly pinched her hand. Smiling down at him, she continued. "I need to thank B&T Construction for their wonderful renovations. Doug, where are you?" She panned the room. Doug waved his hand in the air. "Please give that man a round of applause. He took all my sketches and notes back to his team. And as you can see, they did a fantastic job." Applause erupted. Emma smiled and nodded at Doug. She took a deep breath. No one here knew Matt, but she didn't know what he'd told people as he'd mingled. Not wanting to look ungrateful, she added, "Also from B&T, I want to thank Matt for making sure my dream became a reality. Thanks, Matt." She raised her arm and waved it in his direction. He raised his beer and nodded her way. He added a wide smile and a wink as everyone applauded him.

"I also need to thank my family. My sister Shea, her husband, Rob, my best friend Brandi, and her husband Ben. Their love and support kept me going." She blew kisses to each of them.

"My biggest thank you goes to my husband. Jack, come up here with me." She watched Jack join her on the stairs. Her heart pounded faster as he slid his arm around her. "This man is my inspiration for everything in my life. He is my world. Thank you so much, baby." She tilted her head up as Jack leaned down. Their lips meeting in a sweet kiss as the crowd awed in unison.

"If you've purchased a painting, please see me at the counter before you leave. Jack will help you if you need it. And once again," Emma placed her hand on her chest, "Thank you all so much from the bottom of my heart for welcoming me into your community with such grace and warmth." Applause erupted as Jack led Emma down the few stairs.

Sitting behind the counter as she checked out the purchased paintings, Brandi helped bubble wrap each one, while Ben and Jack carried the larger paintings out to the cars if asked.

With the last of her customers checked out, Emma asked Brandi, "Do you mind taking the wrap up there?" She pointed to the loft.

"No problem, Em. Is there anything else that needs to go up there?" Brandi gathered the bubble wrap and walked toward the stairs leading to the loft.

"That's all, thanks."

"Congratulations, Em," she heard Matt say. She met his gaze as she swallowed quickly.

"Thanks, Matt," she said and looked around for Jack. Not seeing him, she bit her cheek and folded her hands together on the counter. "I hope you enjoyed the evening."

"I did. It brought back a lot of great memories. I miss that time." His smile turned down.

Sighing, she looked around for Shea. She glanced up toward the loft and saw Brandi descending the stairs.

"I'll stop in next time I'm down this way. If that's okay." He covered her folded hands with his and squeezed.

"Sure, Matt. It's fine." She tried to pull her hands from the counter, but Matt tightened his grip. Her eyes searched for Jack again. She watched Brandi pause on her way down the stairs, her heart drumming rapidly.

After scanning the gallery, Matt walked behind the counter and stood beside Emma. She froze. Like a slow-motion movie, she saw Matt lean closer to her. Her pulse raced, she tried to move. She couldn't. His lips grazed her cheek. He softly pinched her hands and whispered, "I'll always love you." Then Matt turned and walked away.

Her eyes blinked as she sat in a statue-like state. She felt hands on her shoulders and someone holding her hands.

"Emma. Emma." She heard Jack's voice but couldn't speak. "Emma!" She felt him shake her.

"Jack...," she looked to her side and saw Brandi and Shea.

"Emma, what's wrong? You're scaring me." Jack embraced her.

143

Pushing back from him, she shook her head quickly. "I'm okay. Is everyone gone?" She looked at her best friend and sister.

"Yes, Em. Are you sure you're all right?" Shea asked.

"I'm fine. I promise." She smiled at her sister.

"Okay, then we'll see you and Jack at home." Shea and Brandi each touched her shoulder and left the gallery.

"It's time to lock up. Richard and his crew finished cleaning up and have left. Now that it's just us, are you sure you're okay, love?" Jack cupped her face gently. Rubbing his thumbs across her cheeks, he brushed his lips to hers. "Emma, please tell me if something is wrong."

"Nothing's wrong, Jack. Matt stopped by the counter before he left. He surprised me, that's all. It's nothing." She slid off the stool and grabbed the counter. "I'm exhausted. Take me home, baby." Jack slipped his arm around her waist, and they walked toward the door. She flicked the lights off and exited her gallery. Turning, Emma locked the door, then slipped her arm through Jack's as he led her to their car.

CHAPTER 25

Staring out the passenger side window, Emma heard Matt's voice in her mind. "I'll always love you." His vow played over and over. Not knowing if she should tell Jack, she swallowed hard and felt her heart racing. She played with her wedding rings as her mind stayed on repeat.

She swore her love for Jack knew no bounds, he filled her every desire, her every need. So why did Matt's pledge of his love make her anxious? Was he up to something like Jack said? Did Matt keep tabs on her all this time? *No way, Matt isn't like that. He wouldn't stalk me like that.* "I'll always love you." Again, and again.

Shaking her head wildly to stop Matt's voice in her mind, she raked her hands through her hair. *Get out of my head, Matt. Get the fuck out of my head.*

"Emma. What's wrong?" Jack asked as he drove them home.

Blowing out a breath, she kept staring out the side window, not wanting him to see her watery eyes. "It's nothing," she insisted. Her grand opening of her new gallery went off without a hitch. She sold a lot of her paintings. She met a lot of nice people, her family and friends were with her, supporting her. How could she let Matt's words torment her like this? "I'll always love you." She shivered as his words whispered in her mind.

"Ahh!" She smacked her hands to her cheeks and yelled, "Fuck me!" Covering her face completely, she did all she could to stifle her cries.

"Em, please look at me." Jack slid his hand onto her neck, gently massaging it. "Will you tell me what's bothering you? I can't help you if I don't know what it is." He took her hand in his.

"Jack." She glanced at him, then bowed her head to her chest. "I can't," she whispered.

"What can't you do? Em, you're scaring me." Jack squeezed her hand.

Shaking her head from side to side, she pulled her hand free and clasped it with her other, laying them in her lap. She raised her head and breathed deeply.

"Please don't take this the wrong way," she said softly.

"I promise, I won't. Emma, you can tell me anything."

"Matt said something to me tonight before he left. I…." She let out a breath and wrung her hands together in her lap. Twisting her wedding rings, she looked at Jack. "Baby, I love you. You know that. I'd never betray you. I swear. No matter what Matt says. You're my heart."

"I know, love. And you're mine. What did he say that has you so messed up?" Jack asked.

"Matt said he'd always love me."

Pulling the car over, Jack put it in park and turned to face Emma. He reached for her hands and brought them to his chest. Holding her hand tight, he said, "I know he will. And he can love you all he wants, but you're *my* wife, forever. I won't ever trust him like you do, Em. But I trust you completely. This isn't an issue for us. He's been in your life since y'all were kids. I saw Brandi and Ben talking with him, it looked like they were having a great time. I get it. I don't expect him to ever stop loving you. I never will." He tugged her hands to his lips and kissed them tenderly.

"Jack, I…" Her head fell to her chest again as tears tumbled into her lap. Sniffling, she raised her head and looked into Jack's soft blue eyes. She saw his undying love for her. *How in God's name is this man so understanding?* "I don't know why you love me so much. And why you risked everything to be with me. And…" Jack leaned into her and kissed her quiet.

Releasing her hands, he cupped her face. "Emma Brooke Bryant. I love you because you are my soulmate. I knew it the moment I saw you. When I decided to pursue you, I didn't have any second thoughts." He brushed her tears from her cheeks, then leaned in and kissed her again.

"But Jack…"

"No buts, Emma. I have no regrets about anything I or we have done." He held her face in his hands, gazing intently into her sapphire eyes.

"But…"

Leaning over the center console, he silenced her with his kiss again. When their kiss ended, he placed his index finger over her lips. Shaking his head slowly, he said, "None."

Taking his hand, she threaded their fingers together. He managed to put the car in drive with his left hand and drove them home.

When they arrived home, Jack came around the car and held his hand for her. He pulled her into him and embraced her tightly. Tilting her head up, she smiled and squeezed him. "I love you, baby. Every part of you is perfect."

He leaned down and met her lips with his, kissing her deeply. Taking her hand, he led her into their home.

"Where have you been? I've been worried," Shea said as Emma and Jack came inside.

"I drove slow." Jack patted Shea's shoulder as he passed by her. Shea turned and watched him walked toward the bedroom.

"Emma?" Shea turned back to her sister.

"What?" Emma dropped her clutch purse on the bench seat and walked over to the liquor cabinet. "Want one?" she asked and brought out a bottle of whiskey.

"Sure, with ice, please." Shea pulled out a chair and took a seat.

"Hey, where were you and Jack?" Brandi asked as she joined Emma and Shea.

"Jack drove slow." Shea rolled her eyes.

Emma poured her and Shea each a glass with ice and whiskey. Handing her sister the glass, she smiled and sat next to her. "I'd offer you one, Brandi, but I know you don't drink. There's Diet coke in the fridge if you want one."

"I'm good. Spill it, Emma." Brandi tapped her fingers on the table and glared at her best friend.

Emma's eyes slammed shut and she huffed out a breath. "Why do you think something is wrong?" She looked at Shea then Brandi.

"Because it took you and Jack way too long to get home. And that's some bullshit about driving slowly. Spill it." Shea took Emma's hand and squeezed it.

Sighing, Emma raked her hand through her hair and threw back her drink. She stood and went to the counter. Grabbing the bottle of whiskey, she returned to the table and sat back down. She poured herself another glass full, then looked at her sister.

"Alright. We pulled over and talked for a few minutes." Emma sipped on her drink.

"About?" Brandi asked

"We talked about what happened when Matt left tonight. Jack was worried." Taking another sip, she hoped Shea and Brandi wouldn't keep pushing for more information.

"What happened? I mean we all saw how you seemed stunned after he left. Did he say something to you that upset you, Em?" Shea asked.

Sighing again, Emma folded her hands in her lap and looked past her sister and best friend.

"Emma," Brandi began. "I saw Matt get close to you just before he left. I assumed he wished you well. Did he say something else? Something that hurt you?"

Staring at the wall behind Brandi, Emma's eyes came together, and she drew in a breath.

"Emma?" Shea tugged on Emma's arm. When she didn't respond, Shea tugged harder. "Emma!" Shea yelled.

Blinking quickly, Emma looked at Shea. "Yes, Matt said something to me, but it wasn't hurtful at all." She paused and rubbed her neck.

"Then what was it?" Brandi asked.

"It doesn't matter what Matt said to me. I told Jack what Matt said, and we talked it out. Jack doesn't trust him and never will. But Jack knows I love him and won't ever stop. He knows I won't betray him, ever." She wiped her nose with the back of her hand and sipped her drink.

"You're not going to tell us what Matt said, are you?" Shea asked.

"No." Emma looked directly at Shea and pursed her lips, shaking her head from side to side slowly.

"Okay. As long as you and Jack are good, then I won't bring it up again. I love you, Emma." Shea rose from her chair and walked behind Emma. Embracing her shoulders, she hugged Emma.

"Thanks. I love you both. I want to go to bed. It's been a long day." Emma stood and hugged her sister, then Brandi. "See y'all in the morning. We can hang out by the pool tomorrow and have a celebration of the gallery's opening."

"Sounds good, sleep well, Em." Brandi and Shea walked ahead of Emma as she finished her drink and placed the glass in the sink.

After a long and incredibly exciting day, Emma opened their bedroom door quietly. "Oh, damn," she squealed when Jack swept her off her feet, rolling her dainty body against his firm pecs. His mouth covered hers, his tongue plunging into her warm mouth to wrestle with hers.

Carrying her to their bed, he laid her down gently. His hands found the zipper to her dress and, unzipping it, he tugged it from her arms. She cupped his face and brought him to her, falling back onto the bed. Their lips crashed together, their tongues twisting wildly as they scooted further up the bed.

Sitting back on his knees, Jack removed Emma's dress, her black lace bra, and panties. He stood and stripped naked as she watched. Her eyes beamed when he crawled onto her, his long, hard cock grazing across her inner thigh. "Baby, make love to me and complete my perfect night." She drew him to her, kissing him deeply as he entered her.

Penetrating her wet pussy with ease, he moved his hips slowly, making her moan with each thrust into her. She grabbed his broad shoulders and dug in her nails, wrapping her legs around his waist.

His warm breath on her shoulder sent jolts of ecstasy to her core. "God, Jack. You're so fucking amazing," she purred.

"You feel so good, love. So damn good." Jack's slow rhythm sent her to the outer edges of infinity. He kissed her long and deep as his dick pulsated inside of her center.

Moving her body with his, she held his face in her hands. The moonlight shining through the bedroom window gave enough light for her to see his seductive blue hues gazing into hers. "You're absolutely spectacular, my sweet." She wrapped her arms around his

149

neck and pulled him to her, melding their lips into a scintillatingly sensuous kiss. Swiping her tongue across his soft lips, she tasted every inch of his warm mouth, moaning over and over as he made love to her.

Jack's thrust became faster as his arms tightened around her. "You're driving me crazy, Em. Jesus, love. I'm coming."

Gently grabbing his face, she said, "Look at me, baby." Their eyes met, she moaned, "Yes, Jack. God, oh God, Jackson!" Her legs clamped hard around his waist as her release came.

"Emma," Jack growled and buried his face into her shoulder. She felt his cock spill his cum into her.

Kissing his cheek, she feathered her fingers through his soft brown hair, resting her hand on the back of his slick neck. He laid to her side, pulling her body into the curve of his. She felt his lips kiss her ear. He whispered, "I love you."

Tugging his arms around her tighter, she kissed his knuckles. "I love you too, baby."

CHAPTER 26

Waking up in Jack's warm embrace, Emma knew her life couldn't get any more perfect. She felt him move as she rolled to face him. "Good morning, beautiful." He nuzzled his nose against her hair, breathing her in.

"Good morning, gorgeous." She snuggled into him. "We should probably get up and see what our house guests are doing," she said, caressing his soft skin.

"Maybe. I'd rather stay in bed with you, love."

"Me too, baby. But they'll be leaving soon, and you can chase me around the house all day long." She kissed his full lips.

Giving into her, Jack kissed her back. "Promise?"

"I promise, my sweet."

They showered quickly and threw on some comfortable clothes for the day.

When Emma opened their bedroom door, the aroma of bacon filled her nose. "Shea," she called out as she walked into the kitchen.

"Good morning to you too, Em." Shea turned and faced Emma, spatula in hand.

"Good morning. What is all this?" Emma waved her arm over the spread of food sitting on the island bar.

"It's breakfast. What else would it be?" Shea said and turned back to the large skillet of eggs to which she'd been tending.

"I can see that." Emma walked toward her sister. Wrapping her arms around Shea, she laid her head on her shoulder. "Thank you so much. You're the best sister ever."

Patting Emma's arms, Shea said, "I know." They both enjoyed a good laugh. "Can you set the table for me?"

"I can do that." Emma released her embrace of Shea and went to the cabinet where the dishes were. Gathering everything she needed, she went to the dining room and set the table.

"Hey, girl." Brandi said when she saw Emma.

"Morning, Brandi. Did you sleep well?" Emma asked as she continued her task.

"Yeah. We both passed out when we hit the bed. Ben's still waking up. Can I help with anything?"

"Ask the boss." Emma nodded toward the kitchen.

"Okay. I'll see what Shea needs." Brandi left Emma in the dining room.

When breakfast was ready, Shea called out to the men, "Robert, Bennett, Jackson!" Each of them appeared quickly from the family room. "Breakfast is ready." Shea pointed toward the dining room, and they all walked that way.

Everyone took their seats and began dishing up the eggs, bacon, sausage, biscuits, and gravy Shea had made.

"Shea, you've outdone yourself. This all looks delicious." Jack raised his coffee mug her way.

"Thank you, Jack. Are you sure I can't show Emma a few things?" She smiled at Emma.

"No, she has other talents that keep me happy." Jack winked at Rob.

Sliding her hand onto his thigh, Emma pinched it gently. He smiled at her and placed his hand over hers, squeezing it. He leaned toward her, and she met him with a sweet kiss.

"Y'all never stop, do you?" Brandi asked.

Emma straightened herself in her seat and said, "Nope."

***

After cleaning up from breakfast, Emma insisted they change into their swimsuits and relax in the pool and spa. It was rather warm day for January even in Florida, but with the cool nights, she still needed to turn the heater on the pool to help take what little chill there was from it.

Laying on inflatable lounge chairs, Emma, Brandi, and Shea floated together in the pool. "Where'd Jack go?" Emma asked when she didn't see him in the spa with Ben and Rob.

"I'm right here," he said as he walked toward everyone holding a bottle of champagne in one hand and six flutes in the other. "To celebrate Emma's successful grand opening of EB's Gallery." Sitting the flutes on the table close to the spa, he popped the champagne cork and poured the sparkling liquid in each flute. Passing one to Rob then Ben, Jack carried the other three to Emma, Shea, and Brandi.

"Thank you, baby." Emma grazed his hand with hers and smiled.

Jack stood by the side of the pool, raising his glass. "To my talented and beautiful wife. Congratulations on your successful grand opening last night. I can't wait to see your next exhibition. To Emma and EB's Gallery." Jack waved his flute in the air.

"To Emma!" Everyone said in unison and sipped on their champagne.

Jack slipped into the pool next to Emma's float. She placed her glass in the holder and held his face in her hands. Leaning over the side of the floating chair, she kissed him. "Oh, Jack!" She screamed when he pulled her into the water with him. They went under the water together, then popped up. Emma wrapped her legs around his waist. With her arm hooked across his shoulder she caressed his cheek and kissed him again. "Thank you. I love you." She laid her head on his shoulder as he walked toward where the spa was at the shallow end of the pool.

Emma, Jack, Shea, Rob, Brandi, and Ben spent the rest of Sunday morning lounging in the spa. Sipping on the rest of the champagne, Emma and Brandi reminisced about their exhibitions at BE Unique.

"Do you miss it?" Emma asked Brandi.

"A little, but we love it in North Carolina, and I've got a decent number of clients up there. It's not the same, but we did the right thing selling our gallery, Em." Brandi shifted her eyes toward Jack.

Emma glanced at him and noticed he seemed disconnected to their conversation. He'd brought his phone out with him and she saw he was thumbing through his emails.

"Hey, Jack. Everything okay?" she asked.

Turning to Emma, he said, "Yeah, yeah. All good." He laid his phone down on the rim of the spa and slipped his arm over her shoulder.

After spending most of the day relaxing and reminiscing out on the lanai, Emma saw Shea glance at the clock hanging on the house.

"Oh, look. It's almost time for dinner." Shea stepped out of the spa and found her towel. "Any ideas?" she asked as she walked toward the French door that led to the family room.

"Shea, please relax and let us order dinner." Emma grabbed her towel once she stepped out of the spa and walked toward her sister. "I insist. Right, Jack?" He didn't answer her right away. Turning, she saw him back on his phone. "Jack," she called to him.

Placing his phone down, he said, "Sorry, love. What did you say?"

"Please tell my sister that we are ordering dinner for everyone. She needs to relax."

"Shea," Jack began. "I think Emma's right. You're a wonderful cook, but you deserve a break. We'll order dinner." Jack got out of the spa and wrapped his towel around his waist. Following Emma into their bedroom, he hugged her from behind. "I'm so proud of you." He leaned down and kissed her cheek.

"Thank you." She turned and faced him. "Is there something going on with work?"

"No, why?" he asked as he walked into the bathroom to change.

"You were on your phone a lot. Did our conversation about BE Unique bother you?"

"Of course not," he said.

Emma sensed something bothered Jack and she needed to know what it was. "Jack."

"Yes, love." He turned and faced her.

"I know something is eating at you. Is it because your parents didn't show up last night?"

"Emma, we've been through this. They chose not to come to your grand opening. It's their loss. They missed out on an amazing evening and a brilliant artist's debut in the community." He sat on the end of the bed, holding his arms for her.

154

She walked between his legs and wrapped her arms around his neck. He embraced her tenderly and kissed her shoulder. Sitting on his thigh, she looked into his saddened blue eyes.

"Jack, I know they'll come around soon. Your mom sounds so nice. She'll convince your dad." Emma held Jack's gaze, shaking her head. "When you talk with your mom again, tell her we'll meet with them someplace where they feel comfortable. If it's at their house, that's okay. As long as I've got you, I'll go anywhere." She leaned into him and kissed his soft lips. Holding his face in her hands, she said, "I can't wait to meet them."

"I love your positive and hopeful attitude, Em. And I hope you're right. It would be nice to see them again. Be a family again." Jack's eyes came together as he sighed.

"We will, baby. And soon, very soon." She kissed him again.

Emma needed to convince Jack that his parents would come around soon. She'd keep asking him to reach out until they'd agree. Somehow, someway, and someday she knew she'd see them.

Joining Shea, Rob, Brandi, and Ben in the family room, Emma took care of ordering dinner. Shea and Brandi set the dining room table for dinner. Forty-five minutes later, the doorbell rang, and Jack answered it.

She kept a close eye on him. She knew deep down he was hurt by his parents continued refusal to meet her.

"Dinner!" Emma called out, helping Jack carry the bags of food into the dining room and placed them on the table. Everyone took their seats as Jack handed out the takeout containers to them.

CHAPTER 27

In the early morning hours of Monday, Emma jolted upright when Jack's phone rang. He glanced at it and looked at her, his eyes squinting, his lips tight.

"Maybe your parents returned early and…" she trailed off. It was much too early for a phone call of anything other than bad news.

Watching him as he went to the bathroom to take the call, she felt a cold chill travel through her entire body. Shaking her hands and squeezing her eyes closed, she sat on the edge of the bed. She wanted to know who called, but she also wanted to give Jack privacy in case it was patient related.

Needing to settle herself, she walked out into the family room and thought about knocking on Shea's bedroom door but didn't want to wake her sister if it wasn't necessary. Instead, she lifted an artist weekly magazine from the holder by the sofa and paged through it. Glancing up every second or so to look toward their bedroom door, she tried to read an article to distract herself. Nothing worked. She looked at her watch and realized Jack had been on the phone for over thirty minutes. Nothing good came of a phone call this early, lasting this long.

Her heart raced as she rose from the sofa and walked toward their bedroom. She about tripped as she got close to the door, pushing all the horrible thoughts from her mind.

Jack opened the bedroom door, walking right by Emma. She caught her breath, knowing for sure the news was awful. "Jack," she called out, going to him. His face was ghostly white. "Baby, what's wrong?" She grabbed his hand and held it to her heart.

Watching him closely, his chest rose and fell several times before speaking. "That was the police." Jack's eyes slammed shut, and his hand swiped under his nose. As his head fell to his chest, Emma tugged on his arm and led him to the sofa.

Sitting next to him, Emma asked. "What happened?" Her pulse raced as she clenched her jaw, waiting for Jack to continue.

His chin trembling, his head shaking from side to side, he lifted his eyes to Emma and said, "My parents were killed in a car accident." Stopping again to catch his breath, he fell onto her lap.

Emma's mouth dropped. "Oh my, God. Jack. I'm so sorry."

Pushing himself up from her lap, he embraced her tightly. She sensed him pulling on his inner strength. "I have to go to the coroner's office… to confirm…." Jack sucked in a deep breath, his cheeks red, as were his eyes. "They need me to confirm their identities. Please, Emma. Please come with me." Tears now flowed freely down his puffy cheeks.

"Of course. Whatever you need from me, I'm here." Emma placed both of her hands on his forearm, squeezing softly. "Let me tell Shea, then we can leave."

Placing his hand over hers, his eyes met hers. "Okay, love. I'm going to need your strength to get through this. I…" Jack collapsed back onto her lap, sobbing heavier than before.

Sucking in her lower lip and blinking quickly, Emma was taken aback by Jack's strong emotions. He'd rarely spoken of his parents after they'd moved in together. She'd known their relationship was strained because of the divorce and their marriage. But of late, Jack and his mom had reconnected. Her words fumbled in her mind. Not wanting to ask Jack an insensitive question, she decided to wait for him to offer anything about his and his parent's relationship. She'd tread lightly in the days ahead. Being there for Jack was her top priority.

Attempting to lift Jack from her lap, Emma gently wiped his cheeks. He tilted his face upward, his blue eyes puffy and bloodshot. He slowly sat upright beside her. Her heart shattered for him. She sucked in a breath and corralled all her strength for her husband. *My God, he's devastated by this. I need to know more. No! Not now.*

Shaking her head, she slipped her arms around Jack, embracing him tightly. "I've got you, Jack. I'll help you deal with all of this. It won't be easy, baby. I didn't lose my mom in an accident, but when

157

she passed, it was the hardest day of my life. She was my biggest fan." Cupping his face, she turned it to hers. "Please tell me what to do, what you need from me." Her lips grazed his cheek.

She drew her eyebrows together, the corners of her lips tugging down. She'd lost her in-laws she'd never got the chance to meet. Jack had tried to make them see how much she meant to him, how much he loved her, but in the end, his father never agreed to meet her.

Pulling in a breath, she rose from the sofa. Extending her hand to him, she wiggled her fingers to get his attention. "C'mon, babe."

Jack stood, hunching his shoulders. His chin touched his chest as he embraced Emma, and they walked toward their bedroom to get dressed and leave.

"I love you. We'll get through this together. I promise."

His face drawn and his cheeks splotchy, he gave her a weak smile.

While Jack changed, Emma went to the guest bedroom where Shea and Rob were staying.

Knocking on the door, Emma waited. The door opened slowly, and Shea appeared, her hair disheveled. "Hey, what's up?"

"Um, Jack received a call from the police..." Emma began.

"Oh my, God. Emma, what happened?" Shea grasped Emma's hands.

"His parents were in a car accident. Shea..." Emma's head fell to her chest, her hair covering her face. She took in a breath, flipped her hair from her face, and said, "Shea, they're gone." Emma's eyes grew wide, and her mouth turned down. Tears streamed over her cheeks for people she would never meet.

"What can I do? How's Jack? Please, Em. Let me help."

"We're going to the coroner's office now. Will you let Brandi and Ben know?"

"I will. Where's Jack?" Shea took Emma's hands again and led her to the family room.

Jack stood waiting for Emma. Shea walked over to him and embraced him. "I'm so sorry." Shea said. Jack hugged her and patted her back.

Emma went to their bedroom and threw on jeans and a top. Joining Jack and Shea in the family room, she slipped her hand into Jack's.

"We should go. I'll fill you in when we get back." Emma touched Shea's shoulder.

"Drive carefully. I love you both." Shea said, her cheeks damp as she swiped her hand across her face.

"We will, thanks." Emma hugged Shea. Turning back to Jack, she threaded her fingers with his and walked to the garage to leave.

In the dark of the early morning hours, Emma drove across town to the coroner's office. When they arrived, Emma grasped Jack's hand tightly. Walking with heavy steps, they entered the building and went to the desk. Emma stood back and waited for Jack.

After a few minutes, they followed the attendant down a long, dank hallway, passing several doors before coming to one near the end. When they stopped, Jack gripped her hand tighter.

"Are you ready, Dr. Bryant?" the attendant asked.

His breath short and quick, Jack's voice sounded flat as he said, "I am."

Crying inside for him, Emma put her free hand on his arm. The door creaked and echoed when the attendant opened it. Seeing the covered bodies lying on two metal tables, she gasped.

The attendant waited, and when the coroner came into the dark room, the attendant left. Jack shuffled his feet as they went further into the room. Shivering when she stood next to him, she rubbed her hand up and down her arm. He paused before going to the table where she knew his father laid. Squeezing his hand, she walked with him. He glanced down at her, his eyes blank, empty, unfamiliar. Needing to stay strong for Jack, Emma hid her fright and stood by his side as he went right up to the table.

"Dr. Bryant?" The coroner lifted his eyes to Jack, and Jack nodded, pinching Emma's hand hard.

The coroner lifted the first white sheet. Jack's chest rose and fell with one long breath. A deep sigh followed as he let go of Emma's hand and brushed his father's cheek.

Watching him intently, she held her breath for a beat. His emotions for his father came out right before her eyes. *Oh, my Lord. Pull yourself together, Em. Jack's going to need every ounce of strength you've got.*

Taking Jack's hand again, she tugged on his arm gently. He looked her way, tears pooling in his wet dull eyes. He squeezed her hand, but she felt him weaken. Nodding 'yes' to the coroner, tears on the edge of his brims, Jack watched the coroner replace the white sheet. Emma fought back her own tears; she had to be strong for him now.

Knowing the next body lying on the cold metal table was his mom, Emma held Jack around his waist. Again, the coroner looked at Jack and asked, "Are you ready?"

Jack nodded in the affirmative, his body weakening as the sheet slowly revealed his mom.

Emma tried her very best to hold Jack as he grabbed the edge of the metal table. She stepped closer along with him. He nodded, 'yes,' again his tears flowing.

With his hand shaking, Jack tenderly brushed his mom's cheek. He carefully leaned down and kissed her forehead, sniffling loudly as he stood upright.

They all turned and left that awful room. When they returned to the front desk, Jack signed some papers, shook the coroner's hand, and said, "Thank you, sir."

"Of course, Dr. Bryant. I'm very sorry for your loss."

Bowing his head, Jack slowly walked to their car, guided by her hand. Emma dug the keys from her purse and opened the passenger's door for Jack. Turning on the car, she drove them home in silence.

CHAPTER 28

When they got home, Emma made Jack lie down and try to rest. She pulled his shoes from his feet and used both her arms to hoist his legs onto the bed. "Rest, baby. I'll make some coffee and we can talk in a bit." Leaning over him, she kissed him tenderly. "I love you." She smiled as she watched him turn onto his side and curl his towering body into a ball. The wall of tears she'd kept at bay released down her cheeks. Emma went to the bathroom and found a box of tissues. Blotting her eyes and wiping her nose, she sucked in breath after breath to compose herself.

Before leaving their bedroom, she walked to Jack's side of the bed. His breathing was still short and rough, but his eyes were closed. She left their room, leaving the door ajar so she could hear if he got up.

Plopping onto the sofa, she looked at her watch. *Holy God, it's 5:00 a.m.* She dragged her hands through her hair and smacked her face. Exhausted and saddened by what she'd just witnessed, she rose from the sofa and walked into the kitchen. She made a pot of extra dark coffee and an espresso for good measure.

Leaning against the counter, she waited for the coffee to finish brewing. Emma jumped when she felt a hand on her shoulder. Spinning around, she faced Brandi. Her eyes came together, and the corners of her mouth turned down as she walked into her best friend's waiting arms.

"I'm so sorry, Em. How's Jack?"

Sniffling as she stood back from Brandi, Emma wiped her face with a tissue. "He's devastated. I mean… Oh fuck. I don't know."

She yanked her hair up, twisted it around and shoved a wayward pencil on the counter through it.

"How are you?" Brandi squeezed Emma's arm softly.

"I'm okay. Shocked, really, but it's Jack I'm worried about. I made him lie down and rest." Emma walked to where she could see their bedroom, then turned back to Brandi.

"He's going to need you now more than ever, Em. This is a big loss."

"Yeah. I don't even know how to ask him questions that aren't insensitive. I mean, his dad absolutely refused to meet me. He even refused to talk to Jack. His mom was reaching out to him by text. And he'd called her a few times to ask them to see us. She said she wanted to meet me, but she couldn't go against Jack's dad. And I understand. I'd never go against Jack's wishes. I'd do all I could to change his mind, but in the end, I'd stand by Jack on anything." Emma looked toward her bedroom again, then went and poured herself a coffee and dumped the espresso shot in.

"Well, at least his mom tried. I'm sorry you never got to meet them. Listen, whatever you and Jack need, we're here. I'm going to call and cancel my appointments for the next week or so. Ben will have his assistant cover the office. We're staying." Brandi grabbed Emma's hand and held it between hers.

Tears flowed down Emma's cheeks as she collapsed into Brandi's arms. "Thank you," she whispered against Brandi's shoulder. Feeling another hand on her, Emma stood back from Brandi and turned to see Shea.

"Hey, how's Jack?" Shea asked.

"He's not good. He's resting now." Emma nodded toward her bedroom door.

"Good, he's going to need his strength. Em, Rob, and I talked, and we're changing our flights home. We called RJ and Amelia and told them what happened. They both send their love. We're here for you and Jack." Shea circled her finger around her and Brandi.

Covering her face, Emma leaned into Shea. The three women hugged one another. Lifting her head from Shea's shoulder, Emma looked at her and Brandi. "Thank you so much. I love you." She pulled Shea and Brandi back into another hug. Then she heard Jack clear his throat.

"Jack," Emma gasped and walked toward him. "Baby, how are you?"

Scratching his face, then his head, he closed his eyes. Drawing in a deep breath, he brought Emma close. "I don't know, love." He shook his head. Raking his hand through his hair over and over, he looked at Shea and Brandi. "I'm glad y'all are here."

"Oh, Jack. We wouldn't be anywhere else." Shea walked over and hugged him.

"Yeah, Ben and I will stay for as long as you and Emma need us to." Brandi came closer, then Jack held out his hand to her. She took a couple of steps and placed her hand in Jack's. She nodded slowly and gave him a kind smile. Jack pulled Brandi in and hugged her quickly.

Turning back to Emma, he asked, "Will you call the center for me, Em?"

"Yes, I will. Go and take a shower. It'll help relax you, even just a little. I'm sure your colleagues will understand." She nudged him gently.

Embracing her tenderly, he leaned down and met her soft lips with his, kissing her deeply. She sighed quietly inside as he stroked her hair. "Thank you for taking care of me. You really are my rock. I love you."

"I love you more than you'll ever know." Walking with Jack toward the bedroom, she found his phone on the nightstand. She waited until Jack stepped into the shower, then went back to the family room. She opened it with his code and thumbed to the center's number.

A few rings sounded before a woman's voice answered. "RG Orthopedic Center. This is Terri. How may I help you?"

"Good morning, Terri. This is Emma Bryant, Dr. Bryant's wife. I need to speak with Dr. Ruben or Dr. Grayson, please. It's urgent."

"Of course, Mrs. Bryant. I'll put you right through to Dr. Grayson."

"Thank you." Emma waited until she heard Dr. Grayson answer.

"Mrs. Bryant, how may I help you? Terri said this is urgent. What's wrong?" he asked.

"Yes, Dr. Grayson. I'm afraid I have bad news to pass along. Jack's parents died in a car accident."

"Oh my. I'm so sorry, Mrs. Bryant. Please tell Jack to take whatever time he needs. I'll have his PA cover his appointments. Is there anything you and Jack need? Anything at all, please let us know."

Emma brought her hand to her chest and sucked back a breath. "Thank you so much, Dr. Grayson. Jack will need several days to take care of this unfortunate event. I'll have him give you a call when he has a minute."

"Whatever you and Jack need, please don't hesitate to ask. I'll pass this sad news on to everyone here. Terri will help you if there is anything you need. Please give Jack our condolences, Mrs. Bryant."

"I will and thank you all so much. Goodbye." Wiping her face with a tissue, Emma went to their bedroom. She dressed and brushed on some light makeup.

Hearing the water still running in the shower, she kept the bedroom door open and walked back to the kitchen. Rob and Ben had joined Shea and Brandi while she'd been on the phone. She walked over to the foursome.

"Hey, y'all. I think Jack may want to go to the lawyer's office and get this over with."

"Okay, Emma. Don't worry about us. We'll take care of things here. I'll go shopping and get some groceries." Shea grabbed a notepad and began to make a list.

"Thank you, Shea." Emma let out a long breath. "It's going to be a rough few days, weeks, and months. But we'll be fine." Emma turned when she heard the bedroom door close.

Ben and Rob both stood and walked toward Jack. "Hey, man. We're so sorry for your loss. Whatever you need. We got you, brother." Rob grabbed Jack and practically bear hugged him.

Ben stood beside them, and when Rob let Jack go, he stepped in. "Yeah, Jack, I'm really sorry. We'll all be here for as long as you need us. I'm sure Brandi has already said that, but I wanted you to hear it from me."

Jack's head fell to his chest as he dragged his hand through his hair. He rubbed his neck and leaned against the counter. "Thank you all. Emma, did you call the center?" he asked.

"Yes. I spoke with Dr. Grayson. He said to take all the time you need and if there's anything we need, to call and Terri will help." She covered his hand with hers.

His head hung. His hand rubbed along his neck again. He sighed heavily as he threaded his fingers with hers. Pulling her hand to his lips, he kissed it softly. He looked around at their family and friends. "I don't know what I'd do without you, Emma. Or any of y'all."

"You'll never have to worry about that, Jack. I'll be by your side always," Emma said.

"Yes, we're all here for you." Brandi motioned her hand around everyone.

"Jack, how 'bout something to eat?"

"Thank you, Shea. But I'm not hungry." He looked at Emma. "Maybe after we take care of this funeral stuff, okay?" He pinched his eyes together and rubbed his forehead.

"Sure. Whatever you want." She glanced as her watch and said, "We should get going. It's a bit of a drive to the lawyer's office." She hugged Shea, Rob, Brandi, and Ben.

"Yeah, it is. Are you ready?" he asked.

"I am." Emma grasped Jack's hand, and they walked out of the kitchen, to the garage. Getting into her car, she took his hand again. "I love you."

Smiling weakly, he brought her hand to his lips and kissed it softly.

CHAPTER 29

Arriving at the lawyer's office, she watched Jack rub his face and suck in a breath before turning the car off and stepping out. Emma's heart sank as she ran her hand over his forearm when they walked toward the building. Turning to her, his brow furrowed, he tried to smile.

She clasped his hand in hers as they entered the lobby of the grand office building that held the offices for his parents' lawyer. Jack walked to the receptionist's desk as Emma took a seat and waited.

Before he could sit, a young woman's voice called out. "Dr. Bryant?"

"Yes," Jack said. Emma rose from the chair and followed him and the woman. The young woman took them to a corner office with tall glass windows. A large mahogany desk sat in the center with a black leather chair behind it. Two leather chairs were opposite.

Taking a seat, Jack leaned forward, his head in his hand. Emma knelt down in front of him and grasped his wrists. "If this is too much right now. I'm sure we can reschedule." She leaned in and tried to see his face.

Keeping his hands tight against his face, Jack shook his head slowly from side to side.

"Okay, baby. How ever you want to do this. It's fine." She rose and drug the other leather chair closer to his. She narrowed the space between them so she could hold his hand and give him comfort. When he leaned back in his chair, she took his hand and intertwined their fingers.

Glancing around the lawyer's opulent office, Emma felt a knot in her chest. She'd remembered all the attempts to ask his parents to see them she'd asked Jack to make. She'd wanted to meet them, get to know her in-laws. Bring them around to liking her. She wanted them to be a part of their lives.

Raking her hand through her hair, her head pounded with a raging headache, but she had to be in that office with Jack. He'd asked her to come with him. She tried to meditate for a minute. Her breaths pained her, she closed her eyes.

Jack softly pinched her hand. Turning to him, she pulled herself together and gave him her sweet smile. "We'll get through this." She gently tugged on his hand.

"I know we will, love." He closed his eyes and let out a breath. "Thank you for loving me."

"You don't need to thank me. I wish I could turn back time and make this all go away. Try harder to convince your parents to meet with us." She sighed heavily "Jack, I...,"

A lanky older gentleman in a suit entered through a side door. "Dr. Bryant, Mrs. Bryant, I'm Sam Case, the attorney for Mr. and Mrs. Charles Bryant's estate." He extended his hand to each of them. After shaking hands, they each took their seats. Looking at Jack, Sam said, "I'm sorry for your loss."

"Thank you, Mr. Case," Jack said, sitting taller in the chair. Emma watched him carefully, ready for whatever happened.

"Your parents have everything in order. You're the executor of their estate. As their only child, they've left everything to you." He opened the large folder and laid a pen on the desk. "I need a signature from you, and the rest will fall into place."

Picking up the pen, Jack signed the papers quickly and laid the pen on the desk. He pushed the papers toward Sam.

"I believe we are done. You'll need to fulfill their wishes for the funeral services with the church. It's all just a formality. My condolences to you both again," Sam said and pushed his chair back as he stood and extended his hand to Jack again.

"Thank you for everything, Mr. Case." Jack stood and shook Sam's hand. Standing next to Jack, Emma nodded and clasped Jack's hand in hers, sensing his emotions coming on. She knew he was on the verge of a breakdown.

Walking to the car, Jack turned to Emma and asked, "Do you mind if we go by the center? I want to speak with Dr. Grayson."

"I don't mind. I can wait in the lobby while you talk with him."

"I'd like you to be with me, Em." Jack's gaze went deep into her.

"Okay, I'll be by your side," Emma said and got in the car.

At RG Orthopedic Center, Jack spoke with Mandy at the check-in-desk while Emma stood beside him. Mandy pressed a few numbers on the phone. Emma heard her ask if Dr. Grayson was available to see Jack. Mandy's head nodded up and down as she listened to whoever was on the other end. She turned to Jack and said, "Dr. Grayson will be right out."

Jack smiled. "Thanks, Mandy." He took Emma's hand in his and walked toward a chair. Before they reached it, a man's voice called out, "Jack, Mrs. Bryant." Jack turned toward the man. "Please come with me. We can talk in private in my office." Dr. Grayson held the large door for them to walk through. Hooking her arm through Jack's, she followed Dr. Grayson down a long corridor, passing many small exam rooms. Large pictures hung all along the corridor. She assumed these were pictures of Jack's colleagues. Her heart warmed when she noticed Jack's. He sat holding a woman's arm, smiling his charming smile. Quivering a little, she remembered how his smile and his touch made her hot as hell when he'd been her doctor.

Taking seats across from Dr. Grayson in his office, Emma patted Jack's hand as she tugged her chair closer to his.

"Jack, Mrs. Bryant, please accept my and the entire center's condolences. I can't imagine the pain you must be going through." Leaning forward, Dr. Grayson clasped his hands on his desk.

"Thank you, Paul. Emma and I appreciate your understanding of the unfortunate incident. I'll take care of my parents' funeral this week and be back to work by Monday." Jack turned to Emma. She saw his determined look and didn't object.

"Take all the time you need, Jack. Kay can handle your appointments. I checked your surgery schedule and noticed you have next Thursday booked. We can move them if you need off through the week," Paul said.

"I'll be fine to return to work on Monday. It'll help my mind to keep busy and not dwell on this. I'll have the closure I need with the funeral." Emma watched Jack closely as his chest rose, and he held his breath after mentioning the funeral. She patted his hand again, and he let out the breath, smiling at her.

"Be sure to call Terri when you know the time and date of your parents' funeral. My wife and I would like to be there for you. Terri will let everyone here know as well."

"Emma or I will call later. We're going to the church when we leave here." Jack pushed back his chair and extended his hand to Paul. "Thanks again for your understanding." The two men shook hands. Emma nodded to Paul as she took Jack's hand in hers, and they walked back out the long corridor to the waiting area.

Leaving the center, Jack drove to the church to make all the funeral arrangements. Knowing this wasn't going to be easy for him, she touched his arm. He glanced her way and forced a pinched smile. His eyes were drawn together, his skin paler than usual. Emma worried that all of this heartbreak would crush Jack. She knew his will was strong but losing both parents suddenly would weaken even the strongest of men.

Wishing she could magically take his pain from him, she held his hand in hers, caressing his arm to soothe him.

"Are you ready, my sweet?"

"As ready as I'll ever be, love. Let's get this done," Jack said as he put the car in park. Opening the car door, she looked up and saw Jack waiting for her, his hand out for her to take. Placing her hand in his, they walked to the double doors of the church. He pushed open the right-side door and let Emma walk in first. Feeling his hand on her lower back, she walked alongside him to the church office.

Knocking on the office door, Jack slowly opened it and looked inside. A woman said, "Please come in."

They entered the small office where a petite lady with gray hair and black rimmed glasses sat behind the desk. Clearing his throat, Jack asked, "May we see the pastor, please?"

Scooting her chair back, the woman said, "Wait right here. I'll go and find Pastor Frank for you. Who may I say is calling on him?" She looked at Jack, then Emma.

"I'm Dr. Bryant, and this is my wife, Emma."

"Wait here. I'll be back in a few minutes."

Jack and Emma each took seats in the metal folding chairs. He fumbled with his fingers, and his foot tapped against the tile floor. Emma touched his knee to try and calm him.

The door swung open, and a man dressed in typical pastor clothing said, "I'm Pastor Frank. Will you please follow me to my office? We can talk there."

They both stood and followed Pastor Frank to the other side of the church. In the rather large office sat a medium-sized brown desk and chair, as well as filled bookshelves lining the walls. She took a seat next to Jack and listened as the two men planned the funeral.

After an hour of going over the premade plans, Jack looked at Emma with tired, droopy eyes. The viewings would be from nine to ten on Friday morning with the full church service to follow, beginning a little after ten. Depending on how many people attended the church service, they would set the funeral time between twelve-thirty to one in the afternoon. The processional would drive them around the block, to the cemetery across the street.

"I'll have the local police help with traffic, and the church will take care of the flowers. Dr. Bryant, your parents did things the right way. These final details were all they couldn't do. They were prepared."

"Thank you, Pastor Frank. Emma and I will be here at eight-thirty on Friday morning." Jack shook Pastor Frank's hand and led Emma out of the church.

CHAPTER 30

"Jack, I think you should lie down and rest for a while." Emma nudged him toward their bedroom. "We haven't eaten all day. I'll ask Shea to make something in a little bit."

His shoulders slumped as he smiled at her weakly. "Emma, I..."

Jack fell hard against the counter. She clutched his body to hold him upright, trying with all her might. But her small frame couldn't hold his towering body. He slid to the floor, crumbling like a Jenga stack when the wrong piece was pulled out.

"Jack! Jack!" Emma patted his pale and heated cheeks.

Entering, Shea yelled, "Rob, Ben! Come in here. Now, hurry!"

Sitting with Jack on the floor, Emma peered up. Her brow wrinkled, she bit her lip and her eyes glassed over as she stared at her young husband's crumpled body.

Moaning and sighing, he sat against the bar. Her eyes wide, she held his hand. "Baby, are you okay?"

"Jack, man. C'mon, open those eyes," Rob said as he knelt on the floor on the other side of Jack.

Sucking in several fast and shallow breaths, Jack wiped his face and dragged his hands through his hair. "Yeah, I'm okay. I guess it all just hit me." He paused as his head fell to his chest. His head swayed from side to side before looking at Emma again. His eyes blinked slowly. He appeared to almost pass out, then he touched her face. "I need your strength to get me through Friday and the rest of our lives together." He draped his arms over her dainty shoulders, embracing her body. He breathed heavily against her neck. "I need you, love." His lips softly grazed her cheek. He held her face in his soft hands and gazed into her blue eyes. Seeing his pain, she drew him to her and hugged him hard.

"I'm here forever, baby. Whatever you need I will give it to you. Always. I love you and always will." She gripped his shoulders tight, holding him up. "Can you take a shower?" she asked. "Let Rob and Ben help you stand."

Pulling in a deep breath and exhaling it all the way out, Jack looked at both men. Nodding, he let them lift him into a standing position.

Shea came to Jack's side. "Let me check your pulse."

"I'll be fine," he tried to convince Shea.

"Okay, maybe, but let me check your pulse right now, please." Shea took Jack's wrist in her hand and looked at her watch. "It's a little fast, ninety-six. Jack, you need to take a cool shower and lie down." Shea stared at Emma, her eyebrows drawn together.

Emma nodded. She knew Shea was concerned about Jack, so she led him to their bathroom. She turned on the shower, and asked, "Will you be okay?"

"I'll be fine, love." He pulled her into him and squeezed her lovingly.

She helped him undress, then she leaned against the rim of the tub and waited for several minutes. She needed to be sure he'd be okay in the shower alone. She smiled when she saw him form a heart with his hands. She blew him a kiss before leaving the bathroom.

Walking to the family room, Emma fell into a chair and rested her head on the back. Staring at the ceiling for a few seconds before she leaned forward and held her face in her hands. Her shoulders bounced as the sobs released from her tired and frail body.

"Hey, Em. Talk to me. What do you need?" Brandi asked.

Shaking her head, she looked at Brandi. Her cheeks were tear-stained, her eyes bloodshot, and what little makeup she'd worn had smeared.

Brandi held a tissue for Emma. Taking it, she wiped her eyes dry and sat back in the chair. Letting go of a breath, she said, "I've never seen him so vulnerable. So out of control of his body."

"He'll be okay. Find your strength, girl. He's going to need you to be the strong one through this entire process. I'm here, Shea's here. Let it all out to us. We love you." Brandi took Emma's hand and gave it a gentle squeeze.

"Thanks, Brandi." Emma looked toward their bedroom. She rose from the chair and hugged Brandi. "I'm going to check on him. Will you ask Shea to make something in a little while? Anything is fine. Something simple. Oh, shit. I almost forgot. Here's the funeral information." Emma dug in her pocket and handed Brandi a slip of paper.

"Okay, I'll pass this onto Shea and Rob. Now go be with Jack." Brandi nudged Emma. She turned and walked to her bedroom.

Seeing Jack sleeping calmly on their bed, Emma went to his bedside and leaned over him, to kiss his cheek. She walked into the bathroom, catching her reflection in the mirror, she sighed. Dark circles, crow's feet and frown lines appeared prominently. The stress of worrying about Jack came out on her face.

She drew a bath for herself, pouring in lavender oil and lighting lavender candles around the tub. Slipping out of her clothes, she slid her tired body into the soft warm water. The only thing missing from her bath was Jack. She closed her eyes and dreamt of him sharing her relaxing bath. In her dream she was lying in his warm embrace as he tenderly kissed her shoulders.

A few minutes passed as she daydreamed of her husband when she felt the water move. Her eyes popped open. She smiled and watched as Jack slid into the tub with her. Smiling weakly, he brought her between his legs and wrapped his arms around her. He leaned down and kissed her shoulders. Her heart burst with love. *How does this man know exactly when I need him?*

She twisted her neck and tilted her head up to look at him. Her hand brushed his slightly puffy cheeks. He held her face in his hand, leaning down again, he kissed her. "Do you mind if I join you?" He smiled his sweet smile, then kissed her before she could reply.

When their kiss ended, she snuggled her body into his. Taking his arms, she wrapped hers over his and held them tight. "I don't mind at all."

CHAPTER 31

Emma clutched Jack's hand as they walked into the church. Jack wore a black suit, white shirt, and a thin black tie. Emma wore a simple knee-length black dress and flats.

Her heart broke for him. He was about to go through an extremely painful day. She would summon all her strength and be right by his side through it all.

The pastor stepped toward them. "Dr. and Mrs. Bryant, please follow me." He escorted Jack and Emma to the front of the church. Shea, Rob, Brandi, and Ben all waited at the back. Jack stopped before reaching the two caskets. Feeling him weaken, Emma slid her arm around his waist. She looked up at him and saw his eyes blinking quickly. She choked back her own tears and stood strong, holding his huge body tightly with all her might.

Reaching into her dress pocket, she pulled out a few tissues and handed them to him. He blotted his eyes as they moved closer to his father's casket. Jack's shoulders slumped as he placed his hand on his father. Her heart crumbling inside, she drew in a deep breath when she met his gaze and saw his tears rolling down his cheeks. Tightening her grip on him, she placed her hand on his while he quietly said goodbye to his dad.

Stepping toward his mother's casket, Jack's shoulders slumped deeper, and his chin fell to his chest. Dabbing her eyes and swiping her nose with a tissue, she blew out a breath and kept a firm hold on Jack.

Pausing again before reaching the casket, he dragged in a breath and held it. She rubbed his arm, encouraging him to exhale.

Their eyes met again, his stare blank and empty. *Oh my, God. Please give me the strength to get him through this. Please.*

Jack grabbed the lower end of his mother's casket, his knees buckling, and Emma couldn't hold his towering body. She tried to embrace him again. Out of the corner of her eye, she saw Ben and Rob rushing to her aid. They assisted in lifting Jack upright.

She squeezed his arm and whispered, "I'm here. Lean on me. I love you."

Patting her hand and smiling weakly, he glanced at Rob, then at Ben and back to Emma. "I'm okay." He drew in several deep breaths and walked the few steps to the head of the casket. Jack grasped the edge, his knuckles white.

"I'll miss you, Mom. Rest well." His body shook as he leaned down and kissed his mom's forehead. Emma stroked his back and felt his knees weaken again, but she was able to hold him. Embracing her, Jack led them to the front pew, closest to his parents' caskets.

Their family sat in the second pew right behind Emma and Jack. She felt a hand on her shoulder and turned to see Shea. Patting her sister's hand, she gave her a weak smile.

At 9:00 a.m., people began filing into the church for the viewing. Everyone slowly went to each casket and then to Jack. His aunt Cheryl came to him first. He stood and embraced her, holding his aunt for several minutes. She reached for Emma's hand, tears streaming down her face. Emma took it and squeezed it softly. She watched as Cheryl slid into a pew behind them.

Each person gave Jack their sympathies and condolences. Shaking hands with those that offered theirs, Jack thanked them. Emma smiled politely and nodded to the visitors.

The pastor took his place on the stage behind the two caskets. A deafening silence encompassed the church as he waved his arms for the congregation to stand in prayer. Standing and holding Jack's hand in hers, Emma gripped his bicep and tugged slightly. He glanced her way, his lips forming a pained smile, his eyebrows coming together. She tightened her fingers around his as the pastor said, "Amen."

As the congregation began taking their seats, a creaking noise came from the back of the church. Emma turned and tensed when she saw Jenna, Jack's ex-wife. Her grip on Jack's bicep released as her hand trailed down his jacket. Murmuring filled the church as the congregation turned and faced the pastor again, but Emma stared at Jenna as she slowly entered the church. Their eyes met. Jenna's eyes pinched together, her mouth a thin line. Emma didn't show any emotion. Her face hot, she felt Jack embrace her tightly. She looked up at him and saw his mouth gaping.

Turning her gaze back to Jenna, Emma released Jack's hand and cupped her mouth to stifle a cry when she caught sight of the wide-eyed child holding Jenna's hand. What Kaitlyn had said to Jack in New York City came back to Emma in that moment. Kaitlyn's anger finally made sense to Emma. Jenna must have told her friends that Jack left her and the baby. Jenna didn't tell them that she told Jack the baby was gone.

Emma met the boy's blue eyes, and she knew immediately he was Jack's son. Her heart pounded fiercely. Her legs felt like jelly as she held onto Jack to steady herself. Her eyes glazed over while the knife in her chest sliced her heart. After a few seconds, it felt as though her heart laid in shreds inside her chest.

She grasped Jack's hand as he stood stoic, staring at Jenna and the boy. The beautiful little boy. Dressed in a suit, he was the mini twin to Jack.

Squeezing Emma's hand, he drew her even closer to him. She felt him shaking as they turned and sat back down in the pew. Two hands squeezed Emma's shoulders. She glanced quickly to either side and saw Brandi and Shea leaning forward, their eyes wide and heads shaking.

Trying to gather her thoughts on Jenna having the nerve to show up at a funeral with the child she claimed she lost, Emma sat staring straight ahead. Her mind whirled. *How could she come here? How could she lie about the baby? Oh my, God. The baby!* She raised her eyes to check on Jack. He sat still, staring forward, his mouth in a thin line.

A child would change things for them. *If he's Jack's.* She knew he was Jack's. Her mind always liked to play tricks on her. The child wasn't a threat to their young marriage. He'd be a wonderful addition to their lives. She'd find a way for it all to work out. *If he's Jack's.*

Dropping her head to her chest, she screamed at the voice in her head, *Stop already. He's Jacks! There's no doubt that boy is Jacks.*

Bringing her attention back to Jack, she noticed his breathing had quickened. Dragging her hand through her hair and fighting the intense ache inside her, she slipped her hand in his. She tried to quiet him with her touch, but his body shook, and his tears flowed freely as the pastor spoke about the Bryant's as wonderful, loving parents to their only son, Dr. Jackson Bryant. They were proud of his accomplishments.

Jack leaned on Emma and held her close to him as the pastor spoke about his parents' contributions to the local Veteran's charities, the children's hospital, and Jack's mom volunteering at the women's shelter. She slammed her eyes shut when she heard Jenna's sobs.

Her heartache went deeper the more she learned about her in-laws. How she'd wished they'd met her. Just once would've been enough for her. She didn't know how to deal with her loss. She hurt for never talking to them, but her biggest hurt was how they hurt Jack by refusing to meet her.

Finally, the congregation said the Lord's Prayer. Clasping his hand, Emma stayed by his side as they followed the caskets down the aisle and as they waited on the church steps while the pall bearers placed his parents into the hearses.

With her sister and best friend beside her, she stood with Jack as they received each person when they exited the church. As the line of people shortened, Emma noticed Jenna at the end, holding Jack's son. Her pulse quickened as Jenna stepped closer. She couldn't take Jack's hand as he shook each one's hand, so she slid her arm across his waist. He looked down at her, then caught sight of Jenna. Emma felt his body tense. She pinched his hip to calm him.

Twisting her wedding rings when Jenna got close to them, she stared blankly at Jenna as she skipped by her and straight to Jack, she breathed slow and deliberate. She moved her gaze from Jenna to the sweet little boy on Jenna's hip. A happy smile formed on his face and his soft blue eyes warmed Emma's heart.

"I'm so sorry, Jack," Jenna said.

"Thank you, Jenna," Jack said and shook her hand.

177

Emma held her breath as she watched them walk down the church steps and to Jenna's car. *Why now? Why come to Jack's parents' funeral? Are you here to show Jack his son and take him from Jack again?* Emma shook her head to quiet the voices in her mind.

She slipped her arm through Jack's and walked to the limousine waiting for them behind the hearses.

Holding his hand while riding in the limousine around the block, then to the cemetery, Emma pushed the thoughts of what might happen afterwards with his sudden son out of her mind. She had to focus on Jack. Everything else could wait.

Stepping out of the limo at the graveyard, they walked hand in hand and sat in the two chairs by the caskets. Emma swayed from side to side, darting her gaze at the people encircling them.

Two hands clamped on Emma's shoulders again. She knew without looking that Shea stood behind her, calming her. Shaking her head to make her mind stop overthinking, she smiled at Jack. He rested his hand on his leg, palm up, and she laid hers in it, watching as his fingers engulfed hers. She placed her other hand on top of his. Resting her head against his shoulder, she sensed his dismayed emotions.

After placing flowers on each casket, Jack sat beside Emma again, and the pastor continued with a few more passages of scripture, then finished his part of the funeral services.

The pastor nodded for Jack to stand and address those in attendance. He rose and turned to face everyone.

Clearing his throat, he said, "Thank you all for coming today and paying your respects to my parents. I know they're smiling wherever they are." He dabbed his eyes with a tissue. "There will be a reception back at the church for anyone wanting to attend."

Jack and Emma rode in the limousine back to the church. Caressing his arm as he stared out the car window, she asked, "Are you up for going back to the church? I'm sure everyone would understand if we went home, Jack."

Pulling in a deep breath, he turned and faced her. "I know they would, but I need to be there for Mom and Dad. They'd want me to be there." He picked up her hand and kissed it softly.

"Okay. I'll go where you go." She squeezed his hand. "What about Jenna? Are you going to talk to her if she's back at the church?" Her eyes came together, and her heart slowed.

An uncomfortable silence filled the limo as Jack looked out the window again.

"Jack." Emma touched his leg.

"Yes, Emma. I want to talk to her. He's my son. I hope you understand." He raised her hand from his leg and pressed it to his chest.

"Of course, I do. I'm here with you for everything." She leaned against his arm as he brought her hand to his lips and kissed it tenderly.

"Thanks, love. I don't think I'd make it through today without you."

Stepping out of the limousine when they arrived back at the church, Emma scanned the crowd of people standing outside. Not seeing Jenna, she wondered if she had come to show Jack his son, then leave.

As they walked toward the large building that held the reception, Emma held his hand. They entered the large room, followed by Shea, Rob, Brandi, and Ben. The church ladies' group had provided the food and drink. The men's group had set up all the tables and chairs. Emma made a note to be sure they made a nice donation to the church.

Looking at Shea, Emma's eyes pinched, and her mouth set into a thin line. She shook her head slowly, trying to convey to Shea that she didn't want to talk about what had happened at the church. Shea nodded.

As the room filled with all the people who had known and loved Jack's parents, Emma's heart tightened with her own grief once again. A tear slipped from her eye and hit the table they stood at. She quickly wiped it away. Jack stood next to her talking with an old friend of his dad's.

A woman came up to Jack and said, "I'm Peg. Your mom and I shared coffee every week. She was such a sweet lady. And boy, was she proud of you, Jack."

Jack smiled and said, "Thank you. It's nice to meet you, Peg." Tugging on Emma's arm, he gently brought her closer to him. "This is my wife, Emma. Emma, this is Peg. A friend of Mom's."

"It's nice to meet you. I wish it were under different, more pleasant circumstances." Emma smiled at Peg.

"Yes, dear. Me too. Christy told me a lot about Jack. She beamed whenever she talked about him." Peg reached into her pocket and pulled out a ball of tissues. Patting her face with it, she said, "Oh, sorry for that. I'm going to miss her. May she and Charles rest in peace."

"We all pray for them." Emma's eyes caught Jenna coming in through the back door of the reception area. She quickly turned her eyes back to Peg and said, "Will you excuse me, please?"

"Of course, I should be going. My condolences to you both." Peg held Emma and Jack's hands for a second, then walked away.

"Emma, where are you going?" Jack asked.

"You need to come with me. Jenna just came in. We should talk to her. No, wait. You go and talk to her, Jack." Emma's eyes pleaded with him. Her heart pounded and blood rose to her face.

Huffing out a breath, Jack panned the room. He held Emma's hand in his and said, "I'll talk to her. Do you mind waiting here for me? I think it's best if I do this alone. I'll find out what the hell is going on."

"It's fine. I'll wait here for you. I love you." She gripped his hand tight.

"I love you too. And if that boy is my son…" He trailed off as he looked at her.

"We'll figure it out. Together."

He tilted her chin up and kissed her softly.

Her eyes trailed after him as he walked to the other side of the room and into a hallway. She walked over to where Shea, Brandi, and the guys were.

"What the…?" Brandi slapped her hand to her mouth.

"I don't know yet. Jack is going to talk with Jenna right now," Emma said and twisted a few strands of her hair.

"Em, I thought you said she'd lost the baby." Shea looked quizzically at Emma.

"Yes, that's what Jenna told Jack. Obviously, she lied. That boy is Jack's twin."

"Yeah, no shit… oh, crap." Brandi covered her mouth again.

Emma's glare followed Jenna as she followed Jack down the same hallway with the boy on her hip. Trying to control her anger

180

with Jenna for lying about losing the baby, she closed her eyes and counted to herself. "I'll be right back."

"Emma, no…" Shea's voice trailed after her as Emma walked away. Her mind went in all kinds of directions, thinking about Jack missing so many of the little boy's firsts.

Slowing her pace when she entered the hallway, she stepped lightly as she got closer to a room with its door slightly ajar. She trusted Jack completely. It was Jenna she didn't trust at all.

She stopped in her tracks when she heard Jack's loud, irate voice. "Jenna, you texted me for God's sake. You texted me to tell me you lost our baby. A text!"

"You gave me no choice, Jack," Jenna said.

"What the hell does that mean?" Jack's voice rose.

Grasping at her chest, Emma inched closer to the door. She wanted to see inside, but instead, she leaned against the wall and listened.

"When you refused to come back home, I went to the condo and sat at the table with *her*. I knew I had no chance of winning you back. So, I made the decision to lie to you about Jordan…"

Jordan, what a beautiful name for that little boy. He's the innocent one in all this mess. Emma took a step toward the door. Slowly she peeked inside while she held onto the door frame. Seeing Jordan playing with a few toy trucks on the carpeted floor, her heart instantly filled with love for him. She caught his eyes and saw him smile at her. *Jack's smile. Jack's eyes. Jack's hair.*

Pulling in a breath, she blinked slowly as she smiled back at him. She'd never seen a child this beautiful. She couldn't move. He caught her in his trance just like Jack had done. This little boy completely mesmerized her.

"Where the hell did you go to have my son?" Jack's bellowing voice shook Emma from the trance she'd been caught in. She glanced up in the direction of Jack's voice and saw his face red and his flailing arms.

Jenna stood with her arms crossed as she spoke, "I went where I knew you'd never look for me." Jenna walked toward her son.

Falling back against the wall and out of sight, Emma's chest rose and fell rapidly. She needed fresh air, but her heart kept her right there.

Emma peeked into the room again to see the boy. Jenna stood beside him, her hands on her hips.

"Dammit, Jenna," Jack said. "You had no right to lie to me about losing our baby. We need to figure this out, but not here. I'll text you. I want to be in my son's life. I'll speak with a lawyer."

"No. Not since you married her." Jenna's words cut Emma deeply. She covered her mouth to silence herself. As Jenna squatted to pick up Jordan, he glanced Emma's way and smiled at her again. Smiling back, she winked at him as her heart melted.

This wasn't right. Jordan deserved to know his father and Jack deserved to know his son. Emma cringed when Jenna said, "No, Jack. I'll fight you. You can't have my son."

"Jenna!" Jack yelled. She stormed past Emma and into the large room. Jack came running after her. He stopped when he saw Emma.

Looking up at him, she saw his raw pain. His eyes pulled together, his nostrils flaring, his face red. He swiped his hand across his mouth and looked at the floor.

"Jack." Emma reached for him. He fell into her arms and began to cry. His huge body engulfed hers as she did all she could to hold him. "We'll fight for your son. You have the right to see him. Whatever we need to do, we'll do. I promise." She hugged him tighter as he continued to cry. His body jerked with each short breath he took. "C'mon, let's go home and sort this out. We'll find the best custody lawyer we can. We'll get you visitation at the very least. Shared custody would be better, and we'll go for that too. Jordan deserves to know you. He does." Emma touched Jack's cheek. Feeling the wetness, she leaned him against the wall and opened her purse. Bringing out some tissues, she blotted his face. He took the tissues from Emma, dried his eyes, and blew his nose.

"Thank you, love. Thank you for saying all that. I know how…"

"No, Jack." Emma interrupted him. "We don't know anything yet. It'll be fine. I promise. Now let's go home." She slid her arm around his waist and led him out of the hallway to the large room. After finding the pastor and the head of the women's and men's groups to thank them, Emma and Jack left the church, followed by Shea, Rob, Brandi, and Ben. Silence lingered in the car as she drove them home.

182

CHAPTER 32

Throwing his suit jacket on the sofa, Jack stomped over to the liquor cabinet. Emma watched as he brought out two glasses and a bottle of bourbon. "Want one?" he asked.

"Sure, just one though." Emma hopped onto the barstool, laying her purse beside her. She watched Shea and Rob go to their bedroom, and Brandi and Ben retreated to theirs. She appreciated them giving her and Jack some privacy and knew if Jack got too loud, Rob and Ben would help calm him down.

Before handing her the glass, he shot back the drink he'd poured himself and refilled the tumbler.

"Hey, baby. Take it easy." She watched Jack slug his second drink before she took a sip of hers, then he poured himself a third.

"I'm fine," he bit at her sharply. Her head fell to her chest. He'd never spoken to her that way but considering all he'd been through with the funerals and Jenna showing up with their very much alive son, she gave him room to vent. She could take it.

With tears welling up, she said to him, "I love you. When you're ready to talk, I'm here. I'm always here for you."

Jack poured his third shot down his throat, then made another. Pulling in a deep breath, Emma's eyes widened. She dragged her hand through her hair. Darting her gaze around the room, she decided to ask, "Would you care to talk about what happened?"

"No." His tone still sharp, he tossed back drink number four. When he began to pour a fifth drink, Emma hopped down from the stool and grabbed the bottle.

"I think you've had enough. You'll get sick, baby. Please, Jack. No more." She held the bottle of bourbon behind her back.

Slumping his shoulders, he rubbed his face fiercely and pushed out a hard breath. He leaned his elbows on the counter, and with his eyes pulled close, he looked at her, then dropped his gaze to his hands.

She ran her hands across his shoulder blades. "Talk to me. We can get through anything together. I promise we can." Emma tugged on Jack's arm, trying to get him to look at her.

"I don't want to talk, Em. Not now. I don't know what to say." His gaze came back and met hers. His eyes were bloodshot and puffy. She went to the sink and dampened a cool washcloth for him.

"C'mon. Lie on the bed and cover your eyes with this. I'll hold you until you're ready to talk." Emma took Jack's hand and led him to their bedroom. Climbing into bed with him, she placed the washcloth across his splotchy face. She laid beside him, resting her arm across his stomach. Placing his hand on top of hers, he gave it a gentle pinch.

"Rest, baby. We have the rest of our lives to talk." She kissed his shoulder, squeezed his side, and closed her eyes.

***

Waking to the sun kissing her face, Emma rolled over to greet Jack as she usually did. Seeing the bed empty, she shot up and looked around their bedroom. She listened to hear if he'd gone to take a shower. She realized she was still in her black dress from the funeral, and they'd slept through the night. Glancing at the alarm clock, she saw it read seven-thirty. She rubbed her eyes and went on a search for Jack.

Finding him in the kitchen with Shea and Rob, she walked toward them. Jack held a coffee mug, and she hoped it was a coffee on which he was sipping. She slipped her arms around him and said, "Good morning, gorgeous."

"Good morning, beautiful," Jack said in his sweet velvety voice she loved so much.

"Oh, you two," Shea said. Emma smiled at her sister and winked.

"What?" Emma shrugged. "Is there more coffee?" she asked.

"Yes," Shea answered.

Emma walked over to the counter and poured herself a cup full. Returning to sit next to Jack, she held her hand out to Shea. "Thanks for staying and being here for Jack and me."

"Of course. We're family and that's what family does." Shea squeezed Emma's hand. "But now we need to get our things together. Do y'all need me to help with anything today?"

"No, go and do what you need to do. Jack and I are fine. Right?" Emma touched Jack's arm. He nodded.

"Okay. Well, if you do, just yell and I'll come running." Shea smiled and went with Rob to their bedroom.

Turning to Jack, she caressed his arm. He smiled and asked, "Did you sleep well, love?"

"I guess. Did you?" She blew on the steaming coffee in her mug.

"No. I kept seeing my parents, then my son." He stopped and held his breath. Placing his coffee cup on the counter, he scratched his scruffy face, then puffed out a breath. Taking her hand in his, he kissed it softly. "Emma, my son is alive. How could she do that? How could she lie to me like that? How…" His head fell to his chest.

Grabbing a tissue when she noticed his tears, she handed it to him and then rubbed his shoulder. "I don't know, Jack. I don't know."

Jack blotted his eyes and blew his nose. Straightening himself, he brought Emma between his legs, and held her around her waist. "I need to talk to Jenna. I need my son. I *want* him. Emma, where do I start? Who do I call?"

Holding him by his broad shoulders, she tried to answer all his questions. "You could try to talk to Jenna first. Maybe she'll be open to sharing custody with you? If she refuses, tell her you're seeing a lawyer." Not knowing how Jenna would respond to Jack wanting to see Jordan, Emma felt talking with Jenna first would show her Jack was open to being flexible. If Jenna refused, then Jack would need to force his rights as Jordan's father.

"You're probably right. I did search for attorneys already. I want to be prepared." Jack looked at Emma and showed her the list he'd made.

"And that's fine. We should be prepared. I'm hoping Jenna is reasonable and agrees with joint custody." She shrugged. Holding his chin up with her hand, she brushed her lips across his. "We'll find a way to have Jordan in our lives. I promise." She threw her arms around his neck and hugged him tightly. "Why don't you call Jenna, and I'll see if Shea wants to make breakfast. Okay?" Emma asked.

"Okay, love." He kissed her quickly, then walked into the family room.

Emma went to their bedroom and changed into more comfortable clothes. She returned to the kitchen and watched as Jack spoke with Jenna. He paced the family room, at times his arms going like he was conducting a choir. A few minutes in, he stopped in the middle of the room, his hand on his hip, and shook his head. His voice fluctuated from his normal tone to very angry and loud. She winced when she heard him yell, "Goddammit, Jenna, you fucking lied to me about our son!" She'd never heard him utter that word even in the heat of passion or whenever he'd been irate. Silence came from the family room as Jack listened to Jenna. His facial expressions told Emma all she needed to know. His eyes rolled, his lips pursed, and his jaw clenched several times. The veins on his neck bulged when he yelled.

Walking toward the spare bedroom where Shea and Rob were, she knocked.

"Hey, Em. Is everything okay?" Shea asked.

"Um, yeah. He's on the phone with Jenna." Emma bowed her head. She huffed out a breath, then looked at her sister again. "Do you mind making breakfast? Or I can order if you're too busy," Emma rambled on.

"Give me a few more minutes to finish packing, and I'll be right there." Shea rubbed Emma's arm.

"Thanks. I seriously hit the jackpot when it comes to sisters." Emma blew Shea a kiss, then went back to the kitchen.

Joining Emma again, Jack placed his hand on hers. "Well, that was pleasant." He hung his head.

"Tell me what she said, please." Emma lifted Jack's chin up to try and read him.

"Jenna refuses to share custody of Jordan. She said she'll fight me. She'll bring up our affair. I told her to go right ahead. Then I'd tell the judge that she lied to me and said she lost our baby. That she

186

left me thinking my child had died." He drew in and huffed out a breath.

"What did she say to that?" Emma asked.

"She backed off a little, but she refuses to share custody. She will allow me to see Jordan…" He paused as he looked at Emma. His eyes pinched shut, his lips in a thin line.

"What, Jack?" She took his hand and tugged on it.

"She won't let Jordan come here. I have to go to them. Just me." His head fell to his chest again. "I'm sorry, Emma. Please let me figure this out. I need to see my son." He reached for her.

Letting him pull her to him, she held her breath and blinked quickly. She knew Jenna would do anything to break them up. She'd try every trick in the book, but Emma knew Jack had rights and being married to her made no difference.

"Okay. But you need to see a lawyer. Just because we're married has no bearing on you sharing custody or having Jordan come here. I'm his stepmom. I want to get to know him too. It's not fair, Jack." Tears pooled in her eyes.

Cupping her face, he said, "I know, love. I'll make an appointment and we can go together. But please let me go and see Jordan this one time alone."

Relenting, she said, "Okay. You need to see your son. I love you, Jack. I'll do whatever you need. But you can't let her use your child to control you. I won't let Jenna come between us. We've come to damn far to let her ruin this." Emma circled her finger between them. "She won't destroy us. I promise you!" Emma stood back from him with her hands on her hips, looking at Jack, waiting for him to speak.

Nodding, Jack reached for her hand. "She won't. She can't. No one can. I love you." Jack pulled Emma toward him, embracing her petite body, locking his arms around her. "I love you, Emma Bryant. Only you."

CHAPTER 33

After Jack left for his visit with his son, and Shea and Rob went home, Emma sat at the kitchen table drinking her coffee. Staring at her phone, she felt helpless. She pulled her knees to her chest and hugged herself.

"Morning," Brandi said when she joined Emma.

"Hey." Emma rose from her seat and went to refill her coffee. She leaned against the counter while Brandi found a Diet Coke. "When are y'all driving back to North Carolina?"

"We don't know. Maybe tomorrow or the next day. If that's okay with you and Jack." Brandi looked at Emma over the top of her soda can.

"Yeah, it's fine. I could use the company."

"That's what I told Ben. We've got things covered up there, so no worries. We'll head back soon." Brandi stood beside Emma and squeezed her arm. "I wish things were better. I think I'm still in shock over what Jenna did. I would've never thought she'd lie. I mean, I know how devastated she was when Jack left her, but to lie about losing the baby? That's not right. Just not right at all."

They walked to the dining room and pulled out chairs to sit in. She looked at Brandi as she sat down. "That little boy is innocent. He deserves to know his dad, and Jack deserves to know Jordan."

"And he will, Em. Jack will move mountains to be in the boy's life. You're going to make an amazing stepmom. I know you love that boy already. He looks exactly like Jack. It's crazy how much though. I don't see anything of Jenna in him. He's young enough that he won't remember this shit going on. That's the good thing.

188

You and Jack have a battle to fight, but I think you'll be fine." Brandi patted Emma's hand.

"Thanks, I hope so. Jack's been through so damn much. He grieved the loss of his child, then his parents. Only to find out his child is alive. I cannot imagine what the fuck is going through his mind. Oh, Christ." Emma let out a breath and fell back against her chair.

"It's definitely a lot for him, but he's got you in his corner." Brandi patted Emma's hand and smiled.

"Yes, he does." Emma paused, then said, "So, I saw you talking with Matt at the gallery. I'm glad y'all are still tight."

"Yeah, it was great to see him again. It almost felt like old times."

"He's happy, I can tell." Emma smiled warmly.

"Okay, Em. I know that look. What did Matt say to you?" Brandi grabbed Emma's hand and tugged.

"It doesn't matter what Matt said. I love Jack. He's my life now. Him and Jordan," Emma stated firmly.

"Nice try but tell me. I know he said something to you. With everything that's happened since the exhibition, you've not had a chance to think about it, and I can tell he said something that's still with you. C'mon, girl. It'll be our secret. Promise," Brandi pushed.

Sighing, Emma looked up, then back to Brandi. "Alright, Matt said he'll always love me. He'll stop in when he's down here for work. And he hopes we can be friends." Emma closed her eyes, waiting for Brandi's response.

"I'm not surprised. He's been in love with you since tenth grade. A love like that never ends. Y'all were friends for years. Maybe you can be again. Just tell Jack if Matt does stop in. Don't keep that from him, ever," Brandi said.

"All true and I'd love to be friends with him again, but I don't think that's what he really wants." Emma shook her head. "The way he kept touching me and brushing his hand against mine. He was quite flirty. More than the Matt I remember." She sipped on her coffee. "And I'll always tell Jack everything. I chose to end my marriage and be with Jack. Jack is who I will spend the rest of my life with. No matter what. It's me and Jack forever." Emma crossed her heart with her fingers.

"I know, Em. I see the love between you too and it's beautiful. I'm so happy for you." Brandi pushed back her chair. "I'm going to go and start packing some of our things we won't need. That way there's less to do when we decide to head home."

"Okay. Jack should be back soon. He still needs to go to his parent's house and decide what he's keeping and what is being donated. I'll be in my studio, sketching or painting."

Brandi leaned down and kissed Emma's cheek. "Love you, girl."

Emma squeezed Brandi's hand and turned to her. "Love you too, bestie."

She watched her best friend walk toward the spare bedroom. Once Brandi closed the door, Emma went to her studio and brought out her sketch pad and pencils. Sitting on the puffy cushion chair in the corner by the window, she put pencil to paper and began to sketch Jordan. Normally, she'd use a photo to draw people, but this little boy's image was burnt into her memory so vividly, she easily drew him as he'd sat on the floor in the room at the church.

After drawing him, Emma laid the sketch pad on the desk, then opened an easel. She clipped the drawing to it and turned on the lamp. Going to the closet, she pulled out the paints to use. Blue, dark-brown, white, and gray for the walls of the room.

Within minutes, Jordan Bryant became her latest work of art. She stood back and tapped her lips with the end of the paintbrush, then grabbed her phone. Opening it to the journal app, she began to type:

PRECIOUS

A precious little child.
One that was thought to be lost forever.
But you are very much alive,
Very much loved.
A precious gift.

Emma stepped up to the easel once again. Dabbing the black paint with her thin paintbrush, she wrote the poem to the right and slightly below Jordan. She filled in the blank spaces with whisps of colors she'd used to paint him instead of the gray she'd originally

190

planned. Grabbing a tube of yellow paint, she plopped a bit onto the palette and lightly drew faint yellow streaks on the painting.

Taking a step back, she bit the inside of her cheek. Nodding in approval of her piece, she picked up another thin paintbrush, dabbed it in the black paint, and signed her name to the bottom left corner, *EB Taylor.*

CHAPTER 34

Lying in bed with Jack that evening, Emma asked him about his visit with Jenna and his son.

Turning on his side, facing her, he caressed her arm. "It went okay. Jenna named him after me. My son's full name is Jordan Jackson. She calls him JJ." He paused and brushed her cheek. "She actually apologized for leaving the church like she had. I don't know if she's spoken with a lawyer or if her parents or friends talked her down, but she's open to talking."

Emma's eyes glazed over as she placed her hand on his chest. Looking up at him, she smiled. "Oh my, God. His name fits him perfectly. He's your twin, Jack." She paused as an ache ran through her. *Jordan Jackson Bryant. JJ. Wow.* She shut her eyes hard, then opened them and caught Jack's baby blues smiling down at her.

"Are you okay, love?" He threaded his fingers through her long blonde locks.

"Yes, baby. I'm fine." She moved closer to him and kissed his firm chest. "I'm happy she's changed her attitude. She messed up when she lied and left suddenly. Leaving you to think the baby had been miscarried."

"That's why I think she's spoken to someone. She was way too nice. All she asked was that we move ahead slowly. She wants what's best for our son, Em. And I've agreed to that."

"What does that mean? Doesn't she live back home?" Emma sat up, crossing her legs in front of her.

"Actually, she lives about two hours from here. After she had Jordan, she didn't want to run into us, so she moved. Two hours is too far away for my liking, but it's better than four hours." Jack scooted up and leaned against the headboard. He placed his hand palm up on his thigh and smiled playfully.

Walking her hand into his, she watched as his fingers swallowed hers. The warmth of his skin touching hers sent soothing pulses throughout her body. She wanted to know more about her stepson, so she asked, "How did Jordan react to you?"

"He was shy and held onto Jenna. Then we all sat on the floor. Jenna brought out his toys, and I played with him. She tried to explain to him who I was. She kept calling me, 'Daddy' when speaking to Jordan about me." Jack's eyes became glassy. "He's a wonderful little boy, and I can't wait for you to meet him. I know you'll love him as your own." He squeezed her hand gently.

"Oh, Jack. I'm so glad it went well. And I cannot wait to meet him too. I won't push. I'll follow your lead. Maybe this little boy will bring us all together. Maybe we can be friends again. Me and Jenna, that is." Emma's eyes came together, and the corner of her mouth pinched as she bit her cheek.

"That would be the best thing for Jordan." He drew her closer to him and embraced her tenderly. "No matter what happened between me and Jenna, it's all over. Jordan is all that matters now." He kissed the top of her head and held her.

***

Squinting when the sun hit her eyes, Emma snuggled her body with Jack's. His arms tightened tenderly around her. His lips traveled along her shoulder blades, his warm breath giving her sensual explosions that traveled throughout her entire body. Wanting him so badly, she rolled to face him. Before she could speak, his mouth crashed onto hers. His tongue plunged past her soft lips, twisting with hers. Her body melded with his as he slid himself between her legs.

Burying his hard cock deep inside her, he moaned as he engulfed her shoulders with his hands. As he pumped his hips, his mouth covered her perfectly sized breast. She arched her back to meet his passion. Smacking the bed, she gripped the sheets tightly when her first orgasm came. Just one of many she knew he'd bring her to. He always did.

Not playing favorites, his mouth moved from one breast to the other in a seamless motion. She blended her fingers through his soft brown hair over and over as he kissed her body. Cupping his cheeks, she lifted his devilishly handsome face up. "Good morning, gorgeous." She wet her lips and leaned into his full ones. "Baby, my God, you make my days perfect when you make love to me at the start."

Jack's sinful smile filled his face as his body slapped against hers with a thrust so powerful, she grasped his broad shoulders, dug in her fingertips, and held on. His hard cock throbbed inside her. Her center walls clenched around him. She wrapped her legs around his waist and enjoyed her ride to the outer bounds of glory when his hot juice sprayed inside her.

Collapsing onto her, his body trembled with bliss. His lips touched her neck, then her cheek, and finally her mouth. After their kiss ended, he propped himself on his elbows. His scintillating blue eyes caught hers. "Good morning, my beauty." His mouth captured hers as he sealed their morning of love making with a passionate kiss.

Lying together afterwards, Emma asked, "Are you going to go to your parent's house today to go through their things?"

"I guess I should. Will you come with me?"

"Of course. I'll do whatever you need me to do." She kissed his firm pecs, then laid her cheek on his chest. She listened to his heartbeat. It drummed in rhythm with hers.

***

After showering, Jack and Emma dressed and found Brandi and Ben in the kitchen.

"About time y'all get up," Brandi teased.

Smiling at her best friend, she walked over to the coffee pot and poured her and Jack each a cup. Walking to the bar where Jack had taken a stool, she placed his cup in front of him. She looked at Ben and said, "Thanks for making coffee."

"You're welcome, Emma." Ben smiled and nodded.

"Hey, Em. Do you guys need us to stay any longer?" Brandi asked.

Emma looked at Jack. When he shook his head, Emma said, "No. We're good. I think Jack and I are going over to his parent's place today and take care of that." She placed her hand on Jack's, squeezing it gently. Tilting his head down, he smiled sweetly at her.

"Then we'll pack our things and get on the road." Brandi opened the lower cabinet and tossed her Diet Coke can in the trash, then walked to Ben and tugged on his arm.

Standing, Ben slid his phone into his pocket. "Okay," he said and walked to the guest room with Brandi.

Emma caressed Jack's arm and pinched his elbow as she noticed him in deep thought. "Hey, baby, what are you thinking about?" She slipped off the stool and stood next to him.

"A lot. I'm not looking forward to going through my parent's things. It's so final." His eyes closed slowly. He drew her between his legs. Embracing her, he held her lovingly.

Laying her head on his shoulder, she embraced him with all her strength. She felt his body slump onto her. His heartbeat slowing as she caressed his back. "Baby, we don't have to do this today," Emma said, holding him tenderly.

After a minute or two, Jack raised his head and caught her concerned gaze. His head shaking slowly, he sighed. "I wish…" he dropped his head to his chest. Dragging his fingers through his hair, he continued, "I wish I didn't have to do this at all. I wish the accident never happened. But my biggest regret…" his voice cracked. Emma lifted his chin up. She noticed his tearful stare.

"No regrets, baby. No." She stepped as close as she could and embraced him tight.

His arms held her gently, his head laid on her shoulder. "I wish… you had… met them, love," he choked out. His arms tightened around her. She heard him sniffle, felt his chin trembling against her shoulder.

Emma never wanted Jack to feel any kind of pain ever again. He'd been through too much recently. She stood tall and moved her hands to his shoulders. Looking him deep in his sorrowful but stunning blue eyes, she said, "You're going to get through this. I'll help you with everything."

His smile weak, he said, "Thank you." He leaned down and kissed her softly. "Let's get this done. I need to get this last bit of closure."

"Are you sure, Jack?" she asked.

"Yes, I'm sure." He stood from the stool and brought her hand to his lips. He kissed her palm, then intertwined their fingers.

"Okay, baby. Do you know what you want to keep of your parent's? Are there any special items?"

"Just photos to share with Jordan when he's old enough to understand who they are to him." Jack softly brushed her cheek. "How did I get so damn lucky marrying you?"

"I'm the lucky one." She leaned in and kissed his sweet lips. Pulling back quickly, she gasped and covered her mouth. "Oh my, God. Jack, did you ask Jenna if she took Jordan to meet your parents? Would she do that behind your back? Would they agree to keep Jordan a secret from you?" Emma's eyes grew wide, and her heart raced. "Oh, fuck. Jack, you must ask Jenna if she did this." She knew Jack's dad wanted nothing to do with them because of her. She knew he'd keep this from Jack and use it as leverage if he could've. She'd never know just how far Jack's dad would have gone now that he was dead. But she hoped his mom would never hurt Jack like that.

"No, I don't think my parents would do that." He scratched his chin and tilted his head. "Well, my mom wouldn't have. Now my dad... I don't know. But I'll ask Jenna. I could always tell when she lied, so she won't be able to hide it if she did take Jordan to meet my parents."

"I'd wait to ask her anything right now. We want to stay on her good side, so she doesn't try and use Jordan as a pawn. So, let's keep this between us for now. We can ask her once the custody arrangements are agreed upon. Okay?" Emma asked.

"Okay." Jack raised his head and turned Emma around to face behind her.

"Oh, hey. Are you all packed and ready to hit the road?" she asked Brandi.

"We are. Please keep us updated on everything." Brandi tucked her hands in her pockets.

"We will. Thank you both so much for staying and being here with us." Emma hooked her arm through Jack's.

"Yeah, thanks. It means a lot to me y'all stayed. And I know it meant a lot to Emma."

"No problem. Glad we could rearrange things to be able to stay." Ben took a couple of steps toward them. Holding out his hand, he said, "Take care, man. If there's anything, and I mean anything, call or text us." Ben and Jack shook hands, then Ben hugged Emma.

"I will, thanks." Jack nodded and smiled.

"Well, Em. I'll talk to you soon. I'll get the photos I took from your grand opening to you as soon as I go through them back home," Brandi said.

"Christ." Emma puffed out a breath. "I completely forgot about the photos. It feels like that night was ages ago, but it was only eight days." She ran her fingers through her hair and blinked slowly. "Can't wait to see them." She stepped toward Brandi, her arms open wide.

Hugging her best friend, Emma held on for a few minutes. Once their hug broke, Brandi held Emma's shoulders. "It's all going to be great. Your gallery is amazing. And now you'll have a young protégé to introduce your love of painting to. Have fun with him." Brandi squeezed Emma's shoulders and they shared one last embrace.

Jack and Emma walked Brandi and Ben out to their SUV. Waving, they watched them drive off, then they went back inside and got ready to go to Jack's parent's house.

CHAPTER 35

She sat in Jack's car outside of his parents' home, her mouth agape. Before her eyes sat a huge two-story, impeccably landscaped home. Using her hand, Emma closed her mouth and then blinked rapidly. She couldn't imagine the money it took to have a home like that.

She and Jack's home was very nice and large enough to accommodate family and friends. But what sat before her was like a castle in her eyes. She shook her head and pulled in a deep breath. She knew Jack hadn't grown up in this house; she'd seen his childhood home before they married. She'd never asked what his dad had done for a living, but by the looks of things, he'd made tons of money. And that explained all the traveling his parents had done.

"So, yeah, my dad loved big things," Jack said out of the blue.

"Um, yeah. This is… wow…" Emma unbuckled her seatbelt and stepped out of the car. Walking to the front door, she looked up at Jack. "What did your dad do for a living, babe?"

"He was an investor. And like Midas, everything he touched turned to gold—or green, as in money." Jack unlocked the double front doors and swung them open for her to walk in.

Gasping when she walked inside, she grabbed his arm to keep from fainting. She'd only seen homes like this on TV. Before her was a dual staircase wrapping around to meet on the second floor. "Jesus, Jack. This is astounding. And it was just your mom and dad living here?" she asked, turning around and around, looking at as much as she could take in.

"Yep. Just them. Oh, and the staff." He shrugged.

"Wait, what staff? Where are they?" Her eyes as wide as they'd go. Her mind blown. She raked her hand through her hair and cupped her own cheeks.

"They were taken care of by my parent's final arrangements. They all received severance and a glowing recommendation. It was already in motion once their lawyer was notified of their deaths. I didn't need to do a thing. They really did take care of all their final details." He walked toward a set of double doors to the left. Swinging them open, he showed her the elegant dining room complete with an oval pine table and ten chairs.

Her mouth dropped open again as she entered the dining room. A matching China cabinet and buffet sat against the far wall. In each corner stood tall candelabras with wine-colored candles in them. The table held a wine-colored runner from end to end. Four paintings hung on the walls. Emma was sure none of them were hers. But she checked them out anyway.

The room to the right was a library. Wall-to-wall books and magazines. She didn't take the time to find out what her in-laws liked to read. All of them would go to local libraries as donations.

When they entered the kitchen, she needed to hold onto Jack again. She didn't cook much, but the kitchen she'd just walked into blew her away. The stove was an industrial kitchen type. The double ovens and the commercial-sized refrigerator matched the teak cabinetry. She walked to a set of thin double doors and pulled them open. "Holy crap, Jack. This pantry is a small store," she said and walked inside.

Scanning the shelves, she saw everything from boxed macaroni and cheese to caviar in cans. "Blech." She stuck out her tongue and went on checking out the supply of staples. Seeing boxed cereal that was more for kids, a knot formed in her gut. She froze, standing in the middle of the pantry, and wondered why people of their age would want that type of cereal. *Oh my, God, no! Please no. Jenna would not be that cruel.*

Turning to exit the pantry and find Jack, Emma caught sight of the baby food. Her heart stopped. She shook her head slowly from side to side. Her body tensed as she walked out of the pantry and found Jack standing in the kitchen. Her eyes wide, she opened her mouth to speak, but nothing came out. She looked away from him as she felt a chill pass through her. Her eyebrows folding inward and nose crinkling, she stumbled and grabbed the counter.

"Emma, what's wrong?"

Not caring about seeing the rest of the house, she grabbed his hand. "Come with me." She yanked his arm hard and scurried out of the kitchen toward the staircase that would lead them to the second floor. For Jack's sake, she hoped beyond hope that they wouldn't find what she feared they would.

With Jack in tow, she rushed up the stairs. "Emma, what is wrong?"

When they reached the landing, she didn't know which door to choose first. The double doors to their left were obviously the master suite, so she turned and drug Jack to the right. Seeing five doors along the hallway, she chose the one the furthest away from the master suite.

Before she could open the door, Jack grabbed her other hand and turned her to face him. Holding her shoulders, he asked her again, "Emma, what the hell is wrong?"

The burn of bile came to her throat. She didn't have the heart to say what she feared was in the bedroom behind the door before them. She shuddered as she felt her heart tighten sharply. She broke Jack's gaze and turned toward the door. Twisting the doorknob, she slowly opened the door and prayed silently, *Please be empty. Please be fucking empty.* She drew in a breath then peeked inside. She yanked the bedroom door closed and froze.

"Em, please tell me what's wrong?" Jack asked.

"Baby." Emma drew in a deep breath, then exhaled slowly. "I'm so sorry." She swung open the door and let him go in first.

Jack stopped dead in his tracks. Grabbing him when she saw him bend over, she led him to the bed. She held his hands tightly in hers. His head fell to his chest, and his breathing became short and fast.

"Why?" He looked at her, his eyes drawn together, his mouth turned down. "Why didn't my mom tell me? Did my parents hate me that much?" He shook his head. His eyes slammed shut but tears escaped down his face.

Emma softly wiped his cheeks. "I don't know. You can blame me. It's me your dad hated not you." She caressed his shoulders.

Bringing his eyes back to hers, he tried to make sense of seeing the crib. "But maybe Jenna just brought Jordan to meet them right before the accident…" He fell back onto the bed and stared at the ceiling. "Em, she didn't come here to hide my son from me, did she?"

"I don't know, Jack. I'm so sorry, but if Jenna tries to keep Jordan from you now, you have this as evidence that she intentionally kept him from you yet brought him to your parents. I'm going to take pictures, so we have this in case we need it." She brought out her phone from her purse and snapped several photos of the crib and close-ups of the frame.

Pulling himself up, he said, "Emma, I…, I don't know what to do. I can't yell at them; they're dead. I can't say anything about this to Jenna; she'll take my son and run like she already did. I can't risk losing him again." Jack's body went limp, and she rushed back to his side.

Holding him, she whispered, "We'll act like everything's fine. You need to keep it together to fight for joint custody. We'll use these photos only if we need to. A last resort if Jenna becomes hostile." Emma pushed Jack's towering body upright and looked into his bloodshot eyes. "This is a lot to deal with, but your parents may have gone along with Jenna's terms. We don't know what she told them. She may have lied to them. We just don't know."

Sitting on the bed, she held his hands in hers. Her heart ached with a pain she'd never felt before. Jenna betrayed Jack by hiding herself and Jordan at Jack's parent's home. Emma wondered how Jenna managed to convince them to keep her secret.

"Emma," Jack said.

"Yes, baby." She turned slightly to face him and looked into his dazed eyes.

"I missed my son's first everything. His laugh, his first time rolling over, crawling, walking. When he spoke his first word." Losing control of his emotions, he sobbed. His body shaking, while Emma held him.

Her thoughts went to Jordan and everything Jack had missed. They'd have to make memories with Jordan of other firsts. She couldn't wait to get to know him. He looked exactly like Jack, and she wondered just how much more like Jack he was. She already loved the little guy, and she hoped he'd warm up to her quickly.

She'd be patient and let Jack handle Jenna. She'd be by his side when he asked her to be. She'd let him know how much she loved Jordan.

"Jack, let's go home." She stood between his legs and tugged on him. Hugging her around her waist, his head rested between her breasts. She threaded her fingers through his hair. Tilting his head upward, she kissed his soft lips. "C'mon."

Jack slowly rose from the bed, staring at the crib. His body jerked as she led him out of the bedroom. "How could she? How could they?" Jack slammed the door shut when he and Emma left the room. "Emma. I'm done here. I don't want anything."

"Are you sure, Jack?" She glanced up into his empty stare.

"Yes. I'm sure." He took her hands and led her back to the staircase and down the stairs. He took one final look around his parents' house, then opened the front doors and let Emma exit. He yanked both doors with all his might and locked them.

When they got in the car, she asked, "Are you okay?" She leaned her head to see him.

Keeping his eyes on the mansion before them, he said, "I'm fine. I've got you and that makes all of this…" He waved his hand toward his parents' house. "Being with you makes everything better. You're all I need, Emma." He clasped her hand, bringing it to his lips, he kissed it. Then they rode home in silence.

CHAPTER 36

Sitting in the loft of her gallery, Emma's phone chirped with Matt's sound. She tapped her phone awake and read his text: **Hey, Em. I'm in town. May I stop by?**

She knew she shouldn't entertain Matt's company even though she believed he wasn't being deceitful. She knew Jack didn't trust Matt at all. She read the text again and thought, *Why not? Maybe he'll bring me a coffee. I could use one.* She let out a laugh, then sent Matt a text back: **Sure, but only for a few minutes. I'm busy.** She wasn't *that* busy, but she didn't want Jack to stop in and find Matt here with her.

Matt: **Great, be there in a few. Coffee?**

Emma: **Yes, thanks.**

She'd been working on another poem painting she'd written for JJ. She only had the poem partially done and wasn't sure what to draw for the frame. Tapping her lips with her pencil, she read the poem aloud:

JORDAN (JJ)

Jordan Jackson Bryant.
The most beautiful little boy I've ever seen.
A mini mirror image of Daddy.

Grabbing her sketch pad, she drew a mirror. Then she drew a caricature of Jack inside the mirror and a caricature of JJ sitting slightly off center of it. Drawing them as similar as she could from memory, Emma smiled when she looked at her finished drawing.

Reaching for her colored pencils, she chose a navy-blue pencil to write her poem. Just as she began to write, the bell over the gallery's entrance rang.

"Hi, Emma," Matt said, looking up at her coming down the loft stairs.

"Hi, Matt. Thanks," She nodded as she took the coffee in hand. "What brings you back to south Florida? Another job?" she asked, taking a seat on the stool behind the counter. She didn't want Matt to get comfortable up in the loft and stay too long.

Rubbing his neck, he cleared his throat. "No, I'm down here scouting buildings. My partners want to open an office here and one in Jacksonville." He raised his eyes to her.

"Oh, okay." She straightened her spine and folded her arms across her body. "That's really exciting. Congratulations on your company's successes. I'm sure you'll find someone to run the office down here." She reached for her coffee.

"That's the plan. I don't want to move here. I like it on the west coast of Florida. But with an office down here, I'll be in and out of town more often. Hope I can stop in." He peeked at her over his coffee cup.

"We'll see, Matt. If there's nothing else, I need to get back to my piece I was working on when you came in." She pointed up toward the loft.

"Yeah, sure. I just wanted to say hi." He tossed his coffee cup into the trash and wiped his hands down his jeans. "I'll leave you to your work." He slowly stepped toward the door.

"Matt, wait." Emma hopped off the stool and joined him at the front door. "Thanks again for this." She swung her arm around the gallery.

"You're welcome, again, Em." He opened the door and stepped outside. Turning, he reached for her hand. Bringing it to his lips, he kissed the back of it. "I'm only a call or text away. If you're ever in need of a friend."

Bowing her head as she stood in the doorway, she pulled her hand back. Taking a step toward Matt, she opened her arms and hugged him. His embrace tightened and pulled her as close as he could. She patted his back to let him know to let her go.

"Bye, Matt. It was good seeing you again."

"Bye, Em. Take care." Matt turned and walked toward his car.

Watching Matt walk away, she caught sight of Jenna across the street with her phone out. She waved to get her attention, but Jenna ducked into the drug store.

Emma looked both ways and hurriedly crossed the street and entered the drug store. Looking up and down each aisle, she spotted Jenna in the shampoo aisle.

"Hey, Jenna," Emma said.

"Oh, hey." Jenna didn't look Emma's way.

"Um, did you take a picture of me and Matt?" Emma raked her hand through her hair and scratched the back of her neck. "What you think you saw… with Matt and me… that was…" She paused and glanced around.

"What if I did? What was it, Emma? Are you cheating on Jack with Matt now?" Jenna blurted out.

"Jesus, fuck, Jenna. No!" She shook her head and drew in a breath. "I'd never cheat on Jack. Matt stopped by my gallery to wish me well and say goodbye."

Rolling her eyes, Jenna bit out, "Oh, you only cheat once, right?" Jenna's words stung. Knives cut Emma's heart to pieces. She'd hoped they could be friends, but she realized friends wouldn't be possible with Jenna. She'd be respectful of Jenna because she was Jordan's mother. She'd be civil when they had to be together.

"Jenna, I know Jack and I caused you a lot of pain, but…"

Jenna waved her hand in Emma's face. "Just stop. Don't apologize. I don't want to hear it."

Emma stepped back a few steps. "I'll ask you again, did you take a picture to try and show Jack?"

Opening her phone, Jenna showed Emma the picture of Matt embracing her. "There you are in the arms of your ex-husband." Jenna smirked as she stared through Emma.

"Please delete it. What you saw was a friendly goodbye hug. Nothing more. I won't let you hurt Jack with that photo. I'll tell him you have it. I'll tell him Matt came by the gallery. I don't keep secrets from Jack. I don't *lie* to Jack." Emma glared at Jenna.

Jenna turned away from Emma for a few seconds. Turning back to her, Jenna said, "Emma, we have to find a way to tolerate one another for the rest of our lives. I can do that if you can. For *my son*."

Emma heard the emphasis on 'my son' from Jenna. She bowed her head and cleared her throat. "Yes. I can do that. I can do whatever it takes to make Jack and Jordan happy."

"Okay, then it's settled. I'll delete the photo, watch." She held her phone and Emma watched Jenna press the trash can icon. The photo disappeared. But Emma knew Jenna could have more.

Thinking for a second, she decided to let it go. She'd talk with Jack and let him know about Matt stopping by her gallery. "Thank you, Jenna. And I know you don't want to hear it, but I am sorry for the pain I caused you." She looked up at Jenna. "Truce for Jack and Jordan." Emma held her arm out to Jenna. She looked at it, then shook Emma's hand.

"Truce," Jenna said and walked past Emma, exiting the drug store.

Going back to her gallery, Emma texted Jack: **Please meet me at the gallery after work.**

Jack: **Okay. See you soon, love.**

Next, she sent a text to Matt: **Will you please come back to the gallery around six?**

A few minutes passed before Matt answered: **Sure. Is everything okay?**

Emma: **I'm fine. We- you, me, and Jack need to talk. Thanks.**

Matt: **I'll be there at six.**

Slipping her phone into her pocket, she went up the stairs to her loft. She fell onto the futon, covering her face with her hands. "Fuck!" she yelled at the top of her lungs. Her body shook as she laid on her back. She stared up at the blank ceiling and blew out a long hard breath, releasing some of the tension. Breathing in deeply, holding it, then letting it all out over and over.

She knew bringing Jack and Matt together to talk with them both needed to be done. She had to make it clear to Matt that Jack was who she wants to spend the rest of her life with. She chose him.

She and Matt could be friends and she needs Jack to understand that their friendship will never interfere with their marriage. Her decision to be with Jack is final.

She blew out a long hard breath and looked up at her easel. Seeing her sketch of Jack and Jordan, her heart softened. Her body relaxed and she stopped shaking.

Glancing at her watch, she saw she had a few hours before Jack and Matt would be at her gallery. She grabbed a palette and placed it on the table sitting beside her easel. She brought out all the colors she wanted to use to paint Jack and JJ. Taking her time with each stroke, she painted the two most important people in her life. When she finished, she signed it as she always did, *EB Taylor.*

"Hey, baby," Emma greeted Jack when he came into the gallery. She hopped off her stool, came around to the front of the counter and embraced him around his waist. She pressed her face to his firm chest and held tight. "I'm so happy you got here first."

Holding her shoulders, Jack asked, "Who else is coming, love?"

"Please don't get mad. I need us all to talk."

"Emma, who is it?"

"Matt's coming by. And before you get upset, I asked him to."

"Why? And why do you still have his phone number?"

Dropping her gaze to the floor, she sucked in a deep breath as she remembered she'd forgotten to tell Jack about never deleting Matt's number after their divorce.

"Jack, I never deleted Matt's number. I've had it all this time." She glanced quickly at him, then dropped her eyes back to the floor. Her heart stung.

"Why did you keep his number, Em?" Jack's eyes narrowed.

Raising her eyes to him, she said, "It never dawned on me to delete it after the divorce. I didn't even remember until the gallery was almost done that I had it. He'd asked me if I still had his number. Jack, it's nothing. And in the end, it was good that I had it anyway." She reached for his hand.

Scratching his chin, he asked, "Is there anything else you forgot to tell me?"

"No, Jack. I promise. I'm sorry I forgot to delete his number then forgot to let you know I still had it." She reached for his hand again. Grasping it, she tugged gently. "Baby, I need Matt to know you and I are forever. And I need you to understand Matt and I were

207

once good friends and I'd like to have a friendship with him." Her eyes pulled together as she looked up at Jack.

"Em, I don't know." He shook his head from side to side. "I've told you I don't trust him." He squeezed her hand.

"He's harmless. I know Matt Taylor. I've known him since high school. He won't try to win me back. He knows I love you."

"I still don't trust him."

"Trust me, baby. I love you." Emma embraced Jack with all she had.

"I do, Em. I trust you completely." Jack hugged her tightly.

"Good, because I need to tell you what happened earlier today." She leaned against the counter and ran her hands through her hair.

"What happened, Em?"

"Matt was here..."

"Emma, I..."

"No, please let me finish. He stopped by to let me know B&T is looking for a space down here to open an office..."

"I knew it," Jack said.

Shaking her head from side to side, she said, "Matt isn't moving here. He likes it on the west coast. He also wished me well."

"Okay, so what's the big deal?"

"When I walked outside with him, I hugged him. Then I noticed Jenna across the street with her phone out. I knew she'd taken a picture of me and Matt hugging. So, I confronted her. We had words." Emma's eyes dropped to the floor. "I know she and I will never be friends again. But we did agree to a truce, and she deleted the photo."

"That's fine. Were you worried she'd show me the picture?"

"Yes. And I don't trust her at all. I saw her delete one picture, but I'm sure she took more than one. I told her I was going to tell you everything. And now I have."

"If she shows me the picture, I'll tell her I know all about it. I never expected you to become friends with her again. Being civil with one another when we are all together is good enough." Jack pulled Emma in and hugged her tenderly.

Turning to face the door when the bell clanged, Emma released Jack and clasped her hand with his. "Hi, Matt. Thanks for coming."

"Emma, Jack." Matt nodded at each of them and closed the door.

"Let's go up on the loft where it's more comfortable." Emma tugged on Jack's arm as she led him and Matt up the stairs.

Matt took a seat on the far end of the futon and Jack sat closest to Emma as she pulled up the small cushion chair. Taking Jack's hand in hers and locking their fingers, she looked at Matt. "So, I'm sure you're wondering why on earth would I ask you both to be here. Well…" she paused and pinched her lips together. "Matt, thank you again for making all of this a reality." Emma waved her arm in the air."

"Em, you're welcome, but yeah. Why am I here?" Matt asked.

"Because I need to apologize for all the pain I caused you…"

Jack squeezed her hand, and she turned her eyes to him. He cleared his throat and turned to face Matt. "It's not just Emma who needs to apologize. I know you probably don't want to hear it from me, but I'm sorry for the pain you went through. I fell in love with Emma when she was your wife." Jack looked at the floor, then back to Matt. "And that was wrong. I am sorry."

Matt's brow furrowed as he watched Jack. He glanced at Emma, then back to Jack. "I don't know how to respond to either of you, but all of that is done. It's over." He scratched his chin and raked his hand through his hair. "Emma made the choice to leave me, and it nearly killed me. But I loved her enough to let her go. Then she made the decision to marry and be with you for the rest of her life. I can't change her mind. I'm sure you know that by now." Jack nodded. "What Emma wants, she usually finds a way to get." Matt rubbed his hands down his lap. "But really..." Matt looked directly at Emma. "I want *you* to be happy. If I can help in any way, you know how to reach me, Em."

Blinking rapidly, she sucked in a breath and pinched Jack's hand. She nodded at Matt. "Um…Okay. I didn't expect all of that, Matt. Thank you." She smiled at him.

Looking at his watch, Matt sat on the edge of the futon and said, "If that's all, I have a long drive home. I won't be back down for several months, but if you need anything or something pops up and needs addressed, call me immediately." He pushed himself up from the futon and stepped toward Emma.

Standing, she held her hand out for Matt. "I will, thanks." They shook hands.

They all walked down the stairs to the front door. Jack stood behind Emma with his hands on her shoulders. She patted his hands and stepped toward Matt as he opened the door to leave.

"Take care, Matt. Friends?" She smiled and opened her arms to him.

"Always, Emma." Matt embraced her and hugged her tight. He kissed her hair, then let her go. Looking up to Jack, he extended his hand to him. "Jack, take care of Emma. I won't ever stop caring about her. She'll always be here." Matt patted his chest and smiled at her. She tilted her head as her eyes came together. She held her breath and blinked quickly to try and dry her eyes. Several tears spilled from the brim of her eyes, and she swiped them with her hands.

"I will, I promise." Jack shook Matt's hand firmly.

Emma slipped her arm around Jack as Matt left her gallery.

CHAPTER 37

After spending the day drawing and painting at her gallery, Emma arrived home just before Jack. She changed into shorts and a blouse, ready to go with him to meet his son. Their anniversary trip to New York City was just days away, but meeting Jordan gave Emma the biggest hope things were going to be fine.

On the drive to Jenna's, Emma clasped and unclasped her hands in her lap. She bit her lip as she watched the scenery pass them by. She took in several short breaths when they entered the small town where Jenna and Jordan lived. Jack covered her shaking hands.

"You'll be great, love. There's nothing to be nervous about. Jordan, he's perfect. He'll love you as much as I do." He squeezed her hand gently as he pulled into the driveway of Jenna's house.

Wiping her hands on her shorts once she exited the car, Emma walked around the back of the car and joined Jack. She gripped his bicep with both hands and forced a smile on her face.

He leaned down and kissed her softly. "Relax, Em," he said and led her to the front door.

Standing and waiting for Jenna to answer the door, Emma blew out a breath she'd held much too long. Her nerves got the best of her. She didn't know if they were from meeting JJ or over soon being in Jenna's home for the first time.

Her eyes darted back to the door when she heard it open. Jenna stood before them with JJ on her hip. His arms immediately reached for Jack. Emma's heart filled with joy. Her smile grew wide, and her eyes sparkled as she watched Jack hug and kiss his son. Catching Jenna's gaze, Emma nodded politely.

"Please, come in," Jenna said as she stepped to the side.

"Hey JJ. I brought someone for you to meet," Jack said to JJ as they walked into the house.

There was a warmth inside Jenna's home Emma hadn't expected. She followed Jack and Jenna to the family room to the right of the front door. JJ's toy box and piles of toys were scattered over the floor. Jack carefully sat on the floor and released JJ from his arms.

JJ went to his big truck and pushed it to Jack. Emma watched as the two pushed the toy back and forth.

"Can I get y'all a drink?" Jenna asked, breaking the uncomfortable silence.

Jack looked up, then to Emma. "Sure. Water will do. Em?"

"Yeah, water is fine, thanks, Jenna." Emma smiled, but Jenna just turned and walked out of the room. *Time. Give her time to come around to you. Be happy she allowed you to meet JJ.* Emma let out a sigh and nodded.

While Jenna was gone, JJ brought out another toy, this time a fire truck. He turned and looked at Emma. She smiled and he smiled back and looked at Jack.

"It's okay, buddy. That's Emma. Say hi." Jack scooted and sat beside her, patting the carpet in front of them. JJ hesitantly came toward them, holding his toy out to her. Emma held her hands open for him to lay it there.

"Hi, JJ," Emma said. "It's so nice to meet you." She placed his toy on the floor and held her hand out. She smiled and watched as JJ took slow steps closer to her and placed his hand in hers. Instantly, she loved him. Her heart grew as it filled with a love she'd never felt before. A protective love. She knew from this moment on that she'd always be there for this little boy, no matter what. Even if she and Jenna never became friends again. JJ was all that mattered.

Staring into JJ's sweet blue eyes, she saw Jack staring back at her. He stepped closer, then looked at his dad. Emma turned and saw Jack smiling from ear to ear. He spoke quietly as he said, "It's okay. Emma loves you as much as I do." Jack patted JJ's back.

Sucking in a breath, she blinked rapidly. Then suddenly, small arms embraced her as JJ fell into her lap. Her arms wrapped around his tiny toddler body, and she rocked him from side to side. She kissed his cheek and whispered in his ear, "I love you, little man." Tears snuck from her eyes.

"Mama," JJ said, and she looked up. Seeing Jenna holding two glasses of water, Emma held her hand out for one.

"Thank you," Emma said, she took a quick sip and placed the glass on the table near her.

Jack rose and took the other glass from Jenna. "Thank you for this. Really, Jenna. We are grateful you agreed to let Emma come to meet JJ. You can see he likes her already." Jack waved his arm towards his son and Emma as they played with his toys.

"I can see that." Jenna walked by Jack and sat on the sofa. "JJ." Jenna held her arms and coaxed her son to come to her. He ran into her arms, and she put him on her lap. "Listen, Jack. I know we have a custody hearing in a week or so, but I've been thinking a lot since your parents' tragic deaths." Jenna pursed her lips and wiped her hand on her slacks. "I was wrong to lie to you about Jordan. I'm sorry. I was hurt by what you both did." She looked directly at Emma.

"I'm sorry for that, Jen…" Emma began.

"No, don't, Emma. It's over and done with. I don't know if we can ever be the friends we once were, but you're my son's family now. So that makes you mine too. And I've done things I shouldn't have besides the lying. I'm working through all that now, and I know forgiveness is what I need to begin to do." She paused and drew in a deep breath. Turning to face Jack, she said, "There's a good school close to your house I would like JJ to attend, better than the one here. So, I've decided to move closer to you. I want our son to be a part of both our lives as much as he can be and that means shared custody. When he turns two in June, I'm willing to begin every other week arrangements with you, Jack. But I need those months to adjust to sharing him with you."

Looking at Jack's stunned reaction to Jenna's mini speech, Emma rose from the floor and stood beside him. She gave him a soft pinch on his arm.

"Ah, yes, of course. We can work all of that out. Jenna… I didn't expect you to agree so easily. I mean…"

Jenna's hands shot up. "I know, Jack. But you don't know everything, and I don't know if I'll ever be ready to talk about it. I can see how much JJ loves you. My son is the most important thing in my life. His happiness is my priority. And that means having you and Emma in his life." Jenna kissed Jordan's cheek when he wiggled in her lap. She let him down and he ran straight to Emma, grasping her leg. "He wants you to pick him up." Jenna smiled.

Bending and slipping her hands under JJ's arms, Emma lifted him onto her hip. Memories of carrying Amelia and RJ exactly like that came flooding back to her. She smiled at JJ and touched her nose to his. His tiny lips kissed her cheek, and her heart overflowed with love. She tightened her grip around him and hugged him.

"I have to know, Jenna. Did you take Jordan to see my parents? And if you did, when?" Jack stood beside Emma with his hands on his hips.

Emma's heart clenched, waiting for Jenna's answer.

Watching Jenna's head fall to her chest, Emma knew the answer. She felt Jack's arm slide around her.

"I'm sorry, Jack. I did. That's what I'm working through. I made them keep my secret. I am so sorry for all of that now." Jenna rose from the sofa, her eyes close together, her mouth turned down. "I know it's a lot to ask, but please forgive me for being so selfish." She dropped her gaze to the floor, her shoulders slumped.

Jack stood still beside Emma. An eerie, deafening silence filled the room for several minutes. Emma looked up at Jack, his eyes wide, his mouth open. He raked his hand through his hair. She nudged him gently. He looked at her with a deep sadness covering his face.

"Jesus, Jenna." Jack's voice rose. Emma nudged him again and he paused. He took in several breaths and looked around the room. "That hurts. But I think we've hurt one another enough. And I can't ask my parents why they chose to go along with your demands." Pausing again, he looked at Emma still holding JJ. She smiled up at him and shook her head quickly as she blinked slowly. She hoped he'd drop it, even though she knew how hurt Jack was by Jenna's lies and his parents' secrecy.

"Jack…" Jenna began.

With his hand in the air, he looked at Jenna. His head shaking from side to side, he said, "No. From today forward. We," Jack circled his hand around Emma, JJ, Jenna and back to himself, "We are going to talk about things. No matter what. No more lying. No more secrets. I'm sorry for my past behavior. This little guy right here," Jack reached for JJ and Emma lifted him up to Jack, "Our son is all that matters."

CHAPTER 38

Arriving at home, Jack and Emma walked into the kitchen. She dropped her purse on the table and watched him walk past her. They hadn't spoken on the entire drive home. She knew he was in deep pain and needed to talk about what his parents and Jenna had done.

She went to their bedroom and changed into one of Jack's t-shirts. She wanted to feel him against her skin. Sitting on the bed, she waited for Jack to join her.

After a few minutes he came into their bedroom and laid across their bed. She caressed his shoulders and laid next to him. "We should talk about what Jenna said." Emma tugged on his body, trying to turn him toward her.

Rolling onto his back, he slipped his arm around her and drew her to him. Kissing the top of her head, he said, "I don't know what to say, love. I'm numb."

"Oh, Jack. I'm so sorry. I never thought Jenna would lie about losing the baby, but to ask your parents to keep Jordan from you. I can't... I just can't." She embraced him tightly.

"I don't know what's worse. Jenna lying to me or my parents keeping her secret, her lie." His body jerked and he sniffled.

"Baby, we can't change what she or your parents did. We can only be there for Jordan from now on. I know you'll always have questions, but you'll never get them answered. You need to be the best father for your son." She placed her hands on his chest and rested her chin on them. "I love you and I love your son. We will figure this all out together."

Jack ran his hand through her hair, resting his hand on her shoulder. "I'm so lucky to have you. And my son."

"I'm the lucky one." She kissed his chest and draped her arm across him. Feeling Jack's arms hold her, she closed her eyes and gave in to sleep.

In the morning, Jack readied himself for work, while Emma made coffee and ordered a light breakfast from the corner deli. When it arrived, she placed the bagels and cream cheese on the bar and waited for Jack to join her.

She'd planned to go into her gallery and fill her day with painting. With the success of her first solo exhibition, she needed to create more pieces if she wanted to hold another event next year.

Having a little boy in her life now changed everything. JJ took precedence over everything. She'd thought about hiring an assistant to open the gallery on the weeks she and Jack had JJ with them. She wanted to be a hands-on stepmom. Be with him during the day when Jack had to work. She hadn't spoken with Jack about her plans yet. She needed to be sure that the sharing custody arrangements would work for them and Jenna.

Feeling Jack's arms embrace her from behind, she wrapped her arms over his and squeezed. "Mmm, you feel so good, love." He kissed her cheek, then sat on the stool.

"Jack," she began.

"Emma." He smiled and took her hand in his.

"I think we should invite Jenna to dinner before we go on our anniversary trip to New York next week. She may feel more comfortable when she sees our home. We can show her JJ's room. It's ready for him. She can see all the safety features we've installed, like the gate around the pool and spa. All the doors that lead to the outside have locks up high. Even I have to stretch to reach them." She let out a laugh and pinched his hand.

Taking a sip of his coffee, Jack placed his mug down and rubbed his chin. "I think you're right, Em. I'll send Jenna a text and see when she's free." He pulled out his phone from his pocket and tapped it awake. Thumbing to Jenna's number, he sent her a text. He showed Emma the message: **Good morning. Emma and I would like you and JJ to come over for dinner. What day works for you?**

Laying his phone on the bar, he finished his bagel and coffee. He glanced at Emma as she stared at the phone. "She's probably working, love. When I hear back from her, I'll text you." Jack rose from the stool and pulled Emma from hers. Holding her in a tender embrace, he kissed her hair.

"I know, I just want things to be perfect." Closing her eyes, she shook her head and leaned against the stool.

"You know that's not possible, but we can get damn close to perfect." He cupped her face and brushed her lips with his. He slipped his phone into his pocket, then took her hand and led her to the door to the garage. "I need to get into the center. See you tonight. I love you."

"Okay. I'll be at the gallery all day. I love you too." She tilted her head upward, waiting for her goodbye kiss.

Slipping his hand to the nape of her neck, he leaned down and kissed her deeply. He opened the door and walked toward his car. Emma pushed the button to open the garage for him. Waving as he slid in and drove off.

While painting at her gallery, Emma's phone rang. Answering it, she said, "Hi, baby."

"Hi, love. Jenna texted me back and said any night is okay with her. Do you want to have her come over tonight?"

"Sure. It's a drive for her, so let's do an early dinner. Can you leave work soon?"

"Let me check. Hold on." Emma waited for Jack to come back on the phone. She hoped he could sneak out early. She wanted to talk with Jenna as soon as possible to be sure everything was settled between them. "Emma, I'll leave the center at four and meet you at home."

"Okay. How about pizza for dinner. I'll order it and pick it up on my way home."

"Sounds good. See you soon."

"Bye, baby." Emma locked her phone and laid it on the stand beside her easel. Seeing it was two p.m. already, she finished her painting and cleaned up the workspace.

After ordering their pizza, she turned off the lights and locked the door. Emma left her gallery and drove to their favorite pizza joint. They'd always had it delivered, but since it was on her way home, she stopped in.

When she arrived home, she stuck the pizza in the oven to keep it warm until Jack, Jenna and JJ arrived. Needing something to wet her throat, she reached for her glass and grabbed the whiskey bottle. *Just one will help calm this damn anxiety.*

She poured herself a tumbler full when Jack came through the kitchen door. "Hey, love."

Turning quickly, she downed the booze and placed the glass in the sink. "Hi, baby." She walked toward him and embraced him around his waist. "I missed you." She tilted her head up as he leaned down. Their lips met in a sweet, soft kiss.

"I missed you too." Jack put his backpack in the coat closet then took a seat at the kitchen island. "Are you ready for tonight?" he asked.

"Yes. We need to be sure Jenna is comfortable with JJ coming here every other week soon. I can put all the shit behind us. I'll do whatever it takes to make things civil between Jenna and me. For you and JJ." She hopped onto the stool next to Jack.

Cupping her face, he leaned close to her and brushed her lips with his. "I'm so lucky."

CHAPTER 39

Jack smiled and turned toward the front door when the doorbell rang. "They're here."

Standing, they both went to the door. Jack opened it and said, "Welcome. Come on in." He reached for JJ and Emma smiled when she saw JJ's blue eyes light up as he fell into Jack's arms.

Stepping to Jack's side, Emma smiled at Jenna and said, "Welcome to our home. Please make yourself comfortable, Jenna."

"Thank you." Jenna glanced around and waited for Emma to lead the way.

"We have pizza for dinner. I hope that's okay. I'm not much of a cook, that'd be my sister." Emma shrugged and walked into the kitchen. "Anything to drink?" she asked, opening the oven to retrieve the pizza box.

"Sure, water is fine." Jenna reached into the backpack she'd brought and pulled out a child's sippy cup for JJ. "Here, JJ."

Jack sat his son on a stool next to Jenna. JJ reached for his cup and began drinking. Jack took the stool to JJ's other side.

When Emma turned around with Jenna's water, she drew in a deep breath. Placing the glass on the island bar, she avoided looking at Jenna. She stepped back and felt for the kitchen counter behind her. The sight of seeing Jenna, JJ, and Jack together had taken her aback.

"Em, are you okay?" Jack asked.

Shaking her head, she smiled and said, "I'm fine." She quickly turned her back to them. Her ribs tightened as she felt a quiver in her stomach. She never expected seeing them sitting together would cause her anxiety to spike. She knew Jack loved her and only her, but JJ showing up in their lives changed everything.

Feeling Jack's hands engulf her shoulders, she leaned back against his warm, towering body. He leaned down and kissed her cheek. "Are you sure you're okay, love?"

Emma patted his hands and turned to face him. Looking up into his loving blue eyes, she whispered, "I'm fine, baby." She brushed his cheek and stretched up on her tip toes to kiss his soft lips. "I promise." Her anxiety melted away when Jack hugged her before sitting back down next to his son.

She drew in several deep breaths and said, "Let's all go to the dining room. Jenna, we have a highchair for JJ."

Smiling, Jenna said, "Thanks. He's not quite ready for a booster chair. Soon though." She reached for her son and lifted him onto her hip. They all followed Emma into the dining room.

Placing the pizza and plates on the table, Emma walked back to the kitchen and grabbed her glass from the sink. She poured herself a double and added ice. *Just to shake off the nerves. Mmm.* She sipped down the amber liquid, then went back and joined Jack, Jenna, and JJ for dinner.

After finishing her slice of pizza, Emma leaned back and observed Jack with JJ. He'd cut the slice of pizza for JJ and helped him with the plastic child's fork. Her heart warmed seeing the love between Jack and his son. She looked across the table and caught Jenna staring at her. Emma nodded and smiled politely. Jenna did the same.

"So, Jack," Jenna began. He lifted his attention to her. "What did you and Emma want to talk about?" She sat back in her chair with her hands clasped in her lap.

"We wanted you to see our home. So, you can see where JJ will live for half of his life. We've childproofed it completely. Emma…" Jack stopped when Emma touched his arm.

"Jenna. I'm going to hire an assistant to run the gallery on the weeks JJ is here with us. I don't want to hire a nanny or use a daycare. We thought it best if I were here with him while Jack is at the center. You know he can't work every other week, but I can." Emma leaned forward and folded her arms on the table.

Jenna's eyes grew wide. "Wow, okay. I didn't expect to hear you say that, but now I feel so much better about our joint custody. I did worry about where JJ would be while you both worked. But, thank you, Emma for putting my son first. I know what your gallery means to you and what a sacrifice this is for you." Jenna's smile became warm as she looked at Emma then to Jack. She ran her hand through JJ's brown hair and wrinkled her nose at him.

His sweet giggles sent warmth all through Emma. That little boy would one day bring her and Jenna to a better place. She knew he would.

"It's what's best for JJ, and I'll… No, we," she grasped Jack's hand, "We will always do what's best for him and always put him first."

Jack smiled and leaned over, kissing Emma's cheek he tugged on her hand. "You don't have to worry about a thing while our son is with Emma and me. I promise, Jenna." Jack pushed back his chair and lifted JJ from his highchair. JJ's little arms wrapped around Jack's neck and held on tight.

Emma and Jenna each rose from their seats and followed Jack into the family room. There he placed JJ down in the middle of toys he and Emma had bought for him.

While JJ played, Jenna brought out her phone. "Jack." She looked his way.

Glancing up at her from the floor, he said, "Yes."

"I should've let you listen to this voicemail from your mom I received the day before the accident."

Shaking his head, he looked at Emma, his eyes glassy. "Why didn't you?" he asked, rising from the floor, and sitting next to Emma on the sofa. He grabbed her hand and held it tight.

"You were upset with me for what I did. And I understand why. I was wrong." Jenna's head fell to her chest. She ran her hand through her long blond hair, then looked at Jack again. "You need to hear what your mom said. Please listen." Jenna pushed the play button.

"Jenna dear. Charles and I cannot continue keeping your secret from Jackson. He's our son and lying to him all this time has caused us too much stress." Holding her breath when she heard Christy Bryant's soft, kind voice, Emma's eyes filled with tears. She looked at JJ and smiled. He gave her his sweet smile back. Her heart melted as her eyes drew close together.

222

"Call Jackson today and tell him before I call him when we arrive home tomorrow. He needs to know he has a son. Please, dear. Do the right thing and call Jackson." Jack's grip on Emma's hand tightened as his mom's voice went on. Her heart ached for him. She felt his body shake and tugged her hand free. She slid her arm around him and held him close to her.

"Jordan needs his father as much as he needs his mother. Give our grandson a hug and tell him we'll see him soon and we love him."

When the voicemail ended, Jack sat forward and dragged both his hands through his hair. His head fell to his chest, his breathing short and fast. Emma squeezed his waist, he turned his head and looked at her.

His eyes were filled to the brim with tears. A deafening silence hovered all around while JJ continued to play with his toy cars and trucks, oblivious to the tension in the room. Emma glanced at Jenna. A single tear escaped down Emma's cheek; she quickly swiped it away.

Jenna sat forward with her hands clasped on her knees, watching her son contently playing on the floor. Emma rubbed Jack's shoulders to try and comfort him. He breathed in a deep breath, held it for a beat, then blew it out.

After several long moments, he cleared his throat. "Jenna," he began. Jenna looked at Jack. Emma sat silently beside him, caressing his back. "How long did you make them keep your secret?" Jack's voice was monotone.

"Too long, Jack, and I am sorry for putting them in the middle of our issues." Jenna laid open her hands and pursed her lips. She sighed heavily, then said, "I hope one day you will forgive me for my mistakes. I wasn't thinking clearly, and I regret every lie I ever told you and your parents. I lied to a lot of people and have spent the past year telling them all the truth about what happened between us and why I chose to lie to you about losing our baby." Jenna fell back against the chair and covered her face with her hands.

"Mama," JJ said. He pulled himself up to Jenna and patted her knees.

Bringing him onto her lap, Jenna kissed his cheek. "It's okay JJ. Mama's okay." She wrapped him into a tight hug and kissed him again.

Watching JJ react to Jenna, Emma saw the strong bond between mother and son. She'd hope one day that same bond would form between JJ and Jack.

"I don't know what to say, Jenna," Jack said. "None of us can change any of this. I need some time to absorb it all. Thank you for sharing Mom's voicemail. I could hear in her voice that she was upset and if they hadn't died, she would've told me about Jordan herself." He sucked in a breath and rose from the sofa. Walking toward Jenna, he held his arms out to his son. Instantly, JJ reached for Jack, and he lifted him onto his hip. "I love you, Jordan." Jack kissed his son's cheek and walked with him toward the French doors, leaving Emma with Jenna as he went out onto the lanai.

Standing, Emma walked into the kitchen. She found her glass and poured it full of whiskey. Shaking her head when she gulped down her drink.

"Emma." She spun when she heard Jenna say her name.

"Jenna," Emma said. "Want one?" She tilted her tumbler toward Jenna.

"No thanks. Whiskey isn't my drink." She slid onto a stool and said, "I know we've all been through a lot the past few years. I don't want to rehash it anymore. I want us all to heal." She paused. "I don't know if we can ever be the friends we once were, but I'm willing to be more than just civil to you when we're together. I'll do anything to make my son's life the best. And as he gets older, he'll see and feel the tension between you and me." Stopping again, she closed her eyes and let out a breath. "Can we start over?" Jenna asked.

Leaning against the counter, Emma sipped on her whiskey and listened to Jenna. She'd do anything for that little boy. Anything. "Of course, Jenna. Tonight, you came completely clean with Jack. That had to be hard to do. Hearing Christy's voice made me sad. I never got to meet her or Charles. But you did. You knew them, they were your family for years." Emma stepped toward the island bar. "I'll always regret not finding a way to bring Jack and his parents together before they died. But I can't let that consume me." She walked around and stood next to Jenna. "I will also do anything for JJ. Anything. I love him and I love Jack. They are my world."

"I know that now. So, friends?" Jenna held her hand to Emma.

"Sure, friends." Emma took Jenna's hand and shook it. "Want to see JJ's room?"

"I'd love to, thanks, Emma."

Leading Jenna to the other side of the house, she opened the door and let Jenna enter first. Jenna turned to Emma with her hand over her mouth. "Emma, this is perfect." Jenna walked around the bedroom, checking the crib.

"That will turn into a toddler bed as soon as JJ is ready for it."

"He should be very soon. I have something similar for him at home." Jenna looked at the murals painted on the two walls without windows. "I know you painted these. They're perfect."

Emma had painted forest scenes on each wall. Each with different wild animals, trees, and flowers. She'd hoped the calmness of the wilderness would be soothing for Jordan.

Emma blushed and nodded. "Thank you. I only want the best for your son, Jenna. I promise to love him as my own till the day I die."

"I know you will." Jenna smiled.

They both walked out of JJ's bedroom and went toward the family room. Seeing Jack playing on the floor and hearing JJ's sweet laughter filled Emma's heart with joy. She tugged on Jenna's arm. "C'mon, let's go join the guys." They walked toward Jack and JJ and joined them on the floor.

After an hour, Jenna said, "We should get going. I have an early appointment."

Jack rose from the floor and held his hand for Emma. She slipped her hand in his and stood beside him.

"Dada," JJ said, tugging on Jack's slacks. He bent over and scooped up his son. Emma caressed JJ's arm and he reached for her.

Catching him as he fell from Jack's arms into hers, Emma smothered kisses on JJ's cheeks. His belly laugh immediately melted her heart. His little arms wrapped around her neck. She noticed Jenna smiling as JJ held onto her tightly. She sucked in a breath as her eyes began to fill with happy tears. Her life couldn't get more perfect.

"Mama." JJ reached for Jenna. Stepping toward Jenna, Emma lifted him. Jenna took JJ and sat him on her hip. His smile stretched across his sweet face as he waved to Jack. "Dada." He pointed to Jack.

"Yes, JJ. That's Daddy. Can you say Em…ma?" Jenna said Emma's name slowly for him.

He looked directly at Emma and said, "EmEm."

"Very good, JJ." Jenna squeezed him and nuzzled her nose on his cheek.

Jack slipped his arm around Emma, and she held onto him. Her heart pounding fiercely with happiness. She glanced upward to Jack. He squeezed her gently as they all walked toward the door.

"Thanks for having us. Call me when y'all get back from New York and we'll plan for JJ's next visit. And we can talk about his first week with you." Jenna opened the door. JJ reached for Jack.

Taking JJ into his arms, Jack spun him around and kissed his cheek. "See you soon, JJ. I love you."

Emma held her hands for JJ, and he fell into them. She kissed his cheek. Hugging him tightly, she whispered to him, "I love you." His tiny hand brushed her cheek then he reached for Jenna.

After taking JJ back into her arms, Jenna turned to leave. "Bye y'all"

Standing together arm in arm in the doorway, Jack and Emma waved to JJ and watched as he waved back.

CHAPTER 40

They were back in New York the day before their first anniversary. Back in the very same hotel where they'd married a year ago. The suite had been decorated by the hotel staff in honor of their first anniversary. When Jack opened the door, he swooped her legs out from under her. Emma held onto his broad shoulders as he carried her across the threshold just as he'd done one year ago.

Smiling, she kissed him when he placed her back down on the floor. Then she led him into the bedroom of the suite.

Turning him so his back was to the bed, she nudged him to sit. She wrapped her arms around his neck then jumped onto him, straddling his body. His magnificent blue orbs captured hers. She gazed deep into his soul, falling deeper in love with him with each second that passed.

She crashed her mouth to his. His arms embraced her as they fell to the bed. She kissed him with every ounce of passion and love she had for him, her tongue swirling inside his warm, sweet mouth, twisting with hers. Her appetite for him had not waned at all. If anything, it'd grown more and more insatiable. Twenty-four hours in a day wasn't enough for her. Emma wanted Jack more than the air to breathe.

Flipping them over, Jack leaned on his forearms, resting them on either side of Emma's head. He laid his long, firm body between her soft legs and gazed into her stunning blue eyes. His lips gently touched her cheek, pecked her nose, then covered her mouth. He darted his tongue between her sweet lips.

Emma's hands traveled up and down his back, searching for the hem of his shirt. When she found it, she lifted the cotton polo over his head. Seeing his firm pecs and tight ripples, she tumbled her fingers from his shoulders to the waistband of his slacks. "You're so fucking perfect, Jack. God, so damn perfect." Her tongue slipped out and circled her lips. "So yummy," she purred as Jack rose from the bed and removed his slacks, then his boxers. "Oh, Jesus," she moaned when he crept back onto the bed and on top of her. Her body writhed with desire for him to fuck her. To make her scream his name over and over, to take her to the edges of oblivion and hold her there until her bliss exploded within her.

Raising her arms above her head, she shivered as Jack slowly removed her blouse. He kissed her navel before quickly unhooking her lacy bra and sliding it from her body. His mouth covered a breast as his tongue licked her stiff nipple. He caressed her other breast tenderly, circling her nipple as it pebbled. "Oh my, God," she moaned.

Jack rose up to remove her skirt, and she noticed his full erection. Her heart drummed fiercely. Her body shook. Her pussy ached for him to make love to her. Pulling him back down, she stared into his eyes. "Baby, take me. I want you inside me." Emma wrapped her arms around his neck and brought his lips to hers, kissing him deeply as his hard cock penetrated her. Thrusting gently into her wet pussy, his grip on her shoulders tightened.

"Em, you feel so damn amazing." His thrusts became faster, harder, deeper. Lifting himself from her, he raised her leg over his shoulder and wrapped the other around his waist. He straightened his body as he pushed deeper into her.

Slapping the bed hard when Jack made her come, Emma grasped the sheets and pulled them. He made her come over and over with each plunge.

"God, I love how you feel. So slick and tight. Damn, Emma. I can't hold out much longer. You're driving me crazy."

"Look at me, baby. Come for me. Jack, fill me up. Look at me," Emma screamed as she pulled her body up when he smacked his body into hers with a force like never before.

Holding one another's gaze, their bodies slapped together. She felt his cum spray into her as her core walls clenched around his dick.

228

Falling onto her, his hot breath against her cheek gave her hot chills. She giggled and kissed his damp cheek. Both their bodies glistened as they laid on the bed, their heartbeats pounding fast.

Sliding his hand under her, Jack cupped her breast and gently drew her dainty body into his. Emma covered his hand with hers. Reaching and feeling for his other hand, she brought it to her lips and kissed it. Closing her eyes, she felt his love completely engulf her as she fell asleep.

***

Bright sun rays woke Emma as she felt Jack stirring. Still in his arms, she smiled and hugged him closer. Feeling his soft lips on her shoulder, she rolled to face him.

"Good morning, beautiful, and happy anniversary." Jack kissed Emma.

"Good morning, gorgeous. Happy anniversary, baby." She brushed his cheeks and gazed into his intoxicating baby blues.

Cupping her cheeks, he kissed her again. "I can't explain how happy you've made me. You're my perfect bride, my perfect wife. You're all mine."

"Oh, Jack. I love you." Her breath hitched as she tried not to cry, but Jack had a way with sweet nothings that sent her tear ducts into overdrive. "This past year has been euphoric, surprising, and devastating. But we made it. As long as we're honest with each other, we'll be forever. Even the hard truths must be told. We'll make it through the pain together. I promise." She caressed his cheek as he leaned down and kissed her softly.

Catching his soft blue orbs again, she gazed deep into his soul. Her soul sang out inside her. The melody flowing within her sounded like soft waves crashing on the beach. Like a soft breeze blowing across a field of wildflowers. Like the sun rising from the ocean's horizon, then slowly and peacefully setting back into the ocean surrounded by an astonishingly colorful sky before darkness came.

Without words between them, Jack gently moved himself between Emma's soft legs. They fell open to welcome him there. Her hands caressed his firm pecs, then tumbled down to his glorious ripples and around to his delicious peach-shaped ass. Squeezing him, she smiled as his mouth covered hers. His tongue touched her lips, then retreated, teasing her over and over. She pushed hers into his delectable mouth. Tasting her forever favorite flavor—Jack.

Feeling his hard-as-steel cock slide between her wet folds, she sucked in a breath. Her breasts pushed against his fabulous pecs. Skin to skin, their bodies melded as one.

"Baby," she breathed. Her chest rose and fell quickly as her body devoured his. His lips traveled across her breasts, stopping on each one to taste her sweet skin. A quick nibble on her stiff nipples sent wild sensations to her toes. "Baby," she moaned again. Her hips shot upward as his came down with a force that sent his rigid shaft deeper into her.

Cupping her shoulders tightly, Jack buried his face in her neck. He kissed her dampened skin, licked her salty sweat from her collarbone, and trailed his soft lips against her cheek. His hips continued in their up and down movement. He glided in and out of her pussy with a smooth motion. He kissed her chin, her nose, her cheeks, then crashed his mouth to hers. He dove his tongue between her lips, searching for hers. He lapped up every inch of her mouth as she did his.

Arching her back as his lips traveled along her sleek neck, she let out a whimper. "Oh…" She clamped her hands on his triceps, her fingers barely reaching to his bicep. She gripped him as tight as she could when her bliss exploded inside her. Her legs captured his waist as she yanked him down onto her. "Baby," she moaned breathlessly against his collarbone.

"Yes, love," he whispered as his tongue trailed her earlobe. He gave her a quick nibble, and she shivered beneath him.

Panting, she feathered her fingers through his soft brown hair, then rested her hand on the nape of his neck. His lips barely touched hers as she purred, "Take me to the edge of forever." And she pulled him to her, smashing their mouths together, their tongues ravaging each other's.

Jack's hips slapped against Emma over and over. Her body lurched up as his came down. The sweet sound of making love with him rang throughout the suite as she moaned his name repeatedly. His lips tasted every inch of her smooth sweet skin. They hungrily devoured one another.

After what seemed like hours, Emma cried out, "Oh my, oh my, God. Yes, baby, yes. Harder please." She bit down on her lip when his cock throbbed inside her. His rhythm increased. His grip on her tightened.

"Emma!" Jack growled and a last powerful thrust into her sent her to the edge of forever. Her body quivered. Inside her soul exploded into the most sensual bliss.

"Jack! Jackson!" Her eyes rolled back in her head as she held her breath and gripped him again with her legs and arms. He collapsed onto her, then slid to her side. His lips softly caressed her shoulder. "If you keep that up, we won't get out of bed, baby." Emma winked and ran her finger across his firm pec.

"Fine with me." Jack pushed his still hard dick against her thigh.

Jesus, fuck. I so love him. God, how I love him, her soul spoke to her.

"I don't mind either. And I'll regret saying this, but let's go and get some fresh air. We can continue this tonight. In the shower, in the jacuzzi, on the table, the sofa, and end back here. Deal?" Her smile filled with glee and sin.

"Absolutely, love." Jack leaned over and kissed her before they rose from the bed and showered for their day in the city.

***

As they were about to leave the suite, a knock sounded. Emma turned around and didn't see Jack anywhere. She heard him call out, "Will you get that?"

Raising her eyes in suspicion, she answered the door. When she opened it, all she saw were red roses and white gardenias. The fragrance from the flowers wafted into the suite and encompassed her completely. Knowing this was part of Jack's plan for their day, she bounced on her feet to see the delivery person.

"Mrs. Bryant?" a man's voice asked.

"Yes, I'm here. Please come in." She stepped to the side and allowed the man in. He walked over to the dining room and placed the enormous bouquet on the long table.

Emma followed him and waited as he straightened his uniform. "Congratulations, ma'am." He smiled.

"Thank you so much." She leaned toward the flowers and drew in a deep breath.

"Hey, Frank. Thanks for bringing these up for me," Jack said as he came toward Emma.

"No problem, Dr. Bryant." Frank tilted his head to the right, and the two men moved away from her. She knew Jack had more plans for their day and knew she'd enjoy every surprise he had in store for her.

When Jack walked with Frank to the suite door, he handed him a generous tip. Walking back toward Emma, Jack held his hands out to her. She placed her hands in his, and he brought her into his loving embrace. Pressing her cheek against his chest, she listened to his heart. It beat along with hers as she tilted her head up and he leaned down. Their lips met in a tender kiss.

"These are beautiful." Emma touched a rose and sniffed it.

"Not as beautiful as you, love." He slipped his arm around her waist and swept her off her feet.

"Jack!" she squealed as she grasped his shoulders. "Put me down, please."

Kissing her again, he placed her down, then got their wool coats from the coat closet by the suite door.

"Before we go out, I have something for you." She walked into the bedroom and returned with a gift bag. "Here, baby. Happy anniversary." Her eyes sparkled as she handed him the bag.

Laying their coats over the chair, he peeked inside. "What's this?"

"Open it."

Pulling out the black book, he flipped it open. His lips turned upward as he paged through it. "Em, you look…Wow!" His eyes blinked rapidly as he flipped each page.

"Do you like it?" She squinted and smiled.

"I love this. You're beautiful and so damn hot." He sat the photo book on the table and drew her into him. "I'm the luckiest man alive to have you for my wife." He leaned down and kissed her. Holding her tightly, he slid his tongue between her lips, twisting it with hers.

Gazing into his soft blue eyes after their kiss broke, she said, "I'm happy you like my gift." She wrapped her arms around his waist and squeezed. "You're everything to me, Jack."

"You're everything to me too, love." He kissed her again, then lifted their coats from the back of the chair. "Let me help you into this. After all, it is February in New York City."

She smiled and slipped her arms in each side as Jack lifted the coat onto her body. "Thank you." She picked up her small clutch purse from the entry table and tucked it under her arm. Once Jack had his coat on, she slid her arm through his, and they left the suite for the day.

When Emma stepped outside, she saw a limousine waiting. Turning, she said, "A limo for the day?' She wondered if they'd make it back to the hotel without making love inside it. She hoped not.

The chauffeur stood with the back door open. He waved his arm for Emma to enter. She tucked her head and went into the limo.

"Thanks, George," Jack said before sliding in beside her. Inside the limo was another bouquet of roses and gardenias, as well as a bottle of champagne and two flutes.

Snuggling up against Jack, Emma slipped her hands inside his coat and hugged him tight. His arms embraced her as he kissed the top of her head. "Where are we going?" she asked.

"Just driving around the city. If there's some place you want to stop, just push the button right there." Jack pointed to a blue button to her left.

"So, this is a private tour of New York City? Just us?"

"Yes. Here, let me open this for us." Jack reached for the champagne bottle, and Emma held the flutes for him to fill.

Placing the bottle back into the ice bucket, Jack held his glass out and Emma did the same. "To you, love. For making the first year of our marriage the best year of my life despite everything that happened. You are the shining light of my life." Jack leaned toward her, and they kissed. Tapping his glass, she twisted her arm around his and sipped on the champagne.

Taking a few minutes to gather her thoughts, she bit the inside of her cheek, then held her glass up. "Jack. I remember our first encounter like it was yesterday. You took my breath away when I turned to see who answered me. As my eyes went up your alluring body, my heart pounded so hard. I nearly fainted at the arousing vision you were that night. You still are the tantalizingly, seductive love of my life. I don't regret a thing. I love you, baby." They circled their arms again and sipped more champagne as the limo drove around New York City.

Gazing out the dark windows, Emma noticed a sign for an art gallery. But before she could press the blue button, the limo came to a stop in front of it. Turning, she smiled at Jack. "You planned this stop, didn't you?" She leaned into Jack and kissed him softly.

"Of course, I did. You can't come to New York City again and not go to an art gallery. C'mon, love." Jack held his hand as the chauffeur opened the door for them.

Stepping out of the limo, Emma panned the outside of the Metropolitan Art Museum. A stunning building before her. She took Jack's hand, and they walked toward the entrance.

"Welcome to the Metropolitan Art Museum, Dr. and Mrs. Bryant," the greeter said.

Emma spun to face Jack. "You set this up. Oh my gosh. Jack, I..." She embraced him tightly. Then she read the greeter's name tag: Susan. "Thank you, Susan."

"You're welcome, Mrs. Bryant. Will you and Dr. Bryant please follow me?"

Emma glanced up at Jack again. His eyes shot upward, then he smiled and put his arm around her shoulders as they followed Susan.

They were led to a small office and Susan asked them to wait for their guide, Phil, to meet them here. Within minutes, Phil entered the office. "Sorry for the delay, Dr. Bryant." Looking at Emma, Phil said, "And you must be Mrs. Bryant. It's lovely to meet you." He held his hand for her to shake. "I'll be your guide for the afternoon. If there's any questions, just ask. I've worked here for twenty years. I know all about everything." Phil nodded and waved his arm for Emma and Jack to exit the office ahead of him.

Phil led them around the entire museum, then stopped at a completely empty area. He waved his arm for them to go ahead of him. Emma's eyes came together, and she tugged on Jack's arm. "What did you do?" she asked.

Jack's eyes shot up again, and he shrugged. "I don't know." He squeezed her gently.

"Please wait here. Our director would like to speak with you." Phil left them alone. Emma walked around the empty space, trying to figure out what Jack had up his sleeve.

"Is this EB Taylor?" Emma spun when she heard her professional name said.

She looked at Jack, then at the woman who'd entered the area, then back to Jack. "Yes," Emma said slowly. "That's my professional name for my art."

"It's so good to meet you, EB. I'm Carolyn Westin, the director of art for the museum. I bet you're wondering why Phil brought you to this empty space."

"Please call me Emma. And yes, we are," Emma said, standing close to Jack.

"Okay, Emma. I'd like to invite you to display your art here for a year," Carolyn said.

Blinking quickly as she covered her mouth with her hand and choked back the happy tears welling up in her eyes, Emma glanced up at Jack. His smile covered his face. She looked back at Carolyn and said, "Oh my. Yes, yes. I would love to bring my art here." Her heart beating rapidly, her entire being tingled inside. She'd always dreamt of sharing her art with more than just those that visited BE Unique and her new place, EB's Gallery. "What do I need to do next?" she asked.

"I have all the necessary paperwork here for you to take with you." She smiled as she handed her papers in an envelope. "You've already been approved by the board. Your husband has been planning this for a while." Carolyn nodded toward Jack.

Wanting to jump into his arms and kiss him forever, she grasped his hand instead and squeezed. He smiled his charismatic smile.

Emma took the paperwork and folded it neatly into the inside pocket of her coat. "Thank you, Carolyn, for this opportunity. I'll get these back to you soon." Emma extended her arm to Carolyn, and they shook hands.

"You're welcome, Emma. And happy anniversary." Carolyn smiled at Jack, who nodded at her. "Now I'll have you look around this space and see what you want to bring."

Emma felt as though she was gliding on air as she looked around the empty room with new eyes. Thinking about her inventory she'd had hanging or in storage at her gallery back home, Emma wanted to include her existing sunset and sunrise paintings, and new ones she'd create.

With this new exhibition in New York City, she wanted to create new and exciting pieces. A more modern look to her art. She'd also include some of her personal poem paintings.

Taking Jack's hand in hers, she brought them to her heart. "Jack. This is the sweetest surprise. My God. When did you put this all together?" She held his hands tenderly.

"I contacted them shortly after we got married. I knew it could take some time for the board to accept your work, and since I couldn't send them actual pieces, I sent them photos instead. That made the process take longer, but Carolyn assured me last month you'd be approved before we arrived here yesterday. I hope you're okay with this." His eyebrows rose and he freed his hands, cupping her face and lovingly caressing her cheeks with his thumbs.

Stepping back, a light went off in her mind. "Jack, was that really your nurse that texted you so often? And your nurse at the coffee café?"

Shaking his head slowly and smiling, he confessed, "No, Emma. The text came from Carolyn, I named her Michelle as a cover. And the woman at the café was Carolyn's assistant, Nancy. Please don't be upset at me for my little white lies." Jack clasped his hands together in a praying manner.

"I'm not upset with you, I'm ecstatic about this. For my art to be on display here in New York's Metropolitan Art Museum. Oh my, God, Jack! Baby. I didn't think our life could be more perfect, yet here you are making it just that. I love you."

He took her in his arms and kissed her deeply. After their kiss, he reached inside his jacket and brought out two boxes.

Smiling, she took the long thin box first. Opening it slowly, she gasped when she saw a gold necklace with a diamond encrusted EB. She drew in a deep breath.

Taking the necklace, Jack slipped it around her neck and clasped it. He kissed her.

Next, she opened the smaller box. Her mouth fell open, her eyes grew wide as she tilted her head up to see Jack's smiling face. "Jack," she sighed. The small pink velvet box held a pair of diamond stud earrings. She took each one and put them on.

Pulling her hair up, Jack kissed each earlobe. "God, you're elegant, love. You take my breath away." He pulled her to him and melded his lips to hers.

"Shall we go back to the hotel?" A wickedly sinful grin covered her face.

"Anything for you, love. Anything." Jack took Emma by her hand and led her out of the museum and into the limo.

EPILOGUE

Sitting on the beach, Emma played in the sand with JJ. It was her and Jack's first week with his son. Jenna had agreed to let JJ stay with them earlier than she'd first said, for the first time all week long, and they'd chosen to spend the week at the beach. Late April was always a perfect month to go there as it wasn't extremely hot.

Her heart filled with all the sunshine and happiness she'd ever felt in her life as she and Jack helped JJ build a sandcastle.

"Dada," JJ's sweet voice said as he held out a shovel toward Jack.

"Thanks, buddy." Jack took the shovel and filled the small bucket with sand.

"EmEm." That was the name JJ had begun to call Emma. She didn't want him to call her ma or mama and knew him saying her name would be several more months of spending time with him and her and Jack repeating her name over and over. JJ handed Emma the small rake that had come in the sand bucket they'd bought for him.

"Thank you, JJ," she said and opened her hand for him to place the rake there.

Jack and Emma built a small sandcastle while JJ drove the two cars that had come in the bucket through the rounded mounds of sand Jack had formed for him. Jack told him they were dunes for his cars to run over.

After playing in the sand, Jack stood and brushed his shorts, then held his hand for Emma. She took it and bounced up to him, falling into his arms and embracing him. Tilting her head upward,

238

she puckered her lips. Jack leaned down and kissed her as he held her in his arms.

"Dada, EmEm," JJ called out.

They turned his way. He stood next to the sandcastle they'd built. Emma recognized JJ's mischievous smile and knew what he was about to do. His mischievous grin was his father's.

JJ slowly lifted his leg to stomp on the castle, but Jack swept his son up into his arms. "Oh, no you don't, little man." Jack rolled JJ against his chest and covered him in kisses. JJ's sweet giggles made Emma's heart erupt with joy and her eyes fill with happy tears.

Jack hoisted JJ onto his shoulders, and Emma slid her arm through Jack's as they walked along the shoreline. She tilted her head up as JJ's little hands patted the top of Jack's head like it was a drum. She pinched Jack's arm, and he glanced down at her. His eyes beaming, his captivating smile filled his gorgeous face.

When they turned around to return to their beach blanket, Jack let JJ down from his shoulders, and their boy took Emma's hand first, then he reached for Jack's. Walking between them, JJ bounced and kicked his feet when the waves crashed on them. He giggled whenever the sand flew into the air from his toes.

She'd never dreamed she'd be here. Married to the most perfect man she'd ever met. For her, it hadn't been an easy road to their forever happiness. But here they were on the beach together and with this beautiful little boy who captured her heart just as his father did.

They swung JJ by his arms. His smile was so familiar to her, his eyes the same. Jordan Jackson Bryant was Jack through and through.

The sun had set, and the evening dusk settled all around them as Jack, Emma, and JJ all sat on the beach blanket. Emma laid between Jack's long legs, and JJ leaned back against her. She feathered her fingers through JJ's soft brown hair and listened as his breathing became a slow rhythm. He'd fallen asleep on her. She squeezed Jack's leg to get his attention.

Feeling Jack's lips touch her ear, she shivered. "Baby, JJs asleep. We should go back to the suite and put him to bed." Emma carefully leaned forward, trying not to wake him.

"Okay, love. Let me get him." Jack slid his towering body from under her and rose from the blanket. He gently lifted JJ's sleeping body and cradled him in his arms while Emma shook out the beach blanket and threw it over her arm.

Back in their suite, Jack laid JJ in the portable crib they'd bought and patted him back to sleep. Standing next to Jack, Emma slipped her arm around his waist. "He's so perfect."

They stood beside the crib where JJ laid sleeping. His sweet baby snores filled the room. She held Jack tightly, squeezing him with all her might.

Jack placed one hand on the small of her back and the other on the nape of her neck. He tilted her head up to him. She'd remembered the only other time she'd seen his eyes sparkle so bright. Their wedding day. She knew his heart was filled with love and happiness for her and JJ.

Leaning down, his lips touched hers. He kissed her passionately. His tongue darted into her warm mouth, tangling with hers. She moaned as their kiss went on and on.

Catching her breath after their kiss ended, she said, "I love you. I love your son as though he were mine. I love our life we've made together. You and this little boy are my world. You, Jackson Bryant, are my perfect man." Tears trickled down her cheeks. His lips kissed each of them away.

Holding her in his arms, his gaze holding hers, Jack said, "I love you, Emma Bryant."

JORDAN (JJ)

Jordan Jackson Bryant,
The most beautiful little boy I've ever seen.
A mini mirror image of Daddy.
Your eyes are your daddy's.
Your smile just the same.

JJ, you are a joy, an angel, a love.
Bringing happiness to those who fought battles
before you were born.
Mending bridges between many.
It's a cross you should never bare.

As I watch you grow,
I love you as my own.
Never worry little one,
Daddy and I will always love you.
And never let you down.

EB

THE END

THANK YOU...

To my husband, Randy. For his never-ending love and support throughout this entire process. I love you.

Gail Saladino. For being the best sister-mom. Listening when I needed you to, then giving me motherly advice whether I wanted it or not. You and Joe are my family and I love you both.

My family and friends. I love you all.

Jules Hunter, thanks for listening. And your honest critiques of my work. You've made me a better writer.

Melony Ann, thanks for listening and always being just a message away. You've taught me so much, given me solid advice on writing and the other. You are a gem of a human being.

ABOUT KC SAVAGE

KC lives in Florida with her husband.

She's new to the taboo romance genre.
She loves to write and read forbidden, taboo, cheating
romances.

When she's not busy creating her latest sizzling novel, KC and
her husband spend time with family and planning their next vacation
destination.

Link to follow and keep up with KC:

https://linktr.ee/Kcsavageauthor